THE WRONG WOMAN

J.P. POMARE

HODDER

First published in Great Britain in 2022 by Hodder & Stoughton
An Hachette UK company

1

A CIP catalogue record for this title is available from the British Library

Hardback ISBN 978 1 399 70918 7
eBook ISBN 978 1 399 70312 3

Printed and bound in Great Britain by Clays Ltd, Elcograf S.p.A.

Hodder & Stoughton policy is to use papers that are natural, renewable
and recyclable products and made from wood grown in sustainable
forests. The logging and manufacturing processes are expected to conform
to the environmental regulations of the country of origin.

Hodder & Stoughton Ltd
Carmelite House
50 Victoria Embankment
London EC4Y 0DZ

www.hodder.co.uk

For Pippa Masson,
my agent, friend and therapist

Praise for J.P. Pomare

'An expertly plotted mystery with echoes of Lee Child. I raced through it and missed it once I finished'
Allie Reynolds, author of *Shiver*

'J.P. Pomare keeps you guessing all the way through'
The Times Crime Club

'A magician, whose every plot is like a magic trick'
Michael Robotham, author of *When She Was Good*

'A master of the carefully constructed, impeccably paced psycho-thriller'
The Australian

'Taut and unpredictable'
Chris Hammer, author of *Scrublands*

'Spine-tingling . . . Pomare is able to pull off red herrings galore and crafty, satisfying twists'
Kirkus

'Beautifully written and disturbingly addictive'
Lesley Kara, author of *The Dare*

'Pomare is a writer to watch'
Publishers Weekly

'Clear your schedules, because after reading page one you won't be able to stop . . . A dark, chilling, atmospheric thriller populated with mysterious and wonderfully flawed characters'
Christian White, author of *The Nowhere Child*

Also by J.P. Pomare

Call Me Evie
In The Clearing
The Last Guests

REID
NOW

WANNA KNOW MY greatest strength? The fact I possess a forget-table face. It's true, I swear – just look at me. Late thirties, white, suburban American male – I am the human equivalent of a toast-sliced loaf of white bread. A caricaturist would struggle to find a single feature they could exaggerate on this head of mine and, quite frankly, I wouldn't have it any other way. Handsome men stand out, which means they can't do what I do; and men unfortunate enough to be uglier than me also tend to stand out. So here I am. Somewhere in the middle. Mercifully plain. Perfectly forgettable.

My haircut is unremarkable, shortish back and sides, and there's a hint of stubble on my cheeks. I keep fit, but not too muscular. Maybe the one feature that is in any way distinctive is a slightly crooked nose. Courtesy Ricky Olsen, tenth grade. It'll never be straight again.

I'm invisible in a crowd, but there's still no accounting for the power of the human memory when it comes to facial recognition. You can plan out everything but someone with a keen eye and the memory of a supercomputer will still recognise you. It happens the moment I step into the tiny reception area of the motel.

The woman at the desk says, 'You're back.'

It stops me cold.

I could turn and leave, but of course I don't. I look around just to be sure she's definitely speaking to me. There's no one else other than us two and the people on the TV screen. She's perched on a tattered office chair, looking at me with tired but kind eyes.

'I think you got the wrong guy,' I say, trying my smile on her.

'I don't forget a face. You stayed here before. Two, three years ago?' She frowns, focusing to recall the exact year. 'You look a little different this time around. It was raining.'

Ah. I did stay somewhere after Mom's funeral two years back, almost to the day. I was drunk, I paid cash, left as the sun was still rising, walking out to the highway where my car was parked. I didn't look back.

Mom never told me how bad her lungs had gotten. I should have visited more; I know that now. We spoke a lot on the phone, her mostly calling me, but it wasn't the same as hugging her and seeing her face in person. If only I'd moved her out near me, but she never would have left Manson, and we couldn't have afforded a retirement home in the city. I can barely afford my one-bedroom walk-up in a neighbourhood the real estate agent optimistically called *up-and-coming.*

There were only a dozen people at Mom's funeral, mostly from the home she was in for the last few years of her life, but there were also some familiar faces. When I saw Kay, I was flooded with memories of sitting out the back of her salon with the stacks of old gossip magazines and hair rollers, waiting for Mom to finish work. Marty, the plumber who used to live next door, turned up to the funeral too, still in his blue overalls, but he'd lost his wife recently. For someone to live for sixty years in one town and have so few people show up to her funeral, that was the saddest part of it all. Mom deserved half the town to be there and maybe once that would have been the case. It was my fault the funeral wasn't teeming with mourners. Maybe they'd earthed their pain and anger through her.

When I'd approached the pulpit and said a few words about Mom, I searched the mourners for Dennis. What did I expect? Of course he wasn't there. But still I could see him in his old suit pants with his shirt sleeves rolled up to his elbows.

'Ah, yeah,' I say to the woman in reception. 'Couple years back when my mom passed. You *do* have a good memory. Even I forgot I'd stayed here.'

She just nodded, knowing she was right without me confirming it.

'Anything on the ground floor?' I ask.

'Let me see,' she says, lifting an old ledger onto the counter.

She takes a long time scanning through the pages. I just stand there, casting around for something to say. My eyes settle on the TV again.

'What you watching?'

'I forget what it's called – one of those shows on Netflix,' she says, licking her thumb, turning a page. 'A crime one.'

I smile but don't say anything. She's got Netflix, but not a computer-booking system.

Another page turns. She clears her throat. 'I can give you seven if you want to be on the ground floor. Or fifteen, eighteen and nineteen are free upstairs.'

'You got anything else on ground?'

'No,' she says. 'Something wrong with seven?'

'Superstitious.' It's the truth. Seven's a bad number for me. Dad died when I was seven, and I've avoided it like the plague since.

'You definitely want something down the bottom floor?'

It's easier to make a quick exit on the ground level than one storey up, but I can't tell her this. 'I like the view.'

She gives an emphysemic hack of laughter. 'You like the view of the car park?' she says. 'I won't ask questions.'

'If there's nothing else, I'll take seven.'

I pay cash upfront for a week, pocket the thin receipt that hums out of the register, take the keys and park the Camry out front of my room. Carrying my bag inside, I find an old TV, pilled linen on a bed I know will be too soft, a ceiling fan and a small table. They're all the same, motels like this.

I close the blinds, take a small multi-tool from the inner pocket of my duffel bag and use it to unscrew the vent in the wall between the bathroom and the bedroom. I take a handgun from my bag – a Glock 19, about as close to police issue as you can get – along with a stack of cash, two thousand in total, and push them into the vent. I have a false floor under the mat on the passenger side of the Camry where I could keep the gun and money, but they'll probably be safer hidden in the room.

I sit up against the headboard with my computer on my lap, sinking into the spongy mattress. Someone who recently stayed in this room must have been smoking a pack a day based on the musty air and the way the pillow expels a weak nicotine odour. I look over at the tiny white card displaying a no-smoking sign and smile. Sometimes, the seedier, the better; people mind their own business in places like this.

I connect to a wi-fi hotspot through my phone. I check my emails and start deciding on a plan of attack for the coming days.

The job came to me via email from someone at Crown Insurance early Friday morning. I work mostly for insurance companies, but sometimes for individuals, sometimes for real-estate firms or banks. Sarah Jennings is the name of my contact at Crown. I've never dealt with the company before, but they're big and reputable. It seemed like a simple job and they were offering good money, then I saw the location and my initial interest evaporated. The fee wasn't enough to get me back to the twin towns. I sent a response declining the offer and passed on a few contacts who might have been able to help.

Must have been that no one else wanted to investigate a woman in a coma because soon enough another email landed in my inbox. The offer had gone up, the language was more urgent. They needed someone out there within days.

Sarah followed up with a phone call, offering to pay for half the job upfront. The other half would come when I'd finished the job, and there would be more work in the future, not in Manson or Ethelton but other places. That was the kicker. Five grand, plus expenses, for a week's work. Ten grand if I could find any reason to cancel the claim.

Which is why I'm here. I need the money. In return, Sarah wants daily updates about anything I find. That's not uncommon, especially with something time sensitive. If the job were in the city, it would have been perfect, but out here, in these towns – that's the part that makes me want to reach for a drink. This place is cursed for me.

Here's the bones of the case: it happened four days ago; single-vehicle car crash; one fatality – the passenger; one hospitalised – the driver, who was put into in a coma while she underwent surgery. Crown provided me with what information they had, which wasn't much: the police report, address and occupations of the driver and passenger, that sort of thing. The deceased, Oliver Stiles, was an academic, squeaky clean at a glance. And the driver, Eshana Stiles, his wife, doesn't have anything against her name either. She works for a recruitment company that specialises in tech start-ups. She's thirty-one, no children. No reason, by the looks of it, to deliberately crash her car.

Simple, right? Sometimes insurance jobs are just about ticking boxes. It gets more delicate when someone is hurt though. I'm a mercenary in that sense; coming in to do the dirty work the insurance assessors don't want to do themselves. The assessor can't have interviewed the driver given she's been unconscious since the crash. The hospital would have seen she was insured and her next of kin must have started the claims process.

The police have deemed it an accidental collision due to loss of control of the vehicle likely caused by a lapse in concentration or falling asleep at the wheel. They committed less than half a day to the investigation before releasing a media statement confirming the cause.

They've got bigger fish to fry apparently – I caught the tail end of a report on the radio while I was driving out here. A young woman has been missing the past few days, since the afternoon of the crash. It's the second disappearance in less than a year, with another young woman going missing from her home in August.

Call me a pessimist, but when girls go missing it seldom ends well. And in a quiet place like the twin towns, when big things happen on the same day, I can't help but link them in my mind. That's just how my brain works. In reality, people disappear all the time. More so these days with the opioid crisis. Hell, some people around here would say I disappeared.

This is the sort of rockstar case small-town cops dream of, except the Manson PD doesn't have a rockstar cop. In my time there, I was surrounded by bare-minimum officers, not the above-and-beyond types you see on TV.

I keep searching for information on my case. The insurance payout must be sizeable for Crown to bring me in as a priority; or perhaps they're acting pre-emptively, knowing the bills are coming. But unless I find a smoking gun – emails discussing their plans; witnesses prepared to sign affidavits declaring some sort of conspiracy to write their car off – I can't see how Crown's going to be able to deny paying out on the policy. And if Eshana Stiles dies in hospital, then some other beneficiary will pocket two life-insurance payouts.

I haven't got a lot of personal detail on the couple yet. Oliver Stiles, the deceased, is Gen X, so I assumed his diet of social media would be Facebook, Instagram, Twitter but I'm surprised to find only a LinkedIn profile. He's smiling in his profile picture, which is odd for a serious academic. I suppose he's pretty good-looking. He has a military daddy look with a roguish face, but he's not really my type.

Eshana's online presence is a bit more substantial. The age gap between Oliver and Eshana is interesting. Ten years. And they moved to Ethelton four years ago. To live somewhere quieter? Maybe. Or was it a career move? He may have earned tenure at Sandown College, north of Manson. Whatever the case, it's another unknown I'll investigate.

I keep going, searching for any hint of their lives, anything that might open this investigation up. There is one thing I notice about Eshana's Facebook page that sends a crackle of suspicion through my chest: she hadn't posted for over a year until a few days before the crash.

Looking for a trip somewhere warm and sunny. Maybe Mexico? Any suggestions?

There are only three comments. She doesn't have a great many friends on here and most of her activity is from years ago: updates from an artists' collective; a shared post calling for an end to oil extraction from tar sands.

A comment from someone called Larissa jumps out at me.

Cabo, it's great. You will both love it.

Eshana's response is what interests me most.

Both?

Haha maybe you can leave Oliver behind and I'll come with you. We could make it a ladies trip?

Trouble in the marriage? Or simply the sort of joke anyone might make about their spouse?

I check her friend Larissa's profile – blonde, ski-slope nose, late thirties. I don't recognise her, maybe she's not a twin towns native. I'll have to speak to her at some stage too. If she's a close friend of Eshana's, she might have insight into her mental state in the lead-up to the crash.

Next, I look at the couple's credit scores. They own their house and don't have kids, yet Oliver's credit score is a little lower than I was expecting. Nothing alarming though: 672. And Eshana's is 698.

I search the sale history of their property. No sale price on the real-estate site, but it was listed for two-million dollars in 2018 when they bought it. Not short of a dollar then.

Google Maps tells me the house is sixteen miles northwest of here, out in the Ethelton hills. Big blocks, with tall fences and taller gates. Removed from the usual blights of the twin towns.

I could drive by tomorrow, check the place out. Eshana is in a coma in the hospital, but someone might be minding the house.

I said I'm good at what I do because I'm completely average in appearance, but it's not just that. I have an insatiable appetite to understand. I don't stop until I get to the truth. Even if it's simple, even if it doesn't earn me any more money, I keep at it until I scratch that itch.

I open a new document, start making notes. First, I type out the facts of the case from the police report and any news articles I can find, adding NQR – not quite right – when something is suspicious.

- Car crash between 10.50 and 11.10 pm
- Couple left restaurant, The Pearl, at 10.30 pm
- Brakes were not engaged until car already veering from road (driver fell asleep?) – *NQR*
- Driver on SSRI medication – *interaction with alcohol may be contributing factor?*
- Speed was a factor – but police report suggests car was not travelling above speed limit of forty miles per hour
- Passenger not wearing seatbelt – propelled through windshield, died on impact
- Car totalled – value $32,000
- Car serviced week of crash – *NQR*
- Next of kin, unconfirmed
- Beneficiary unconfirmed – enquiry sent to Crown, no response yet

Here's the first thing that really piques my interest: the route between the home address and the address for The Pearl, the restaurant they ate at, is just a twenty-minute drive according to Google Maps. Why is that important? The crash happened in the middle of the drive, just ten minutes from the restaurant, which means it should have happened before 10.50 pm. So they stopped on the way home? Maybe. Or they drove very slowly in the rain.

Police reports aren't always accurate either. The rely on witnesses recalling what time they arrived at the scene.

I add a note beside 'Car crash between 10.50 and 11.10 pm': '– without stopping on the way, the crash should have been around 10.40 pm'. It's not necessarily a red flag, but enough to warrant further investigation.

I go to a local news site to see how it was reported in the paper. The reporter covering it has done a reasonably thorough job, but she's not uncovered anything new. And no press outside of the area gave the crash any attention at all.

> Police have ruled the collision accidental, with Deputy Chief Cosby releasing the following statement: 'Obviously when members of our community pass away in these circumstances, we want to understand why it happened to prevent it happening again. Tragically, this was a driver error; a mistake any of us could make.'

Cosby made deputy chief? I taste something sour at the back of my throat. I guess the opposite of *no good deed goes unpunished* is equally true.

Most of the other local news articles are about the missing girl. I feel almost dizzy when I see her full name: Maddison Stubbs. The missing girl is Chief Stubbs's daughter.

I remember her from a barbecue at the chief's home years ago. A tiny blonde thing with a gap between her teeth. She was sad because the family cat had just died and no one could coax a smile out of her. She and I played snap, the sort of game you usually regret starting when you want to go drink beer and mingle with your colleagues. But the last thing I wanted to do was upset the daughter of the chief of police, and soon enough she'd forgotten about the recently departed family pet. *One more,* she'd say after each round, and every time I'd let her win again.

No wonder it's Cosby and not Stubbs running point on the crash. The bigger crime is against the chief's family, his only kid.

'That's where all the resources are,' I tell the room. 'They're all distracted.'

A knock at the door.

My eyes instinctively go to the frosted window above the toilet, which leads out to a narrow pathway along the rear fence of the property. I can get out if I need to.

There's another knock.

I stand and silently move towards the door, thinking about the handgun in the vent.

ESHANA
BEFORE

I'M BEAMING AS I drive home from the city. The dance competition went well tonight; a couple of the local girls were competing, and I'd gone along to support them. I'd thought, *Why not?* Oli's been working late more than usual these past few months. It's not the competition results that have me bubbling inside, though. It's my birthday this week and a few days ago, as I was getting Oli's coat ready for the drycleaners, I felt the box in his pocket. I wasn't snooping – I promised him after last time I'd try to temper my suspicions whenever they arose. *Naturally*, I did a little further investigating and when I opened the box, I found a delicate silver chain with a pendant. It was really beautiful.

Oli's always had a good eye, but his previous gifts weren't exactly *me*. One year he got me gold earrings, even though I never wear gold and almost never wear earrings. I'm not sure the silver chain is really my style either, but it's the thought that counts and I'm pleased he's already organised something, that he's thinking about me. It may sound like a low bar but after so many years together, it's nice to know he can still be romantic.

I sent a message to him tonight before I left the city. I haven't heard back. When I get to Ethelton, the rain gets heavier. I pass through town and start up towards the hills. As another mile of black road hisses beneath the car, I call him.

'How far off are you?' he says by way of greeting.

'Hi, husband,' I say. 'Is that any way to answer the phone?'

'Sorry, I'm just thinking of heading to bed early and was wondering if I should wait up. You said eleven, right?'

'I'm five minutes off. I got away a little early.'

'Five?' he says.

'Yeah. Could you put the lights on up the driveway?'

'Right, okay. Sure. I'll see you soon.' He ends the call abruptly.

His car is outside when I pull through the gate and drive up to the house. The bottom level is lit up and there's a light on in the spare room too, which turns off as I watch. Oli must be upstairs.

When I open the door and enter the house, I smell pizza, but my husband, a coeliac with a very particular diet, never eats pizza. No, it's oats and two bananas for breakfast; a green smoothie and three boiled eggs for lunch; salad and tuna for dinner. He's always been like this. And yet now, on the kitchen bench, I see half a pizza sitting in an open box.

The nagging suspicion that something is off is amplified by a lingering fragrance, like one of those flavoured vapes, or a cleaning product, or . . . the sort of cheap perfume I wore at college.

Oli's at the island bench, hands splayed, looking at me.

'Hi,' I say. The word seems to hang in the air.

'How did they go?' he asks.

'Sienna came third in her division. Megan didn't place. They had fun though.'

The buzz of the night has worn off; even my excitement about the necklace has faded.

'Very cool,' he says, reaching for a glass of wine.

'Drinking?' I say.

He raises his eyebrows. 'Is that okay?'

'On a school night?' I tease. Oli almost never touches alcohol midweek.

'It's the only thing that's going to get me through this semester, I swear.' He laughs.

'And pizza?'

'Oh,' he says, rolling his eyes. 'I stayed back, let Marty order our dinner. He forgot I'm coeliac, so I brought my half back thinking you might want a piece.'

I look at him properly now, see his collar open, a patch of colour on his throat, a sheen of sweat up near his hairline.

I place my bag on the table and pour a glass of water from the fridge. 'So when did you get in?'

'A couple hours ago, I suppose.'

I want to mention the scent, a woman's fragrance.

'Can you smell that?' I say, watching his face closely.

He pauses mid sip. 'Smell what?'

I give my head a shake, as though I must be imagining it.

'It smells like perfume,' I say. 'Women's perfume.'

Oli gives his trademark side smirk. 'What are you saying, princess?'

The way the word slides out of his mouth is somehow both endearing and patronising. I can feel the undercurrent. Am I going to let him pull me into an argument over something I think I can smell?

'I don't know,' I say. 'I just thought I smelt something when I got in, that's all.'

'I'm far too busy to be having an affair,' he says. Again, a little laugh. 'And I love you too much, obviously.'

He finishes his wine and places the glass in the sink.

Who said anything about an affair? I think. And is it just his lack of time that's stopping him? Of course not. He's teasing.

'What are you doing tomorrow?' he asks.

'Just the usual. I've got meetings in the morning; I'm interviewing a candidate for the GM role for one of our clients out west. I hope she's good – it's been a nightmare finding someone. I'll try to get some groceries in the afternoon.'

'Sounds good. Well, I might have a shower and head to bed,' he says. 'Early start.'

And like that, the perfume is forgotten, and I'm left with half a cold pizza. I close the box and carry it to the front door. If I don't put it in the trash tonight, I'll be tempted to have a piece tomorrow.

I stumble slightly on the way and the box opens, the pizza hitting the driveway. *Shit.* I crouch down to pick up the pieces and notice something off. I reach out and find the gravel beneath the car is wet. If he's been home for hours, wouldn't there be a dry patch?

I stand and place my hand on the car bonnet to see if it's warm, but it's cool.

I put the pizza box and slices in the trash, fetch Oli's car keys from the hallway and go back out to his car. The rain is just a fine mist now. I open the driver door and lean in and there it is. That same cloying scent.

Oli's already in bed reading when I get to our room upstairs. He doesn't even look up when I enter. I go to the ensuite and take a long hot shower with the bathroom door open. Once upon a time, Oli would see that as an invitation. It seems years ago when we were last so spontaneous.

'Oli . . .' I say from the shower.

'Mmm.'

I press my body to the glass.

'Funny,' he says, turning back to his book.

I feel myself deflating. *Funny* is not what I was going for. Not *sexy* either, but maybe somewhere in the middle.

I thought maybe he'd notice I've slimmed down, or that I had my eyebrows done this week. Maybe he'd say, *Don't tease me.*

And I'd reach up and slowly squeeze my left breast, and he'd say, *Eshana, I'm warning you.* And I'd say, *If your book is more interesting than me, I can take care of myself.* Then he'd throw his book on his bedside table, climb out of bed and have me pressed up against the shower tiles in just a few seconds. But all he gives me is *funny.*

I brush my teeth and keep silent until I'm in bed. I hope he notices my frostiness, but he doesn't say a thing.

I grab the sheet and roll away from him. 'Are you going to be up long?' I say.

'Not too long.'

'Thought you were tired.'

'You're in a mood.'

'You've not made me feel great tonight, Oli,' I say, my back still turned.

I hear his book snap closed. The light clicks off. Then he's holding me from behind.

'I'm sorry,' he says. 'I'm just a little stressed.'

I hear a sound somewhere in the house. A door closing.

'What was that?'

'What?' he says.

'I heard something.' I sit up. 'Where's my phone? Call the police, quick!'

'The police?' he says, and rolls out of bed with a sigh. His light comes on. 'Do you want me to check?'

'I heard something. It might have been the front door.'

'Are you sure?' he whispers. 'You think someone's in the house?'

'I don't know.' Fear grips me.

He strides to the curtains and opens them enough to peer out. 'No cars, I think you're hearing things.'

'I heard something, Oli.'

He goes to his wardrobe. I hear the safe click open and see that he has something in his hand. The gun.

'I'll check the house,' he says. 'Just wait here.'

'I'm scared, Oli.'

'I won't be a second. It's all in your head.'

But if that's true, why did he get the gun? To show me he's taking it seriously?

'Was someone else here tonight, Oli?' I ask.

Even in the dark, I see his brow heavy with scepticism. He gives his head a little twitch, as if shaking off water.

'No, of course not, but I'll go check so you have peace of mind.'

I hear him moving through the house, doors opening and closing, checking each room one at a time.

Finally, he returns. 'All clear,' he says, opening the safe again and depositing the handgun inside. 'Just you and me, but I put the alarm on in the other rooms just in case. Remind me to turn it off when I get up.'

I'm a bad sleeper. When most people claim this, what they really mean is, *I don't prioritise my sleep*, or *I'm a light sleeper*. When I say it, what I mean is I was diagnosed with insomnia as a child. I try to sleep, and the harder I try the less likely it is I'll actually fall asleep. At the worst of times, I might only get three or four hours a night – I might just lie there thinking about the links between sleep deprivation and early onset dementia, or I'll relive any embarrassing moments from my life. Some nights, I just lie there and think about how much work I have to do the next day.

Oli gets worried about me sometimes, awake all night, so when he stirs or wakes, I often pretend to be asleep, staying still and keeping my eyes closed. It was one of those times I was pretending to sleep that my suspicions started last time.

That night, it was already late when I heard Oli receive a text message. I was pretending to sleep with my eyes partially closed when his phone screen lit up on the sheets between us. Before he picked it up, I saw the name on the screen: Taylor. He rolled over and opened the message. Over his shoulder I could make out a photo of a girl, lips pursed at the camera. I didn't say anything.

In the morning, when I checked his phone, the message and image were gone.

Then it happened again: another late-night message. Oli didn't wake this time, but I knew he might if I reached over for his phone, so I did nothing. The following day, I snooped and found he'd blocked out half an hour after lunch on his calendar: *Meeting – Taylor Jones*.

I cleared my own schedule for that day and drove to the campus. My mind conjured images of a young woman straddling my husband on his office chair. I was going to bust in, confront him.

With a thudding heart and light head, I strode the corridors. As I neared Oli's office, I saw a girl – possibly the one from the photo – approach the door, knock, then enter. She was thin and good-looking.

The door closed behind her. I thought about open-door policies at colleges – a strategy to prevent potential harassment. Yet Oli's door was closed. Did I want to hear what was going on behind it? What if it was what I thought it was? Did I want to see?

Eventually, I approached the door and pressed my ear to it gently. It wasn't what I was expecting. It wasn't Oli's voice at all.

'There won't be any disciplinary action, or any record of this. I just want to make it clear that it's not appropriate to contact your lecturer in the evening for anything that's not related to the course.'

Then Oli's voice. 'I really admire your work, Taylor, and I think you're an exceptional student. This blip won't impact on our student-teacher relationship at all.'

'This is mortifying,' a female voice said. 'I'm sorry, I can't—'

I was leaning against the door when it suddenly opened. I stumbled into the room, and there was Oli and the dean of the college, both giving me puzzled looks. The girl gave a sharp inhale. She was crying.

'Eshana?' Oli said. I could tell he was trying to disguise his shock. 'That's right, we've got lunch plans today, haven't we?'

I was drowning in embarrassment, my cheeks seared red and Oli was throwing me a lifebuoy to clutch.

'I won't be a moment, darling,' he added.

I swallowed. 'Oh, umm, take your time. The, ah, booking isn't until two.'

Over our late lunch, Oli explained it all to me. Taylor was a keen student who had become a little obsessed. He did the right thing, reporting it to his superior and setting up a meeting to discuss it.

That was all a couple years ago, and when my shame had reduced from a boil to a simmer, I'd started to wonder whether a leopard could change its spots. But now the suspicion is back. And with it, my insomnia.

•

Oli's gone early the following morning. That normally means he's riding his bike to college, but that's clearly not the case today as his car is gone.

On my way back to our bedroom after eating breakfast, I notice that cheap scent coming from one of the spare bedrooms.

Another woman has been in this house, I'm sure of it now. I step into the room and there, on the edge of the rug, I see the smoking gun. My heart seizes; something clogs my throat.

A hairclip. So small, yet so damning.

REID
NOW

RIGHT AS I'M contemplating squeezing through the bathroom window to the alleyway, I hear a voice.

'Mr Moore? It's May from the front desk.'

I go closer, lean in to the door. Through the peephole I see a short woman in a dressing gown. She's alone.

'Hi,' I say. 'Is something wrong?'

'Would you mind opening up?'

I check through the window and see there's no one with her. I leave the chain on and open the door enough to look out.

'What's up?'

'I'm sorry to do this to you so late at night, but I'm going to need your ID for my records. I forgot to ask.'

'You, uh, forgot to ask?'

'Yeah, I'm sorry.'

'Sure thing,' I say, trying to keep the muscles in my face relaxed.

I close the door to remove the chain before opening it again, then go to my bag and find my driver's licence.

'I don't remember doing this last time,' I say. 'Have you changed policy?'

She looks closely at the licence then hands it back to me.

'You don't need to make a copy or take a photo?' I ask.

'Oh,' she says. 'Umm . . .'

'Look, have I given you reason to be suspicious of me?' I keep an earnest expression. ''Cause I'm just out here on a sales trip. I have a few appointments the next couple weeks and I don't want to put you out. I can find somewhere else—'

'Oh no,' she says, her cheeks wobbling as she shakes her head. 'No, no. It's nothing like that.'

I glance down at her purple slippers and those skin-coloured flight socks that help with varicose veins. She reminds me a little of my mom, later in her life. She seems nice, so maybe there's another reason for this late-night visit.

'Well, what is it?' I ask. I'd thought this would be a good place for privacy with all the potential sex work or drug-taking going on behind the closed doors.

She stares hard at me for a moment. 'Just with things being the way they are in town . . . the young girls going missing and all. The police want us to confirm our guests. They're asking about strangers, you know?'

'Oh yeah. I heard the news about the girl,' I say, wishing I'd given her an alias with one of my fake IDs. Most police don't like private investigators, but the cops in Manson have extra motivation to dislike me. 'If it makes you feel better, I'll get my boss to send something over on a company letterhead confirming why I'm in town.'

'Oh no, that won't be necessary.'

'Well, thank you, I suppose.' I pause, hold her gaze as if asking, *anything else?*

She gets the message. 'Right, well, I'll leave you to it.'

Lying on the bed again, I imagine the worst-case scenario if the police knocked on my door right now.

What else could they do to me that they've not already done? A drowned rat on the floor of my car. A stray bullet on my pillow.

Threatening notes. *Your father would be embarrassed to call a piece of shit like you his son.*

One week – keep your head down, I tell myself. *Do the work, send the daily updates back to Crown. Focus on why you're here.*

Despite trying to reassure myself, my traitorous mind wanders back to Stubbs and his missing daughter. I read another article.

It looks like the chief and his family still live on the small 'lifestyle' farm that I'd visited when I worked with him. It's not far from the Boulevard, and Maddison Stubbs was at home alone the afternoon she was taken. Neighbours reported seeing a white car on their road; the tyre prints were for Bridgestone 225 Turanzas – one of the most common tyres in the country. Chances are most people are riding on Turanzas on their morning drive to work. The kicker is there were no discernible markings on the tyre prints, no distinctive wear, no nails or patches in the tread. The 225 Turanza also happens to be the tyre of choice used on police cars in the county, including, I bet, that of Chief Stubbs. It doesn't take the collective brain power of MENSA to work out the tyre prints they found probably belong to the chief.

There were boot prints to the house, and Mrs Stubbs found three things missing when she got home. Her jewellery box, some cash and her eighteen-year-old daughter.

This sort of horror story isn't the only reason I've never wanted kids. I saw enough of what you can lose, what you can go through, when I was police. You bring this person into the world, you love and care for them through the ups and downs, then something unimaginable happens to them. Years of love, sure, but potentially a lifetime of grief.

I left Manson PD ten years ago, but I still remember every missing person's case we had. In almost all of them, we found the person eventually. Almost all of them were alive, although perhaps not *well*. Most were only 'missing' because they didn't want to see their families; they'd rather smoke crack or meth, or shoot up, or snort oxy. There were a few missing persons cases each year that turned out to be deaths and, of these, most were suicides. I only saw five or so missing persons cases that ended in homicide, and with most of them it took less than forty-eight hours to determine it was a murder. A body turned up, we had suspects, we got convictions.

And then there was Amanda Marley, the young woman who disappeared not once but twice. The first time, she was discovered locked in the basement of her boyfriend's family's holiday home up near the mountains. She'd tried to break up with him, and he'd kidnapped her. She didn't cooperate, refused to testify, but we had enough evidence to convict the boyfriend anyway. Or so we thought. Nic Wojcik was his name, and everyone was surprised to discover he was from Ethelton, from a good Christian family. Even with his family's influence and his city lawyers, the writing was on the wall: Amanda's hair was found in his car; someone had to have had a key to unlock the house. There was enough circumstantial evidence to build a case, and then Wojcik got off on a technicality.

The one grand-slam piece of evidence that would have gotten the case over the line was the witness testimony of a sixteen-year-old drug dealer who was in the area and claimed to have seen Wojcik dragging Amanda Marley to his car. The kid knew Wojcik because he was a regular customer. I was there when we brought the dealer in for questioning. I heard the story myself from his mouth but, unfortunately, sometimes things fall over. The case was tossed out and a month later Amanda Marley was dead.

I could have a drink now. Take the edge off. I've never really minded having a gin alone. Sometimes it's over a solitary drink that my best ideas come to me. But this motel isn't exactly offering a stocked minibar. There's a liquor store up the road, with barred windows and probably a shotgun under the counter. It would be open I'm sure, even this late.

I reach for a trashy magazine instead; the copy of *US Weekly* I picked up at the gas station coming into town. The checkout girl paused for just a moment when I placed it on the counter, as if it was a joke. It might go against my professional ethos of blending in, but I stopped caring about what strangers think of me a long time ago. I like the magazines. I've never cared much about the rich and famous but just turning the pages is an anaesthetic, providing a view into a world of fiction, melodrama. It started when I was a kid in the backroom of that salon.

But tonight it is a small comfort as I wait for sleep in a damp motel room, trying to block out the memories of everything that happened in this town all those years ago.

ESHANA
BEFORE

WHEN PEOPLE ASK how Oli and I met, I usually just say at college because it saves time. The real story always invites more questions, speculation. It wasn't a scandal – that's not why we moved away – it was just easier to start over, build our life together.

Trident College isn't quite Ivy-league level, but it's a good school and the best that offered me a scholarship with my 3.68 GPA. My tuition was covered, along with my accommodation, but for everything else I started working at a restaurant to make money. I learnt to smile on demand, and got okay tips so long as I over-looked the occasional casual sexist remark.

I knew Oli's name before I walked into his class. He was some-thing of a superstar at Trident – just shy of thirty, at least a decade younger than the average professor. He was lecturing in creative writing after having one book of short stories recently published. A book that didn't sell particularly well – one review I'd read called it *fiction for academics who don't like fiction* – but that gave it a sort of street cred. His work was so impenetrable, so full of in-jokes and subtext, that it felt exclusive. We'd all read it and I didn't get what the fuss was about. To me it was just banal observations and moments between characters that seemed to bear no significance.

I didn't *feel* anything other than mild interest, a little like people-watching. Then again, I just assumed I didn't *get it*.

I took Oli's creative writing class in my second year. It had nothing to do with my business degree, but I'd always been interested in literature and writing. My boyfriend at the time, a tall mid-western boy named Tommy, couldn't work out why I would take a creative writing class if I had no interest in being a writer.

My relationship with Oli didn't happen how you might expect. I didn't see him and fall in love. He didn't woo me. It was slow and organic – how love should be.

He wore cool clothes, not like a stuffy professor but like an architect or a barista – fitted chinos, with a loose linen shirt, sleeves rolled up to show the veins in his taut forearms. You could tell he really looked after himself. He drank coffee from a mug while he taught, sometimes pausing mid-sentence to take a sip. Back then he had long hair and, when he was talking, he'd occasionally run his fingers through it and hold his hand for a moment at the back of his head.

I was so taken by him that I found myself neglecting my other subjects. This class, one that other students knew was an easy pass, became my focus. I wanted to impress him. Our first assignment was a composition of one thousand words, and I put everything into it. I shared it with a couple of classmates, including my best friend at the time, Becky, before submitting it and they all loved it. They all thought it could have been published. So when I got back the assignment and saw the C-plus grade I felt like I was going to be sick.

'Did you get your result?' Becky asked when I saw her later.

I just nodded. I was angry, embarrassed.

'Well?' she said. 'Let me guess – A-plus?'

'I don't want to talk about it.'

'What happened?'

I turned to her. 'What did you get?'

'B,' she said. 'I'm happy with that. I don't know what I was expecting.'

The ache in my chest tightened.

'C-plus,' I said.

'What?'

'He gave me a C-plus.'

I might as well have slapped her. 'No, that can't be right!'

It took everything to keep from crying. I sat through the next class feeling dejected, poking holes in everything Oli said and trying to find his flaws. He was just as acerbic, funny, self-deprecating as he usually was, but it came off as unprofessional and annoying to me. I hated him for a few days, then, after two glasses of cheap wine in my room with Becky, I decided to email him for further feedback on my story.

It didn't take long until he replied.

Hi Eshana,

The story was great, it just didn't follow the outline of the assignment. I was hoping for students to exhibit a strong voice. Happy to chat further about it if you would like.

That was it. Short and to the point.

'What are you going to do?' Becky asked.

'I'm going to ignore it.'

'It's bullshit. Your story had a strong voice.'

'No,' I said, thinking about it again. I'd wanted to impress him and had written the best story I could. But I didn't follow the instructions.

I took a sip of my wine. 'I suppose I see his point. I'll just have to stick to the instructions next time.'

The poor grade wasn't mentioned again, but I found myself working harder and harder in Oli's class. Asking questions. Volunteering to read my work aloud.

One day in response to one of my questions, he said, 'Look, Eshana, I'm happy to chat about this further after class but I can't cover it all right now.'

And that was it. That was how it started.

As the others were leaving the room, he came up to me. 'I've got another class to teach now but come by my office at four.'

'Sure,' I said with a smile. 'Sounds good.'

•

'Take a seat,' Oli said, when I turned up. He left the door open.

The room was just like I'd imagined. Books lining shelves; a large wooden desk covered with mess.

I sat down across from him, keeping my knees clamped together. I'd gone back to my room to put on a skirt and apply a little make-up. My black hair was scraped back in a ponytail.

I forced myself to meet his eyes, but he was looking at his laptop.

'This isn't about your questions in class, is it?' he said.

'What do you mean? I just want to know—'

'Eshana, every day you sit there much more attentive than anyone else; you hand your assignments in early; you're a model student. But the questions you ask – you already know the answers.'

'What do you mean?'

He smiled. 'If you're doing it for me, thinking it might help with your grades, then I suggest you stop. I don't care how attentive you are. I just want you to learn.'

In class, he could cut right through you with a single comment. Candid, that's how I would have described his teaching method. It hurt hearing that candidness coming out of his mouth now.

'That might seem harsh but consider it a compliment,' he continued. 'I read your work and think *this isn't the same girl asking me all these questions*. You get it. I don't know what it is – maybe you instinctively want to demonstrate to the other students how clever you are.'

I could feel my face growing hot. My embarrassment was morphing into something else. An anger that was surging up my chest like bile.

'No,' I said. 'I'm not trying to impress you or anyone—'

He raised a hand to cut me off. 'You've seen the way I call out bullshit in my classroom. I'm giving you this feedback privately because I think you're a great writer and your heart is in the right place.'

'Right,' I said, exhaling.

'And you never emailed me back about your mark.'

'I thought your email was a touch dismissive.'

'I'm busy.'

'Well, it didn't warrant a response. I got a bad mark. You explained why.'

'You think the mark was unfair?'

'Not unfair,' I said. 'I just wanted to know what I could have done better.'

'Do you want me to tell you yours was one of the best stories I've read from a freshman student in years?'

I felt small and silly. Like I was wasting his time. 'I want you to be honest.'

'I enjoyed it. It was funny, well written. You wrote like Raymond Carver, which would be great if that was what you were instructed to do.'

'I see.'

'I won't revise the grade.'

'I don't expect you to.' I was still thinking about what he'd just said. *It was funny, well written. Like Raymond Carver.*

'Well, if that's all, I'll see you in class tomorrow,' he said.

I realised I was being dismissed. When I got to the door, he spoke again.

'Eshana.'

'Yes?'

He took his glasses off. 'You've got my attention,' he said, with the hint of a smile. 'You don't need to ask me any more questions.'

Those few words warmed me from the inside. I closed the door and smiled, and couldn't stop smiling until I got back to my room.

•

For the rest of the semester, I stayed back late to talk to Oli about books and short stories. I found myself infatuated with him.

There were rumours that Oli had slept with one or two of his students in the past, but I didn't believe it. I just thought when a man in that position is young and good-looking, people like to speculate. He was flirty and charismatic in class, but he was never inappropriate.

Every time I went with my friends to the student bars, I hoped to see him there. I wanted to bump into him in the street or the quad, somewhere outside of class where we could just be ourselves. But it wasn't until Becky told me she'd seen Oli in a dark dive bar across town with some other lecturers and tutors that a plan formed.

From then on, whenever we went out, I tried to drag my friends to the dive bar where I thought I might bump into Oli. Finally, I got them along on a Friday night and he was there, with a glass of wine in hand.

His eyes settled on mine and before long he had separated himself from his group and was waving me over.

'I expect you've finished your assignment, Eshana. Considering you're out drinking?' he said with a wry smile.

'I'd never want to let you down, Mr Stiles.'

'Professor,' he said.

'Sorry, *Professor* Stiles.'

'I'd prefer it if you just called me Oli, actually.'

I felt wanted, and I wanted him. I was just drunk enough to flirt.

'I better leave before your friends notice we've been talking,' I said. 'I would hate for them to get the wrong idea.'

'They can't tell we're flirting from over there.'

Heat at my hairline. I found myself touching the collar of my blouse.

'I mean, a professor can chat with his student outside of a classroom setting, can't he?' Oli went on. 'I'm more worried about what your boyfriend might think.'

'Well, my boyfriend's not here, Professor.'

His face changed. Was that a flash of disappointment?

'Ah, so there *is* a boyfriend. What a shame. I'll see you in class. Enjoy your night.' Then he was turning away from me, back to where he'd come from.

I didn't want to miss my chance. I stepped forward, touched his hand from behind. He stopped.

'Can I . . . Can I give you my number?' I asked.

He turned back. 'Now what would I do with that?'

'You could send me a message sometime maybe.'

'Sure, you can give me your number,' he said, pausing. I was tempted to fill the silence but I knew more was coming. 'But you won't hear from me, not unless it's related to the course.'

My heart sank. 'I know. I meant—'

'I know what you meant, Eshana. I feel it too, but what would your boyfriend say?'

The fact he respected my relationship only made me want him more.

'It's not so serious with him,' I said. I knew I'd feel rotten about it later, but it was true that whatever I felt for Oli I'd never felt before, not even close. This was different. Strong.

He swallowed, looked past me. 'Okay, I've been there myself. And look, I like you, Eshana. I sense you like me too. If you're saying what I think you're saying, then we can wait. Don't take any of my classes next semester and we'll see what happens, okay?'

He turned and was gone, but he messaged me so I had his number. It was completely innocuous.

Then one day after class, I told him that I wouldn't be taking his course next semester.

I remember the way he wet his lips before he spoke. He looked around the room as people were leaving and said very quietly, 'I am *so* disappointed to hear that. I do hope you keep in touch, Eshana. I'd love to follow your progress.'

'I'm sure we'll cross paths again, *Professor*.'

Then the messages began. Nothing was overt – everything had plausible deniability – but it was still flirty, mildly suggestive.

We met for coffee *to discuss my recent paper*, but of course we both knew what it was: a date.

Another day, we went for a walk together. Then lunch. In the restaurant, I reached across the table and touched the back of his hand with my forefinger, moving it in a circular motion. Our eyes met but neither of us spoke.

Afterwards, he walked me most of the way back to my accommodation. He was careful not to get too close.

Then I saw him at the dive bar again. We were messaging each other from across the room. We got into a taxi together and that was our first kiss, in the back.

When the taxi pulled up outside my accommodation, I said, 'You could sneak in?'

'No,' he said. 'God, I can't wait until next semester. People will still talk, but I don't care.'

'Me either.'

'I've not felt like this before. This is different, isn't it?'

'This is something,' I said, then I kissed him again and climbed out.

•

On the last day of semester, I'd been drinking for hours with friends at a bar. I messaged him and he picked me up and we went to a hotel room.

We hadn't slept together yet, but we'd gotten close. He wanted to take it slow, but I couldn't help myself. It was late and I was drunk, but not too drunk. He ordered a bottle of French champagne to the room but we could barely keep our hands off each other waiting for it to arrive. We got through half a glass each before I was unbuttoning his shirt and pressing my lips hard to his.

We went swimming in the lake the next morning. It was my idea – most men probably wouldn't have even entertained it, but it is still the most effective hangover cure I know. It was so cold that I swam hard, hoping that by chopping through the water, the blood would pump into my arms and legs and warm me up. Oli was still thigh deep at the shore, holding his elbows, when I turned back.

'It's too cold,' he said.

'Just go under, it's not so bad.'

And he did.

Next time it happened in his car, out of town near the mountains. He'd packed bear spray, just in case, and made a picnic. We drank white wine and ate berries and different sorts of cheeses I'd never even heard of before then. We were on a patch of grass, holding hands and talking. I led him to his car, and we put the front seat back far enough for me to climb on to him.

Then things escalated further. The next time it was in his office. The risk of it was thrilling. We both knew the consequences if we were caught. It was so passionate, but somehow we kept ourselves almost silent, with his hand over my mouth, my teeth pressed against his palm.

But for the most part, it happened in hotels away from college, in places no one would see us. One night, we stayed up and talked until almost daybreak. It was like we were living in a novel, our own tiny world. I told him I loved him and it seemed to shock us both.

'Oh,' he said. I'd made a mistake. Why did I say it? He exhaled and looked down at his hands. He was rubbing the knuckle of his ring finger with his thumb.

'I love you too,' he said. 'But things are . . . complicated with me. I should have told you.'

Then I realised something I should have known from the start. It wasn't mentioned in any of the bios I'd read, but suddenly it all made sense. Oli, the love of my life, was already married. I was the other woman.

REID
NOW

IN ETHELTON, I park on the Boulevard at the point where the houses stop and the shopfronts begin. On one side of the road there are restaurants, a Pilates studio, a pet shop, and on the other is manicured parkland. It's the *European* part of the twin towns, although there's nothing distinctly European about it other than outdoor dining and the absence of a Chuck E. Cheese or Dairy Queen or 7-Eleven. People around this part of Ethelton think they're above chain restaurants and fast food.

It's around one hundred yards from my car to the intersection where the crash happened. As I walk, I'm searching the road, the sidewalk, the buildings, even though I'm not entirely sure what I'm looking for.

I note the slight curvature of the road and decide to come back at night to see what it looks like in the dark. But from where I'm standing, you would be pretty unlucky to hit the power pole.

I continue on until I see the tyre marks on the road leading towards the crash site. It's cordoned off with police tape and cones, and where the power pole once stood there is just a base. The tyre marks suggest the driver turned hard towards it, as if aiming for it. She may have dozed off and jerked the wheel down when she woke. Or it's possible she deliberately steered towards the pole. But why brake at all then? Fear? A change of heart? Or what if her husband applied the brakes? He could have grabbed the handbrake and pulled it up?

I can't be certain about any of this without more information.

I walk closer, eyes down on the road. No glass, no blood. Everything's been tidied up.

The spot is marked by a bouquet of flowers decaying in the lukewarm autumn sun, and a book. I crouch down. It has Oliver Stiles's name on the cover – a short-story collection. *An author as well then, not just an academic.* Maybe some of his colleagues from Sandown placed this here.

There's a cafe on the corner. *CCTV?* If there is, the police would have it; maybe that's why they were so quick to rule the crash an accident. A driver asleep at the wheel, waking when the car veers out of control. Then again, if there was CCTV, there'd likely be screengrabs from the footage in the press reports.

I carry my bag across to the cafe and find a seat in the corner closest to the door. It should be safe for me to visit. The police station is on the Manson side of the river so the local cops are more likely to head to Dunkin' Donuts or maybe Papa's cafe in the shopping centre.

I've also taken my usual precautions when it comes to how I look. When I'm out on the job, it boils down to blending in, disappearing in a crowd. Today I'm in blue jeans and a grey sweater, no labels, all plain. My one memorable, removable item is a red Kansas City Chiefs hat, pulled low over my eyes. I doubt I'll need it, but better to be safe than sorry. The idea is that if someone were to describe me to the police, they'll fixate on the hat and not really see the rest of me. And because it's removable, I can dispose of it easily – another way to disappear.

On a recent job, I was tailing a man through a casino because his wife was concerned he was having an affair. He somehow realised he was being followed and sent security after me. If I hadn't been wearing a green tweed coat and reading glasses – both of which ended up shoved down the side of a slot machine – they might have gotten their hands on me. The man, it turned out, wasn't having an affair but he was addicted to gambling.

Fitting in is about how I act too; everything is considered. Down to the smallest detail, like how I sit at the table, with the newspaper spread out open and my laptop beside it. A cursory glance at the real-estate listings shows Ethelton prices have gone up a lot, but Manson has somehow managed to defy the adage that real estate doubles every ten years. The prices don't seem to have moved much since the late 90s.

Contrary to what the media would have you believe, I doubt places like Manson have really gotten any rougher over the years; it's just new strains of the same disease. Poorer, small towns have replaced crack and amphetamines with opioids. The kids do most of their bullying online. Domestic violence hasn't disappeared with advancements in technology. Ethelton might be where all the money is, but they've had their own problems. Not to the same scale as Manson, but there's drug use, suicides, DUIs. The difference is the ugliness is hidden away there. No broken windows on the Boulevard, no boarded-up shops. Almost no graffiti. And even within Ethelton, the class divides are stark: close to town is mostly blue-collar workers, but out in the hills where Oliver and Eshana Stiles live – lived – that's where the money is.

As usual, I search for my ex's name when I'm browsing the local news, but I never see it. Marco fled the twin towns, just like me, but unlike me he fled to a better job and presumably a happier life. Meanwhile, I lost my job, moved to a small apartment in the city and realised I'd never again trust that feeling that I was in love.

When you develop a scepticism about love, the world loses just a little of its lightness. I've not had a functional relationship since Marco. Then again, I've not really wanted one.

I reach into my pocket, stop myself, grasp the rubber band around my wrist, draw it back and let it slap my skin.

'Ouch,' the waiter says, drifting closer.

'Oh,' I say. 'I quit smoking – it's supposed to help.'

'Does it?'

'It's been a few weeks, so I guess it's working.'

The waiter comes over. He's tall, young, with his hair pulled back in a bun. He reminds me of that Irish musician, Hozier. I can see tight biceps within the sleeves of his white t-shirt. *Too young for you, old man.*

'What'll you have?'

He has a nice voice too. It's smooth, vowels sliding into each other and some consonants disappearing entirely. Like the 't' in 'what'll'.

'Black coffee and the omelette,' I say.

'The omelette? Are you sure?' He smiles.

'What? Is it bad?'

'It's boring,' he says.

'One omelette, please.'

He snorts. 'House black coffee okay? Or you want espresso?'

'Black is fine.'

He takes the menu and heads back towards the kitchen. I try to resist but I can't help watching him go. I shouldn't make myself so obvious.

When the omelette comes, it's good and greasy like it ought to be, filled with cheese and fresh tomato. The coffee is strong and gritty, and the waiter refills my cup whenever it drops below half.

When I'm done eating, I make a few notes about the intersection. There's a streetlamp, and traffic lights that hang down from cables. The kerb is low; the car would have mounted it before hitting the pole. Everything seems to be *just* this side of legal. *Under the speed limit*, the police report said. *Blood alcohol 0.071*, just shy of the limit. That's probably two glasses of wine. Eshana Stiles was definitely driving. I wonder what Oliver Stiles's blood alcohol would have been. Could someone have wandered out into the intersection, forcing her to swerve? It was raining, but anyone would see the headlights coming. The tyre marks seem to suggest the car lost control about fifteen yards before the pole. No brakes until the last second. All the possible factors in this crash warrant some level of suspicion.

I stare at the intersection. It's quiet for this time of the day. Back in the city, it would be bustling with morning traffic.

The waiter glides over again and takes my empty plate.

'Compliments to the chef,' I say.

'You can stop pretending now. It was awful, wasn't it?' he says.

'It was perfect. Hit the spot just right.'

He narrows his eyes as if suspicious. 'I'll take your word for it. Can I get you anything else?'

'Sure,' I say. 'A slice of pie, if you have it.' I don't need the sugar, but I suddenly feel like something sweet.

'Apple? Cherry? They're both mediocre.'

I laugh. 'You're hardly selling the menu. Are you sure you really work here?'

'I'm just honest. The granola is great, we've got a passable pecan slice. The pancakes are – well, pancakes are hard to mess up.'

'I feel like pie.'

He shows those dimples again, but with a *hmph*, like he's entertained if not impressed. 'Apple is the slightly more palatable pie.'

'One slice of apple pie, please. No cream.'

I go back to the news articles about the crash.

DRIVING FATALITY BEING TREATED AS ACCIDENT

A collision last Wednesday that resulted in the death of one person and another remaining in a critical condition in hospital is now being viewed as an accident by the Manson PD.

Emergency teams rushed to the single-car crash on the Boulevard, north of Ethelton, at about 11 pm.

At first the crash was treated as suspicious, but investigators have confirmed they believe the crash is the result of driver error, resulting in a loss of control of the vehicle.

Emergency services workers said two critically injured patients were rushed to hospital in separate ambulances. The passenger, Oliver Stiles, died before arrival. His wife, Eshana, who was driving the car, remains in a serious condition.

Manson PD Deputy Chief Cosby urged locals to stay safe on the roads and to not get behind the wheel when tired or intoxicated.

It seems so clear. On the page is a link to an article about one of the missing girls. My brain – or maybe everyone thinks like this – makes links between things even when they're not connected, like some great big net of cause and effect. Two girls, both eighteen at the time of their disappearance. No bodies have been discovered, but in both instances the girls appear to have been taken from their homes. Both gone on a Wednesday, although Kiara King disappeared late at night, Maddison Stubbs in the middle of the day.

The media haven't linked the cases, and to be fair there are differences. Kiara is from Manson; Maddison's from Ethelton. Kiara's family's likely poor; Maddison's is middle class. Kiara disappeared five months ago; Maddison just three days ago. Kiara's bike was missing but nothing else. Whoever took Maddison stole some jewellery and money. Maddison's crime scene seems more typical of an abduction – with the boot prints, you can form a narrative around it. Kiara's appears much more like a runaway. There are signs everywhere and a reward for the return of Maddison, but I've seen almost nothing like that for Kiara.

'You didn't take her, did you?' the waiter says, looking over my shoulder at the screen.

Normally that would bother me, but I don't mind this time.

'Ha,' I tell him. 'I've got an airtight alibi.'

'And what's that?'

'I was in the city.'

'A city boy. Well, here's your pie.' He puts it down in front of me and folds his arms. 'Still, it's horrible, isn't it? Parents must be going through hell.'

'Yeah, it wouldn't be easy.'

'I remember when Kiara King disappeared,' he says. 'The entire town was talking about it, then everyone sort of moved on. Obviously not her family and friends, but everyone else, you know?'

'It's been a bad run for the twin towns.'

'Yeah,' the waiter says, leaning over the back of the chair across from me. 'I hope they've just run away.'

'And what about the car crash? You know anything about the woman in the coma or her husband?' I ask.

'They used to come here, actually. More so him. He would mark papers, at that exact seat.' He nods towards me.

'You knew him?'

'Not well. He was very charming when he wanted to be, but my roommate knew him somehow and didn't like him at all. His wife was nice, she'd leave generous tips and make an effort to talk to you, to everyone, actually. I just hope she pulls through.'

I've stumbled onto something here. 'She must be popular then?'

He shakes his head. 'You're new to town, aren't you?'

'Kind of.'

'I know they liked her at the dance school. Maybe the rest of the town would have liked her too if it wasn't for him.'

'He's not widely admired I take it?'

'Not exactly.' He looks over to a pair of women who have entered the cafe. 'Not everyone was mourning when they found out he'd died. Especially over the other side of the river.'

Then he's gone to serve the newcomers. I do a bit more digging online. Like most private investigators, I pay for access to a number of private databases. I can get mobile phone numbers, addresses, licence plates for most people from the databases, which are continually updated. I pull Oliver's and Eshana's information. They've got a second car registered to Eshana, a white SUV. Neither Eshana nor Oliver have a criminal record. I check the marriage registry to see precisely when Oliver and Eshana got married and discover that Oliver was married before. Annabel Stiles. A quick search shows she hasn't changed her surname back. She's an interior designer in the city. I find a photo of her: dark hair and eyes, tanned skin. He's got a type. Although she's definitely a little older than Eshana.

I decide to make a list.

Visit the restaurant. Speak with friends of the couple. Speak to Annabel Stiles. Visit their home. Visit the hospital. Find the car. Visit the victim's place of work.

Victim – that's a Freudian slip, even if it's only written in my notebook. When did I start to see Oliver Stiles as the victim here? Is there a victim in an accidental collision? Or am I thinking of him as a victim because I sense a crime has been committed?

ESHANA
BEFORE

AS I HEAD back towards the house, I think about me being the other woman when Oli and I first got together.

He told me he'd gotten married too young to the wrong woman. She was controlling and difficult. She wanted children and he didn't. It was never going to work.

'We sleep in the same bed sometimes, and I go back there to pick up stuff, but it's over,' he told me. 'I barely stay at the house at all.'

'You don't want kids?' I'd asked.

'No,' he said, without a hint of hesitation. 'Do you?'

I thought about it. I hadn't really considered *not* having kids, but I knew it was ethically in vogue to shun procreation and protect the planet as well as your lifestyle.

'No,' I said. 'I don't think I do.'

'Our generation doesn't *need* children,' Oli said. 'Robots will look after us in old age and our carbon footprint will be much lower than all the breeders.'

I laughed at that and he knew he was off the hook.

'I want *you*, Eshana,' he went on. 'Not my ex-wife, nor anyone else. This can be whatever you want it to be, but you're the only woman I want.'

Years later, I would understand why the wives and partners of the other faculty members at Trident fell quiet when I entered the room. They all knew and liked Oli's wife; they never got to see what she was like at home with him. Oli told me they would have screaming matches. He said she was controlling and mean but to his colleagues and their partners, I was the villain. I was the home-wrecker.

Oli and I continued to date in private, until the end of my third year of college when he proposed. The divorce had finalised with his ex and I married him. He stayed at Trident for one more year, and I was interning at a recruitment agency until another rumour surfaced: a woman claimed to have had an affair with Oli when she was a student. It wasn't an official complaint but it was a mark against Oli's name.

Then another woman wrote a blogpost for the college paper about a one-night stand with her professor at Trident. Oli wasn't named but everyone assumed it was him.

He told me about those others eventually, confessing to a drunken mistake with an honours student; a fling with a teaching assistant. It was all above board; they weren't *his* students when the affairs happened and it was before he and I got together.

The #metoo movement was just starting to capture the nation's attention and Oli knew he was in the firing line. The job at Sandown came up and we decided to uproot and move to Ethelton four years ago, one year after we got married. There were never any official complaints or an investigation, but we wanted a clean break to escape the rumours.

Oli already knew some of the professors at Sandown. Although it was a less prestigious school, it meant someone like Oli, with his academic reputation, would be one of the stars of the faculty. He never faced any consequences of those earlier affairs at Trident.

Oli had a contact at a tech recruitment company who got me a good job working remotely. I established my own career.

It isn't quite the same living in Ethelton as living in the city, though. I met some people through volunteering at the dance school, and the wives of other professors or professors themselves, but most of the friends I have, I made through my work.

Our kind of work is all meetings online, phone calls, messages and email. Most of my colleagues live out in LA, Denver, San Francisco – places with thriving tech hubs. But some are like me, opting for the quiet life. A few times a year, I drive to the office in the city and catch up with my colleagues in person. Otherwise we see each other at work conferences every year. Last year it was a resort in Miami for two days. The year before we flew into San Antonio for a weekend.

Visiting big cities makes Ethelton feel small and insular. Oli is more popular than me here. He has his academic colleagues, their poker nights, some friends he cycles with in the hills. And of course he works hard, staying late at the college more and more often. There's something admirable about someone committed to their career, even when they don't need the money.

Oli was born into an upper middle-class family, but he made his own money – a lot of it – through luck. When he was at college, he had a roommate who was tech savvy and they stayed in contact for years. Around 2010, he convinced Oli to invest in some obscure digital currency. At the time, it was basically worthless, but Oli was taken by his old roommate's enthusiasm. When the opportunity came up to invest in more bitcoin around 2012, Oli took it and he still holds substantial wealth as digital assets.

When he told me the story, it was with relative nonchalance, but of course he could afford to hold onto the investment all those years through the ups and downs, because if he failed he still had a safety net of generational wealth to land on. He still had his family's contacts to get good work, and he had a solid education.

Oli has his charity project too: a week-long creative-writing workshop with advanced high-school students. He set up the program himself when he arrived at the college and it started off as a way to give back, but quickly blossomed into something bigger. He was profiled by the local newspaper, and kids from the twin towns began applying for the program in droves, but there's only so many spaces.

One or two of those kids might one day go on to sit in Oli's college classes, just how I did all those years ago.

●

As I drive through the gates at home, I can't stop thinking about the hairclip in the bedroom, and that scent. It reminds me that I was once the other woman.

I know deep down that Oli could be seeing someone else. But I've been wrong before. It was mortifying last time, when I stumbled into his office. But *once a cheater always a cheater* – isn't that what they say?

I move through the house searching for any other signs that someone else was here, but the place is spotless.

Oli arrives home in the early afternoon. For once he's not working late, or playing poker, or playing squash. As he makes his way from his car to the front door, I see he's carrying a bouquet of flowers and a bottle of wine. In spite of myself, I smile. A warmth starts in my chest and spreads to my limbs.

I'm waiting for him when the door swings open, his key still in the lock.

'You've got the wrong day,' I say.

'Oh, I know your birthday is Friday, but it's not a surprise if you get flowers and wine on the day, is it?'

I let him kiss me, feel his stubble scratch the corner of my mouth.

'So this is instead of celebrating my birthday?' I ask.

'No, but I've been shit lately. I know that. I want to be better and I want to apologise. I said I'd tidy the house yesterday, but I got a cleaner through instead. I was working late so . . .'

'When did you get a cleaner?'

'Yesterday, before you got home.'

'Oh,' I say, thinking about the perfume smell, the hairclip. Doubt cools my fear and anger. 'Who?'

'May, she cleans at the college. I asked if I could pay her to clean the house and she needed the money.'

He lays the flowers on the bench and reaches under the sink for a vase.

'Right,' I say. 'Well, thanks for this. It's a nice surprise.'

'I've booked a table at Marcel's,' he adds. 'The new French restaurant near the river.'

'I better put on something nicer than this then. When are we booked for?'

'Seven. Go get ready. I've just got some emails to send, then we can head off.'

Marcel's, it sounds expensive. We've never spoken openly about how much money he still has squirrelled away. There was a prenup for me to sign, but I've no idea how much he inherited from his father or made in cryptocurrencies. All I know is it was enough to buy the house his first wife lives in, and then this place in Ethelton, which cost almost two million dollars.

Some writers starve themselves to remain true to their art, refusing to compromise on their approach. Some writers sell out and write romance or crime fiction or clickbait articles, giving up on the idea of literary stardom and Booker prizes. Then there are writers like my husband, who would rather be admired than sell out and can afford to fail because he doesn't need the money.

He's been working on his second collection of short stories for years, without an end in sight, but there's really no need for urgency. He's comfortable in his role teaching students and dispensing advice about the writing world, knowing full well that very few of them will ever make a career out of it.

The privilege of financial security is so far removed from my upbringing that it still feels a little like a fairy tale. I was raised by a solo mother who fell pregnant to another student at medical school. The deck was stacked against her from a young age and having a baby in her final year of college didn't help.

My grandmother helped raise me until she passed away when I was nine. My father, who was on a scholarship, moved back to Denmark when he finished college and we didn't hear from him much at all – which was fine with Mom. She had boyfriends, but nothing lasted more than a couple years. She had me and her work to keep her busy, and she seemed happy enough.

She liked Oli; was glad that I married a kind, caring man and he liked her. When I told my mother in my mid-twenties that Oli and I would never have children, I said the hardest part was that I wouldn't give her a grandchild. She told me she didn't care as long as I was happy and she would always love me, but I could see a hint of sadness in her eyes.

That's what Mom was like; she was a GP and used to others unburdening their worries, pain and sadness on her. She would never do that to me. When she finally told me she was dying, it was only after her own doctor had told her the cancer was terminal and she had just a few months to live.

At first, I felt angry at her for keeping the cancer secret for eighteen months. I thought it was the most selfish thing she had ever done. But mostly I was angry at myself for missing the signs.

Oli took time off and we drove down to stay with her. I was there for most of the final months, working part-time and caring for her. Oli was back and forth. He called in all his favours trying to get her on trials at medical schools. 'We can afford it, Eshana. We can get her in for immunotherapy. Don't worry about the money.'

But of course he didn't understand the stage she was at. All I could do, all anyone could do, was comfort her. So that's what I did for those last three months that dragged out to five.

Then one night, like a tide in the moonlight, her chest fell slowly for the last time and the breath was gone.

It still feels like I'm mourning her. The world feels so lonely now.

At least I have Oli, or I *had* Oli. Now I'm not so sure.

'Eshana Stiles,' he says as I descend the stairs. 'As beautiful as the day I met you.'

And just like that the last of my suspicions evaporate. Oli is *still* the man I married. It was all a false alarm.

I go to him, grab his cheeks and kiss him hard and deep like we used to. He's surprised at first, before he's kissing me back.

REID
NOW

I HEAD TO the restaurant the couple visited on the night of the crash: The Pearl. Back in my hometown, everything seems smaller somehow and the great blue sky seems bigger. The buildings and the brick clocktower in the middle of town might have shrunk since I was a boy. The drugstore, the laundromat that used to be the salon where I spent so many afternoons, the town hall are all half the size I remember them to be and the roads are wider. The old water tower is more dilapidated and has fresh layers of graffiti; a new mobile phone tower stands on the hill coming into town.

If the buildings seem smaller, the events that happened here are just the same. Spikes and mountains on the seismograph of my life. Ten years is a lot of water under the bridge; would my former PD colleagues still harbour such a strong grudge? What about the locals – will they remember what I did?

I know the answer. Few will have forgotten. And I doubt anyone is ready to forgive.

The Pearl is quiet and I find a duty manager setting up tables.

'Hi,' I say.

'Sorry, we don't open for another fifteen minutes,' he says, without looking at me. 'Did you have a booking?'

'No, I'm not here to eat.'

He looks up now, his eyes fix on me. He tilts his head to the side. 'Reid?' he says.

I squeeze my eyes closed as if in pain. I can't help it. Things have changed around here, but so have I. I didn't expect old acquaintances to recognise me.

'Vince Reid, it is you, isn't it?' he says, peering at me like I'm some mythological creature.

'Adrien Bryer,' I say.

We weren't close but I knew him pretty well at high school. When I became a cop, I lost a lot of friends and Adrien was one of them. Our friendship became incompatible given he was a relatively successful merchant of pills, ecstasy and speed in the party scene. He had dreams of being a DJ, touring the world, but now he's managing a restaurant.

'I knew it!' He laughs. 'You're not a cop anymore? I heard you skipped town.'

'Yeah. I'm in the city now but back on business.'

He nudges my shoulder with his fist. 'It's been years.'

'Too long,' I say awkwardly, before cutting to the chase. 'Listen, I'm here about a couple who dined in on Wednesday, actually.'

He raises his hand. 'You don't need to tell me who you're asking about. What's this about then?'

Thankfully, Adrien Bryer is hardly the type of man to go running to the police to tell them I'm in town. 'I'm a PI now, working for an insurance company. Just helping to figure things out.'

He gives me a knowing look. Then turns and flips a table stacked on another down onto its legs.

'Well, I'm glad to see you,' he says. 'I heard all kinds of stories and you just disappeared. And that thing with the girl – you know I didn't see that as your fault. Just one of those things.'

'Thanks,' I say. 'So what can you tell me about the couple?'

'Well, I've actually got work to do so I'll just tell you what I told the cops and the journalist. I can't remember what they ate, or what they talked about. All I remember is the argument.'

'They argued?'

'No, not them. The argument happened with someone off the street. They were sitting near the window and this guy just comes in and starts going at them.' He places his hands on his hips, looking towards the door as if it might jog his memory. 'I don't know what it was about, and it ended pretty suddenly. Candice, the server, rushed to get me and I kicked the man out.'

'You don't know who it was?'

'No. Never seen him before. He was angry though. Getting right in the other guy's face.'

'You got CCTV?'

'Only from inside. The cops have got a copy already.'

'Any chance I can see the footage?'

He looks past me towards the street. 'Why? It was just a crash, right?'

'Probably, but I've got to make sure.'

'Sure of what?'

'Well, sure that the insurance claim is legit. The crash was an accident, for starters.'

He nods. 'Alright, come on.'

We pass by the toilets and the entrance to the kitchen all the way to a locked door. Beyond it is the office: a small windowless room with a safe bolted down in the corner, and an old desktop computer surrounded by a stack of printed menus on thick stock, Post-its and a neat pile of receipts.

Adrien turns the computer on and clicks an icon that's a cartoon detective holding a magnifying glass to his eye. The screen fills with four streams: two inside the restaurant, one along the hallway towards the bathrooms, and one in the office showing us.

Adrien searches by date and pulls up the footage from the night of the crash. As he scrolls, people eat, laugh, chew, move in and out of the doors and to the bathrooms at hyper speed until he reaches the moment he's looking for.

'Here,' he says. 'You can play it from this point and you'll see the argument. I've got to get back to work but let me know when you're done.'

I'm sure he trusts me, but even if he didn't he knows there's a camera above me and no escape.

'Will do.' Then, as he's about to leave: 'Oh, one other thing.'

He turns back, half in, half out the door. 'Shoot.'

'I don't want anyone to know I'm in town. I just want to do my job and clear out.'

He bugs his eyes out, taps his temple. 'I get you, man. My lips are sealed.'

I sit in the seat and zoom in on the couple in the corner. I watch for half an hour; their body language isn't great. Even without sound, I can tell by the way he checks his phone and the fact they barely look at each other that something is off. They're waiting for the bill when the man approaches.

His hood is up, which doesn't help, but I get a good look at his face. He's young, maybe early twenties. White, no facial hair, blue or green eyes. It's hard to tell given the quality of the zoomed image. Jeans and running shoes. I pause on a frame where he's looking towards the bar and see a small tattoo near his collarbone. I can't quite make out what it is.

I rewind, see that he looks through the window as he passes, as if he's looking for them. Anything else? Not that I can see. I let the footage play to the argument.

It starts from afar, and it's clear when Oliver Stiles realises something is amiss. He looks up from the table, catches sight of the newcomer and says something to his wife, probably a warning. He shifts a chair between him and the man.

The man comes closer, towering over Stiles who has backed himself into the corner. He reaches out and grabs Stiles's shirtfront and rams a finger into his cheek.

Adrien comes rushing out; someone from a neighbouring table pulls the hooded figure off Oliver Stiles. It takes three of them to get the attacker away and shove him out the door. He continues jawing at Stiles from the other side of the glass.

Adrien closes and locks the door, turns around with a smile and says something that makes the other diners smile too. But not Oliver and Eshana Stiles. Eshana is staring down at their empty table. Oliver touches her hand; she rips it away.

Adrien comes over, crouches down and speaks to them, before heading back to the bar.

Taking my phone from my pocket, I record the footage for my own records and to share with my contact at Crown. Daily updates, I remind myself.

Who is this man? Within an hour of this argument, Oliver Stiles was dead and Eshana Stiles was placed in a coma with a head injury. What went wrong? What was said?

I screenshot the younger guy's face and zoom in. I don't recognise him at all. My guess of late teens to early twenties was right, though, and he's definitely Caucasian, medium build. He's at least six foot tall.

When I leave, there are some diners in the restaurant. A waiter is serving them and Adrien is behind the bar.

'Thank you,' I say as I pass him. 'I have everything I need.'

'No worries. Hey, come by whenever – we'll grab a drink.'

'Sure,' I say, knowing I won't. I don't want to risk any more exposure than I need to. 'Oh, by the way, what did you say to the couple after he left?'

'What?'

'I saw on the footage you approached and spoke to them.'

'Oh yeah. I just asked if they wanted me to call the police, and he insisted he didn't want me to. He said it was a personal matter. But I told him that the police take threats seriously.'

'Threats? What sort of threats?'

He clears his throat, closes his eyes like an actor preparing for a scene. 'I won't cuss, but it was more or less things like "You're a dead man, I'm going to kill you" and "You thought you got away with it, didn't you?"'

'And you told the cops this?' I ask.

'I did. But obviously it wasn't so important because I didn't hear from them again.'

ESHANA
BEFORE

MANY COUPLES REACH a sagging patch in their relationship. It usually happens when each person wants something slightly different, and no subject is as contentious as sex. As things slow down, that initial blaze turns to a simmer.

We were still in the warm glow of the first few months of marriage when we shared our fantasies. Oli told me he'd never had a threesome, but it was at the very top of his list of fantasies.

Three glasses of wine into that summer afternoon, I joked that maybe at our five-year anniversary I would entertain the idea of inviting a girlfriend to join us in bed.

I thought I saw something change in his eyes. 'Oh, I love you more every day,' he said. 'Five years.'

And that was it. It wasn't supposed to be serious.

As our five-year anniversary got closer, Oli began to remind me of that conversation. He seemed to be joking at first, and I joked along too. Then, about a month out, he started to talk logistics and I knew he was serious.

I would consider myself sex positive. I think when two consenting adults agree to do something in bed it's healthy so long as everyone is on board. As tame as my fantasies were, Oli always indulged me.

And even though I never wanted to share him, I knew that if a threesome made him happy, it would make me happy too. A one-off indulgence.

There was no doubt that the other party would be a woman.

It couldn't be someone we knew. It couldn't be someone from town either, because the last thing you want is to bump into the woman you had a threesome with at the gas station or the supermarket.

After some discussion about Craigslist, Tinder and other avenues, Oli settled on a website I'd never heard of before. It sounded more or less like a marketplace for sex work. I said I would let him choose the other party and he organised everything.

If he was nervous leading up to that night, he didn't show it. I, on the other hand, was a wreck. By the time the woman arrived, I'd already downed half a bottle of wine.

Oli opened the door and kissed her on the cheek.

'I'm Grace,' she said, which I knew was a fake name, but I didn't mind.

She came into the house and looked around at the furniture, the art, the fireplace, which was blazing by that stage. I was struck by how beautiful she was. High cheekbones, blonde hair, tanned skin and big eyes. She was wearing a lot of make-up and I'm not sure she needed so much. I was never that beautiful, and I would have probably been jealous if I wasn't fizzing with nerves. A cloud of perfume followed her deeper into the house. The other thing I noticed was how slight she was and younger than I was expecting.

'Sit, sit,' Oli said, gesturing towards the lounge.

'Would you like a glass of wine?' I offered, then thought that perhaps she wasn't quite of age yet. No, she must be. Oli said she came from an agency. There must be checks and balances.

'Oli, could you join me in the kitchen?' I said.

As I topped up our glasses and poured her one, my hand was trembling. 'Are you sure about this, Oli? You sure you want to go through with it?'

'I'm game if you are,' he said. 'She's beautiful, isn't she?'

'She *is* beautiful.' I knew how much I'd be letting him down if I turned back now. I thought Oli had a type. I thought *I* was his type but she was so different to me. Curvy, thick make-up, fair skin. 'Quite young, don't you think?' I caught his eye then.

'She's twenty-two,' he said. 'I checked.'

I swallowed. 'Okay.'

We went back through.

When I let myself relax after a drink, I came to see it was fun, normal, like a date. She was flirty, and clever. She told us she wanted to be an actor, had had a couple of small roles in the past. She said she loved to do this kind of work and only met with couples to make their dream of a threesome happen. That's what attracted her to us.

Things started in the lounge. We were making out, all three of us. She was a much better kisser than my husband. Slow and teasing, all glossy lips and soft bites.

When she slipped into another room to 'freshen up', I was surprised to discover that she had changed into a short-cut school dress. It gave me a moment of pause. *Had Oli requested this? Was it a bit . . . Was it a kink?*

But I let myself go. I let myself enjoy it all.

•

Why am I thinking of that now while I'm sitting in the waiting area of Holly's office? She practises out of a room above the pet store in Ethelton. The access is from the rear, and it's not as though you can hear kittens in cages or the trade downstairs, but I've always thought it an odd place to put a psychiatrist's office.

Holly's done well with the space. She doesn't have or need a receptionist, but there's a waiting area with magazines and comfortable seats, and a diffuser sending vaporised sandalwood oil into the air. She has generic impressionist prints on the walls, and coming through the speakers is the sort of lyricless music that I assume is intended to stimulate reflection.

'Eshana,' she says, with that smile that is comforting if not entirely warm. 'Come on through.'

I'd been in Ethelton for about a year when I started to see Holly. She's a city transplant like us, opting for the quiet life over the bustle of city living. Now, I see therapy the same way I see servicing my car, but at first it felt so self-indulgent, the sort of thing I might have once scoffed at. But over the years I've come to realise it's important to look after myself and reflect on my insecurities and how I've always needed validation. Oli picked that about me from day one, from all those questions I used to ask in class just to show him I existed. To show him I was paying attention.

I know I can be needy. I have a desire to be liked, and fear being disliked more than anything. Serial people-pleasing. I've tried to make friends in Ethelton, but the folks here are nothing like me. I feel like an outsider, and when I catch up with my old friends I realise how much I miss a normal, busy social calendar.

Holly reminds me that *that's okay.* We work through these issues, we talk about my insomnia, and sometimes we talk about Oli too.

Today she quickly zeroes in on the latest cause of my sleeplessness: the night of my birthday.

'It was lovely,' I tell her. 'A bit like old times. We shared a bottle of wine, ate some nice rich food, then we came home to our bed a little tipsy and hungry for each other.'

'So what went wrong?' she asks.

'Nothing that night, but in the morning I realised something. Oli forgot to give me the necklace. Then days passed and he never gave it to me.'

'The necklace?'

I exhale, realising I hadn't mentioned this last time. 'I found it in his coat pocket a week earlier. I can't stop thinking about it, because when I went back to find it, it wasn't there. And he didn't give it to me.'

'I see,' she says, frowning. 'We have discussed this in the past, Eshana. You're naturally suspicious because of how things started between you and Oliver.'

'You think I'm imagining zebras,' I say. It's one of her sayings: *you hear hoofs beating and you think zebras.*

She smiles. 'I think you are owed an explanation. Perhaps he returned it to the store because he thought you wouldn't like it? Or it's possible he found it and was planning on handing it into the police or lost property. Did he give you another gift?'

'He got me a voucher for a facial at the beauty spa in town, but I still have that nagging feeling.'

'I won't remind you of the last time you were convinced he was having an affair,' Holly says.

I wince as I recall the shame of stumbling into Oli's office at the college. 'This is different.'

'You were convinced then too, Eshana. I'm just saying it can be destructive to catastrophise instead of speaking to him about it. Putting aside this, do you feel safe and happy in your relationship?'

'Sure, mostly.' I shrug.

'That's why communication is so important. We all need to make space and time for important conversations, even when we're busy.'

'Yeah,' I say. 'I know. I just want proof that he's loyal.'

'You might be looking at it the wrong way around. Proof that he's loyal is harder to come by than little things that might pique your suspicion. He's fighting an uphill battle on that front. It's natural to have suspicions, but the only way to move past them is to have the conversation with Oli. Don't attack him or try to catch him out. Just express how you are feeling and why. Make it clear that you're concerned.'

'Okay,' I say. But in my head I know I can't, I won't. Oli won't just *confess* to having an affair.

'Tell him it's coming from me,' she continues. 'Lean on my input. Say, "My therapist thinks it would be healthy for me to externalise my concerns so we can clear things up."'

'Okay,' I say. 'Sounds easy.'

'He will understand,' she says. 'Trust me, it's better to air these things. You don't need to tell him you found the necklace if you don't want to; just let him know how you're feeling. After last time, he'll understand and appreciate that you're coming to him instead of trying to catch him out.'

I look down, and nod. 'Okay, maybe that's a good idea.'

But Holly hasn't allayed my doubts at all.

•

Later that day, I'm sitting in the garden with my laptop, enjoying the sun, when I hear the gate buzzer. We rarely get surprise visitors. I decide to ignore it, except the buzzing comes again.

I go to the intercom near the front door. 'Yes?'

The camera shows a man's face, his nose distorted by the fish-eye lens, his mouth wide, crowded with white teeth.

'Can you open up?' he says. 'I need to talk to Oliver.'

'Oliver's not here actually. He's working.'

'At the college, I suppose?'

'I'm sorry, how do you know my husband?'

I watch him roll his tongue along his bottom lip and his eyes shift right, towards the house. He's young, not much older than twenty, with pockmarked cheeks and dark eyes.

'You're the wife, huh?'

I hesitate.

When I was nine, my mother took me hiking around Gauley River. There was a moment when, seemingly apropos of nothing, she said with urgency, 'Move away quickly, Eshana.' When I asked what was wrong, she just said, 'I want you to go fast through here. Go on, hurry.' Later, she told me she'd seen a snake – probably a copperhead – in the underbrush, but she knew I'd panic if she told me. The snake was already moving away and was unlikely to bite, but she didn't want to take a chance.

At the time, I'd sensed something was wrong by the way she spoke, the fact that danger was just feet away. Why is it I have that same feeling now?

'Look, my husband isn't here. You can come by later if you want to speak with him.'

'Could you pass on a message?' he says.

'Sure.'

'You'll need a pen and a piece of paper.'

We keep a notepad on the chest of drawers in the entrance hall. I reach for it. 'Okay, what is it?'

'Tell him the price has gone up.'

'The price?'

'Just write this down. *Bring seven for Kiara tomorrow.* He'll know what it's about. You got it?'

I can barely respond. 'Okay,' I manage.

He steps back from the intercom and stares up towards the house. I look out through the glass beside the front door and see him down at the gate. He seems to be sizing it up. Of course, anyone young and able-bodied could probably scale the fence if they want to, but I'd have time to lock the doors, call the police and go for Oli's gun. Then what?

At last, the man leaves.

I'm left with two questions: *Who is Kiara?* and *What is happening tomorrow?*

•

I don't mention the visitor or the message when Oli gets home. As we cook dinner together, he seems a little stressed but otherwise himself. He has a glass of wine with the gluten-free spaghetti bolognese.

I consider what Holly said about raising my concerns with him. *Not tonight*, I think.

'How was your day?' I ask.

'Fine. Start of the semester is always busy, everyone is a bit stressed. What did you get up to?'

'I had therapy at eleven, otherwise just work all day.'

He keeps his phone close all evening, even taking it into the bathroom when he showers that night.

I slip in and pick it up from the vanity shelf. He can't see what I'm doing through the steamed glass; I'll just be a flesh-coloured outline, like him. I look at the screen as I brush my teeth, but suddenly a wet hand is on my shoulder. The shower is still running.

'What are you doing?' he says.

I place the phone down, spit out my tooth paste. 'Sorry. I was just checking the time.'

He reaches back into the shower to turn the water off. If I didn't already know he was hiding something, this would confirm it.

In those few seconds I had his phone, I managed to turn on 'Share my location'. Now I'll know exactly where he goes tomorrow. It will make it much easier to follow him so I can find out who Kiara is and what it is he's doing with her.

REID
NOW

WHAT HAPPENS TO a car after a major collision in which someone died? After the police have finished at the site, they might have the vehicle towed and held as evidence, or returned to its owners. If the car is a total wreck and isn't being held as part of an ongoing investigation, it will go to a junkyard where it'll be stripped for parts or crushed into scrap metal. Crown Insurance reported to me that the Stileses' car has been written off. Given Eshana Stiles is incapacitated, it's likely someone else is taking care of her affairs. And that someone must have initiated the claims process, and probably also signed off on the wrecking of the car. It's only been five days since the crash so there's a chance the vehicle is still intact somewhere.

In my own car, I look up all the junkyards in a twenty-mile radius from town. There are five, which is a lot and doesn't give me much hope I'll find the car in a hurry. I call all of them and only one answers; they don't have the car. One of the numbers is disconnected; and I leave voicemails with the other three.

I head towards the Stileses' house. It's unlikely anyone will be there, unless someone's minding the place. It takes ten minutes from Ethelton to get into the hills, where it's all oversized blocks, gates and fences, and views down towards town. The Stileses' house is perhaps the biggest of them all and a six-foot-high stone fence wraps the property.

As I drive past, I see a large black steel-bar gate and an intercom system. I follow the fence along the bend, driving slowly. At times I can glimpse the top story of the house. It's palatial; looks like it recently had a fresh coat of white paint. Thankfully, it's some distance from the neighbours. I'll be surprised if they don't have cameras installed so I'll have to be careful.

I put on dark glasses, a moustache, and the trucker hat from the glove box, then drive back to the gate and intercom. I press the button. It rings and rings but there's no answer. I press it again. Still no answer. It seems the house is empty. Perfect.

I park up around the bend, way off the road in the grass. I pull on black gloves, and shove a balaclava in my pocket along with my phone – switched to airplane mode.

After one long sweeping look along the tree-lined road, I scale the fence. On the other side, I get into the cover of a nearby bush, then crouch-sprint to the corner of the house. There's a large green rainwater tank and I tuck in behind it, staying close to the white weatherboards. I work my way to the back garden. The lawns are all neat and there's a shed nearby. The outdoor setting is tasteful. *So this is how life is on this side of the river.*

I scan the eaves for cameras; nothing, so I start to look around the house. Through the kitchen window I see a stack of mail on the bench. Could be something there.

I'm not above searching mail or garbage if I think it will help resolve a case. This work isn't half as glamorous as blockbuster movies will have you believe. We pee in bottles, we go through trash, we barely eat and when we do it's almost always greasy takeaway food. There's nothing romantic about it. This is gritty work and sometimes we need to break the law to get the job done.

I try the back door; you never know, sometimes you get lucky. The handle turns. It's . . . unlocked.

This is the scary part. I can see the alarm panel on the wall near the front door. If it's armed and I go inside, there really isn't much I can do. I'll have thirty seconds to sprint through the house before clearing out. I'm not worried about the neighbours wandering over; it's the security company that will be on their way in a matter of minutes. That's *if* the alarm is armed.

I recognise the alarm system. There are no red lights, which makes me certain it's unarmed. Does that mean someone is here? Maybe they just didn't hear the intercom.

No, I haven't spotted any other signs of life inside.

I'm about to go from trespassing to unlawful entry.

Slowly, I push the door open and step inside. I go straight to the alarm system to confirm it's unarmed. Then I take a look around.

Other than the small stack of mail on the bench, the kitchen is spotless. There are no dishes in the sink, no dust in sight. Some of the mail is open, beside a pair of reading glasses. Oliver wore glasses in some of the photos I've seen of him, they must be his.

I rifle through the mail: a bank statement, a letter from a charity thanking Eshana for her donation, a bill from the water company. I take photographs of the bank statement, then slide it back inside the open envelope.

I enter the living room and feel like I'm in a shoot for an interior design magazine. The walls are dripping with art; the furniture is styled and probably worth more than my mortgage. If I were a thief, I could make off with some substantial loot. But I'm not a thief. And despite how much I need money, I could never rob a woman's home while she's in a coma. I have *some* principles.

I move through the house room by room, rifling through drawers and wardrobes, being as methodical and as quick as I can be.

If I find anything notable, I'll take a photo, but nothing piques my interest. Nothing until I walk into the bedroom.

The bed is made, and the room is as spotless as the rest of the house. Inside one of the wardrobes there's a squash racquet, running shoes and a headband. There's also a gun safe, unlocked and empty.

Behind it, I find a box. I open it and lift out a school uniform with *Ethelton High* emblazoned on the chest. I lay it on the bed, take photographs of it, then put it back. They don't have children, so why is there a school uniform hidden at the back of Oliver Stiles's wardrobe? I now know this case is much bigger than just the crash.

As I continue through the room, I remind myself that the uniform doesn't necessarily mean what I think it means. But my mind still goes to Kiara and Maddison, the missing girls. Maddison disappeared right before the crash, and Kiara a few months ago.

It's possible the uniform is part of some fantasy role-play, I suppose. It seems too risky to have it somewhere his wife could find it if it's something he's not *supposed* to have. If, for instance, it belongs to one of the missing girls.

I'm letting my imagination get away from me. I need to focus on the task at hand – searching for anything that might undermine the insurance claims for Eshana Stiles and the estate of Oliver Stiles.

The bathroom yields nothing further, other than some 5-HTP pills, which is a mild over-the-counter antidepressant, some Valium and sleeping pills. All things I'd expect to find in an average couple's medicine cabinet.

I can't leave without one last look at the uniform. Is there anything I missed? I check the size, and then examine it for bloodstains or rips. Nothing. I upload the photos to the cloud, then delete them from my device.

What was Maddison Stubbs wearing when she went missing? What was Kiara King wearing?

I go back into the hallway and check another bedroom. Something's slightly off here. It's the first room I've stepped into that isn't spotless. The heavy curtains are half closed; the bed is made but not as neatly as in the other rooms. I see an open book face down on the bedside table. And then, as I step further into the room, a suitcase on the ground.

The unlocked back door, the alarm system turned off. Eshana is in the hospital, so who has been here?

That's when I hear the front door open and I freeze. A silent alarm is my first thought. But whoever it is, they're not a cop or from a security company. I can hear a woman talking loudly on the phone. This suitcase must be hers. This is the room she's staying in. I've got to get out. With my heart slamming, I focus on her voice. She's downstairs in the foyer. Something drops on the floor – shoes or a bag. Then she's moving deeper into the house.

I creep into the hallway, listening, trying to place her movements. Could I climb out a window and flee?

'I just got back.' There's a pause. 'The doctors don't know, that's the thing. They're going to try to slowly bring her out of it.' Another pause. She's talking about Eshana. She must have come from the hospital.

If she moves towards the stairs, I'll go into the master bedroom. I could hide away in the wardrobe, or sneak by if she goes into the room where her suitcase is. For now, I slip on the balaclava.

'If it was a long-term thing, we could always apply for a conservatorship, but I'll look through the house and see what I turn up . . . No, he's not found it yet.'

She goes into the kitchen. *Did I close the back door?*

'Hold on,' she says. 'The door's open. The back door . . . I don't know. I don't remember, but I doubt it . . . Don't overreact, it's probably nothing . . . Okay, maybe just to be safe. I'll call someone now.'

Someone. The police. *Always close the door,* I chide myself.

'I'll call you back.'

I hear a cupboard opening, pots and pans moving. She's searching for a weapon. I suppose that's a good sign. A pan I can escape; a gun is a tougher proposition.

The stairs creaked when I climbed them earlier, will they give me away if I go down them now? I slide in behind the door of the master bedroom.

This woman, whoever she is, has courage. I can hear her opening doors on the lower level, and soon she's coming up the stairs. She doesn't go to her room first, as I predicted, but comes straight into the master.

My heart thumps. If she closes the door, she'll see me. I'll be trapped. I'll have to shove her and run. It's not ideal, but needs must.

She walks straight past me and into the bathroom. I hear her open a drawer. *What is she doing?*

Next she goes to the wardrobes and opens them both, before leaving again. She closes the door behind her and I exhale. Trapped like a bug in a jar.

I hear her move down the hall into the other rooms, and finally she's on the phone again. Her voice murmurs through the wall but with the master door shut I can't make out what she's saying.

Slowly, I reach for the door handle, turn it and open the door just enough to slip through. Down the hall, her bedroom door is closed. She's talking loudly but she won't see me.

I sneak along, pressed to the wall, so low my knees creak. I'm at the top of the stairs, then I take them one at a time. A small whine as I place my foot down. Did she hear? I'm still, waiting to see if the door opens. Then I continue on.

I get downstairs and, with my senses firing, cross the kitchen to the back door. It's locked from the inside. I turn the bolt and the handle at the same time and the door opens with a small gasp. I twist through the gap and close the door behind me. It clicks. Too loud.

Staying close to the house, I sprint to the corner, then into the trees towards the fence. Turning back to look, I see her shape in the window upstairs, phone pressed to her ear mouth moving quickly.

I clamber over the fence, get to my car and throw the door open. I'm on the road, wheels squealing, in a matter of seconds.

The police, who I'm certain she's called, will be coming the most direct route from town. That leaves me with only one option: the long way home.

ESHANA
BEFORE

I'M IN BED, my eyes closed, when Oli leaves the following morning. What my husband doesn't know is that I'm very much awake, and I sent two emails last night rescheduling my morning meetings.

When I hear his car start, I race to get dressed, and I have pulled on jeans and a sweater by the time he passes through the front gate. I snatch my phone and car keys, locking the door on my way out.

Inside my car, I bring the map up on my phone. The blue dot sliding along the road ahead is my husband. It's early, 7.30 am. I think of all the times in the past when he's left this early, before any shops open, hours before his first class.

I follow at a distance, and give him even more room as we get closer to town. I'd hate to pull up behind him at a set of lights.

I see on the map that he's stopped on the main street of Ethelton, near the clocktower. I pull into a spot further back, which allows me to see all along the street from my car.

Oli looks in my direction. I slide a little lower in the seat even though I know it's impossible for him to see my car let alone me inside it. He stops at an ATM. Then after a few moments, he goes across the road to the bakery. A minute or two passes before he comes out carrying a paper bag and a coffee.

He drives off again, and I wait until I see the blue dot cross the bridge a few minutes from here. I expect to see him turn left towards the college, but he turns right, heading south towards Manson. I turn on my ignition and follow.

Manson has about three times the population of Ethelton, but most of them are squeezed into a collection of small urban blocks just off the main drag. The police station and the courthouse are at the start of the drag, not far from the river, but the further along you go, the rougher things get, until you emerge on the other side into pastureland. Oli is heading right into the heart of Manson's residential area.

I stop at a set of lights, and a guy approaches with a brush held up. I shake my head, but he starts to clean my windshield anyway. He's out here early. *He must be desperate*, I think.

I open the centre console, the glove box. I don't have any coins.

I lower my window. 'Excuse me,' I say. 'I'm so sorry, I don't have any change. I'll come back soon.'

He just raises his hand as if to say *it's fine* and wipes the water off with the rubber strip on the back of the brush.

I check the map: Oli has stopped in a side street. I drive on, and see that he's started moving again. He drives out of town for fifteen minutes and I follow, again at a distance. He's five minutes ahead at least.

He stops on a road five miles out from the main drag of Manson. I won't be able to disguise the car or myself if I get too close. Especially out there on the open road.

I park and wait for him to move again. Ten minutes pass. I sit with tension balling up in my chest. I can't help but think the worst. I imagine a drug deal, or prostitution. Soon he's heading back towards me. I turn around quickly and accelerate away so he doesn't come up behind me.

I take a right on the first street and a few minutes later I see him continue on. I exhale, then spin the car around and follow him once more, this time closer.

For ten minutes, he heads back the way he came. His classes start at nine today and it's already eight-thirty, so he hasn't got long. *What is he doing?*

I think about the man who came to the house yesterday. Will Oli get into some kind of trouble because I didn't convey the message? Is it drugs? Or gambling? Or an affair?

He stops again, on the same side street as before. I race through an intersection, barely slowing to check if it's clear. I'm almost there, but he's moving again by the time I arrive. Oli's car is just up ahead. I see someone walking towards a house at the exact spot where Oli stopped. A girl in a school uniform. *Who is she?*

The skin on my chest tightens and I can taste something sour on the back of my tongue. I pull over outside the house and sit there in the car, dropping my face into my hands. I try to slow my breathing, but I can't.

Is she a schoolgirl, or just dressed like one?

That night comes back to me, our fifth anniversary. Heat rushes to my face. Is this anger I feel? Disgust? Disappointment? It's everything, whirling through me all at once.

Then comes denial. I can feel it growing inside: *this can't possibly be what it looks like.* There's a reasonable explanation. There has to be. But what is it?

Perhaps she's a student from Oli's summer school. Students from the local community come to do workshops at the college over the break. That must be it. But . . . if he picked her up and took her somewhere, why?

There's only one way to know for sure. I open the car door and set out towards the house the girl disappeared into.

The gate swings on rusted hinges, and the few feet of lawn between the fence and the house is overgrown. I had friends at school who grew up in homes like this. Mom and I didn't have much money, but we certainly weren't poor. Mom worked hard and set up her own private practice in our neighbourhood.

I knock hard on the front door. I've not prepared what I'm going to say; I just need to know who Oli picked up in his car.

I hear a woman's voice. 'Kiara! Get the door!'

Kiara. That name the man said yesterday.

Footsteps, a lock opening. Then the door swings inward.

It's her. The girl I saw walking along the street just after Oli left. I recognise her from somewhere. It clicks: she came for a few lessons at the dance school a couple years ago. She was a decent dancer if I remember correctly, then one day she just stopped.

The tiny annoyed line in the centre of her forehead disappears the moment she sees me. 'No,' she says, as if it's the only word she's got. The door slams shut.

'Wait,' I say, and knock again. 'I know you.' The door re-opens an inch.

'If you don't leave in ten seconds, I'm opening the side gate and letting Ham out,' she says.

Ham, I assume, is a dog. I turn and stride back to my car, feeling eyes on me all along the street. The other houses, all knitted in tight together like teeth crowded in a mouth.

When I get home, I can't stop thinking about it all. I'm supposed to be working today but my mind is hooked on what I saw this morning. Oli has a big secret. This time the reality appears worse than what I was imagining.

REID
NOW

I TAKE OLD Holden Road all the way out of town on the way to Merrick. I could keep going and lie low out that way for a few hours, maybe even overnight. Surveillance is legal, but entering a property is not and, worst of all, there was a witness.

The adrenaline is still pumping; breaking the law in Manson PD's jurisdiction is not my smartest move. There are two things linking me to that house: what I was wearing and the car – but only if she saw it. I need to get rid of it all. I ditch the fake moustache out the window.

I hear the sirens before I see the lights. Blue and red flashing. My heart pounds. My throat closes. I squeeze the wheel, I could floor it. I could take a risk.

They've got me, though, when it comes to speed. I've got a 2010 Dodge Challenger parked up in a garage in the city – it's the car I drive when I'm off the job. If I was driving that, I'd be tempted to push my foot to the floor. But not in the Camry, not in this car designed for the safe courteous driver.

I indicate, pull over and brace for what's coming.

As an officer approaches my car, I snatch the balaclava up from the seat beside me and shove it under my own seat.

I wind down my window. I know what's about to happen: hands outside of the vehicle, then a slow step from the car. Onto my knees, hands behind my back, cuffed and pressed against the gravel.

'Licence and registration?' the officer says. I don't recognise him.

I'm almost too relieved to move. This is just a traffic stop.

'It's in a compartment on the passenger's side,' I say. 'Can I reach for it?'

He stares for a moment, then says, 'Sure. Nice and slow.'

The car is registered to my name, the insurance too. I lift the floor mat and open the compartment.

'Why do you keep it in there?' he asks.

'I get a lot of break-ins in the city.'

'Up from the big smoke, huh. What brings you to town?'

'Just taking care of a few of my mother's affairs.'

'Sorry to hear,' he says, but he doesn't sound sorry.

'Oh, she passed a couple years ago.' I hand over the registration and my licence.

'Won't be a moment.' He goes back to his car. Most of it is automatic these days, they have computers on board.

I look in the rear-view while I'm waiting and see a second cop riding in the front seat. This time, it's the passenger door that opens. This can't be good.

He comes up the passenger side of my car, a tall, thickset figure. Then I see the underside of a huge police-issue boot, a second before my passenger side mirror smashes.

He comes around the front of the car with a big shit-eating grin. *Sticks*. That's his nickname. Real name, Jarrod Stickland. He's a couple years younger than me; a nasty man with a worse temper.

He saunters over to the driver's window, rests the blade of his forearm on the edge of my door and leans in close.

'We've got you doing sixty-five. We're citing you for that, and it looks like you're missing an exterior wing mirror, so we'll have to write you up for that one too.' He pauses, smiles again. 'Officer Cowell mentioned something about a cavity under the mat on your passenger side. That's the sort of thing a drug dealer has, which is probable cause. We're going to have to search the vehicle, I'm afraid.'

The temperature rises ten degrees.

'Look, I know what this is about,' I say.

'Oh, do you now?'

'I'm just trying to get home, okay.'

'Please step out of the vehicle and place your hands on the hood.'

'Come on, you don't need to do this. Just write me up.' There is one silver lining. They've not mentioned anything about trespassing, or unlawful entry.

'Write you up? *You're* telling *me* how to do my job?'

'No,' I say.

The second cop is coming back. I see his hand hovering down near his holster and can tell he wants so desperately to draw his weapon. I'm not going to give him extra motivation.

Sticks steps back. Slowly, I open the door, climb out and place my hands on the hood.

Sticks cuffs one hand, wrenching it up my spine so it feels like my shoulder might pop out. Then he does the other and tightens the cuffs.

'Legs apart.'

He pats me down, squeezing hard around my ribs and calf muscles so I feel like I could buckle under the sharp pain.

'Take a seat on the edge of the road.'

I do.

Soon I hear him laughing as he tosses the balaclava out of the car towards me. He works through the rest of the car, the trunk.

Sitting on the roadside, I feel the coils of tension tightening inside. I need to phone my lawyer. I need a friend in the force. I think about the only cop I kept in touch with from Manson:

Sid Mosley. Mosley was shipped off to another PD. I assume it was his choice, to get away from this place, although we've never spoken about it. Now and then I get in touch, see how he's going, ask about the wife and kids. We must be close to his jurisdiction out here, but I know if I'm going anywhere it's to the Manson PD.

Sticks finds my lockpicking kit, hurls it onto the gravel in front of me. 'Fuck is this shit?'

My heart is slamming so hard in my chest I feel like I might faint. 'Huh? What is this for, Reid?' he says.

'For picking locks,' I tell him. 'I'm training to be a locksmith.'

'Cute. And the balaclava?'

'Hunting.'

Neither of those things are illegal, but they're enough to bring me in. It's going to be a long day.

A call comes through on Sticks's radio, but I don't catch it. The two officers look at each other.

'Write him up,' Sticks says.

The younger cop starts issuing the citations, printing them out from a handheld device. If I can get out of this with a couple fines and a short stop at a garage to fix the wing mirror, I've been kissed by an angel.

There's urgency in their movements now. Whatever the call was, they've got to get going. I think for a second it might be from the Stiles house, but then I'd be a prime suspect. It must be something else.

'You're not welcome here, Reid,' Sticks says. 'Get the fuck out the twin towns. I'm putting the word out – if I see you in town again, you'll be spending a few days in the Manson Marriot, you understand me?'

He throws me forward on my chest and my face hits the gravel. The cuffs come off and the fines float to the ground in front of me. Boot steps crunch on the road back to the police cruiser and then they're flying away, lights and sirens. Something big has happened.

I lower my face against the stones, feel my chest heave a couple big deep breaths. I feel like I could melt with relief, but after a moment I push myself up. Put my things back in the car, and change into cargo shorts and a plain t-shirt with a hoodie over the top.

I put my previous clothes and the balaclava on the back seat. Then I continue on to Merrick, where I drive to the goodwill store and drop my jeans and my shirt in the donation bin.

Merrick is about as small-town as this part of the country gets. A big man at an ATM is wearing a t-shirt with *I own a gun and I vote* on the back.

Back in Manson, I drive through the Dunkin' Donuts and order a cream cheese bagel with a large coffee. It tastes like dishwater mixed with sugar but I get it down as I drive along. I eat half the bagel, then put the balaclava in the paper bag and shove it deep inside a bin on the corner of Main. The cops already know what I had on me, but it can't hurt to get rid of the evidence. They could come for me again. Especially if the woman at the Stileses' house called the police.

It's unlikely she saw my car, I tell myself, but someone else might have seen it parked near the road's edge. A white Camry with local plates is a good lead for the cops. I could always go home to the city and swap it for my Challenger. Except the Challenger will probably make me stand out. Some cops love to pull over fast cars.

•

By the time I get back to the motel, it's afternoon. I log into my encrypted cloud storage and look at the photos I took at the Stileses' home. I can't stop staring at that school uniform.

Imagine if those two cops had seen these images. Would they suspect me of having something to do with Maddison's disappearance? There's no way they could make the connection – I was at home in the city the night it happened; the CCTV in the lift in my building will confirm it – but they could make my life hell. Manson police are good at spreading rumours.

The fact Oliver Stiles had the uniform in his wardrobe is a big red flag waving in my face. That man definitely had secrets.

ESHANA
BEFORE

I TRY TO smile my way through my afternoon work calls, but I'm distracted, my head somewhere else completely.

My hairdresser calls and I realise I was booked in to get my hair done this morning. I apologise and offer to pay for the time, but she won't accept. I reschedule for next week.

I call Toni to tell her I won't get down to the dance school today to help out. Before she hangs up, I ask the question I've been dying to ask even though I probably shouldn't.

'Toni, do you remember a girl named Kiara?'

'Kiara,' she says slowly.

'She lives in Manson,' I say, hoping to jog her memory.

'Yeah. Kiara . . . King? That was her name. She came along a few times.'

I swallow. 'Yeah, why did she stop?'

'Couldn't pay.' It's a blunt response, and an obvious one. Toni's fees aren't cheap. 'I think the mother had health issues. Why?'

'No reason. I just remember she was a good dancer.'

'Talented, sure. Not a good fit for us, though.'

I can read between the lines. Kiara's a Manson girl. Not many of those come through the dance school.

After the call, I just sit in the lounge with the TV on and my phone in hand, scrolling the day away until it's late enough in the afternoon to open a bottle of wine. Then I become a sponge, soaking up expensive wine and playing Lana Del Rey records, waiting for Oli to come in the door.

I check the blue dot on the map and find that it's gone. He's turned it off. Which means he must know that I turned it on.

•

He doesn't get home until six. 'Hi,' he says, turning to hang up his coat.

I don't respond, I just watch him.

'Eshana, honey?'

'Hi,' I say. I feel heat at the back of my eyes. I'm most of the way through a second bottle of chardonnay and I thought I was ready for this, but maybe I'm not. I draw in slow, steady breaths, trying to stay calm.

He strides to the kitchen, where I'm perched on a stool, my hand gripping the stem of my wine glass. He kisses my cheek, leaves it damp. Places his gym bag and leather work satchel on the bench.

'What do you feel like for dinner?' he says. 'I can defrost something. Or I could duck out to pick something up.' He turns back to me. 'Eshana?'

I can't hold the tears in. I had a plan to confront him but it's draining from me.

'What is it? What's wrong?'

I swallow. 'I know what you did this morning.'

He bites his lips for a moment and his eyes search my face. 'And what is it exactly that I did?'

'I saw you, Oli. You got cash out and you picked up that young girl and took her somewhere.'

His eyes find a spot on the ceiling, as if he's trying to remember. Then he releases a little chuckle and a hint of doubt drips down my spine. 'That's what you saw, is it?'

'Yes,' I say. 'What are you doing with her? She's a schoolgirl.'

'And you turned on *share my location* on my phone to keep track of me? Which, by the way, I wouldn't mind leaving on if it didn't eat through the battery life.'

'Who is she?'

He sighs. Reaches for my wine glass for a sip, but I don't let it go so he fetches his own from the cupboard.

'Her name is Kiara, she came through the high-school program over the summer,' he says, his back to me. He turns and pours himself what's left of the wine. 'But I'm more interested in what you think is going on, Eshana. This has happened before and you still don't trust me.'

Do I say it? Do I tell him what I think?

'My therapist thinks it's important for me to externalise my concerns.'

'But you didn't externalise them,' he says. 'You snooped through my phone and you followed me.'

I steel my resolve. 'I think any woman would be suspicious when her husband leaves early, takes money out from an ATM, picks up a teenager and *parks up* somewhere in a rural part of town, then drops her home.'

'You've still not told me what you think I've done.'

I place my glass down hard enough that I think the stem might break. 'What if some man came and picked me up and took me for a drive – what would you think we were up to, Oli?'

'Well, I wouldn't necessarily think you were fucking him.'

'Stop playing games! What's happening? What are you up to with her?'

'Kiara's mother is dying, Eshana. She has lung cancer and requires expensive targeted drug therapy to stop the tumours from growing and to possibly shrink them.'

'You're telling me this is one of your charity projects?'

He sips his wine thoughtfully. 'I can call her if you'd like. Do you want to speak to her?'

'I already did,' I say.

His face remains neutral but I can see a vein pulsing at his temple.

'Well then, she would have told you. Did you meet Sandy, her mother? Lovely people.'

How he says *lovely* makes me think he believes the opposite. This story also sounds familiar: he tried to help my mom in a similar way. What if it's just a tale he knows will make me empathise with the girl and her family?

'Why don't you transfer the money?' I say. 'Why pay cash?'

'Because they're in debt, every account is overdrawn. The bank would hold any money that lands in their accounts. I pick Kiara up and take her to her grandmother's house – where we stopped.' He gives a wry smile. 'They keep the money out there because of the neighbourhood she lives in and because her brother's a bit of a rough sort. Her grandma helps her pick up the medication.'

Brother. I think of the man who came to the house yesterday, who said the price had gone up.

Oli pulls his phone out and opens a crowdfunding page. I see they only raised a couple hundred dollars. There's a photo of a woman with three young girls around her, her kids. Among them, I see the girl, Kiara.

'She wrote a story about it in the high-school class,' Oli goes on. 'That's how I found out. I thought you of all people would understand.'

A fist of guilt presses against my stomach. But I only reacted how anyone would, right? Or is this another symptom of the way we met; the fact he was married when we got together?

'Why don't you pick up the drugs.'

'I don't have the prescription. Trust me, it's just easier this way. Without my help, Sandy would likely die and there would be three girls without a mother – and let me tell you, her grandmother isn't swimming in cash either.'

'Okay,' I say through a long exhale. 'Well, sorry, I guess. Sorry for doubting you.'

'I know how it looks. I should have told you, but I didn't want you to think it was too much money.'

It's not like Oli to shy away from the glow of altruism. But maybe he's telling the truth. If it's a lie, it's very elaborate. I remind myself that this is what happened last time. I got suspicious; I got ahead of myself; I trusted my instincts even when they were wrong. So why did the girl close the door in my face then?

'How much?' I ask.

'The treatment costs about a thousand dollars a week.'

I almost spit out my wine. 'And we can afford that? How long has it been going on for?'

'Months,' he says. Then smiles. 'But it's working apparently. They don't have insurance.'

I stare down at the last mouthful of wine in my glass, my cheeks burning with shame. 'I'll organise dinner then, shall I?' I say, going to the fridge.

'That reminds me, we should really check our insurances. Make sure we're covered for everything.'

REID
NOW

I WAIT IN the car park near the town hall. It's almost three, which means kids will soon be coming out of school and likely heading straight here for dance class.

The town hall is on the Ethelton side of the river, but it feels like Manson. It's primarily used for community events. It's close to the bridge, and not far from the old coal-fired power station across the river that's been closed for a decade or so but is still an open sore you'd be a fool to poke at. There were three things that kept the twin towns afloat in the nineties: work at that power station, forestry and Sandown College. Now the power station is defunct, and there are only a few jobs in logging. The college is all that's left as far as large employers go and they don't tend to take on the sort of people that worked at the Manson power station.

I think about those years when I was a cop patrolling this town. This car park between the town hall and the picnic area by the river was the spot where minor drug deals happened. Come by late at night on the weekend and it was easy to pick up dealers, if you could be bothered with it. Arresting small-time pushers felt a little like throwing a cup of water on a house fire. They were selling meth back then, the boys in their hoodies and their piece-of-shit cars.

Now I see only a couple of family vans parked around me. Maybe the creep of gentrification has pushed the drug trade all the way across the river.

I glance towards the side entrance to the town hall. Does a single male sitting in a car outside a dance school look suspicious? I'm still hopped up from the run-in with Sticks. I was nearly hauled into the station. I've got to be careful. By now the entire PD will know I'm back.

I climb out of my car and look over towards Manson. A chill breeze rushes up off the water and I turn up the collar of my coat and warm my hands in my pockets as I head to the side door.

I'm peering inside when I hear a voice behind me. 'Can I help you?'

My shoulders hunch instinctively; I'm still rattled. Turning, I see a woman leaning in the alcove beside the door, a cigarette between her fingers.

'Sure,' I say. 'Is this the dance school?'

'*Toni's* Dance School. Yes, it is.'

'And you're Toni?'

She smiles, but it's all mouth; her eyes look exhausted. 'Guilty. You want to enrol your kid?'

'No, no. I'm just investigating the car crash that one of your helpers was involved in. Eshana.'

'Oh,' she says. '*Eshana.*' The word comes out of her mouth like she's exaggerating a foreign accent. 'You're not a local cop?'

I shake my head. 'Not local.'

Technically, I've not lied. It's an old trick: convince someone you're a cop, they almost never ask for your badge. And even if they do, I simply flash my private investigator badge. No one really knows what they're looking at. It's not breaking the law until you explicitly state you're a police officer, or you wear a police uniform.

'Well, I have class,' Toni says, dropping the cigarette beneath the toe of her flat dancing shoe. She pulls a phone out of her bag. 'In fifteen minutes, and I'm setting up until then.'

'I won't keep you long.'

She looks at me with a hard glare, like she's the one interrogating me. 'What are you investigating anyway?'

'Just confirming a few things in the lead-up to the crash.'

'It was an accident, right? That's what the paper said.' She crosses her arms; the skin at the hinge of her elbows folds over the handles of the bag.

'It's something else,' I say. It could be true. I could be investigating Eshana Stiles's taxes for all Toni the dance instructor knows.

'Well, the clock is ticking. Come on.'

I follow her inside. If she's this short with someone she thinks is a cop, what is she like with the mothers and the kids? Do they call her Toni? Or Mrs Toni?

I smile at that. When you're young, only the coolest adults let you call them by their first name, or so I'd thought. Maybe that's how Dennis tricked me into liking him at first. *Call me Dennis. Mr Webb is my dad.*

Toni drops her bag near the stage, which is just a thick piece of polished fibreboard.

'So, Eshana was involved with the dance group?' I ask.

'Yeah, she helped out sometimes.' She uses a set of keys to open a cupboard at the back of the room, and wheels out a sound system. 'Not that I needed it. Mostly stopping and starting the music. She couldn't teach the kids anything I couldn't teach them myself.'

Is that bitterness in her tone, or is she just blunt?

'Right. So how did she get involved?'

'She's friends with Maggie's mom, Larissa, and came with her one day. Like I said, I didn't need her help. She'd talk to the girls sometimes. Bake slices and cookies. She helped with a fundraiser night to cover the costs of getting to the county dance competition. Larissa seemed to get on with her well – not that I let the mothers stick around while we practise.'

'You kick them out?'

'It's the rules. Eshana was different because she was impartial. She wanted all the girls to do well. Dance moms are overbearing.'

'And you have just the one class?'

She's finished setting up now and turns to face me, her fists resting against her hips. I notice a small tattoo on the back of her wrist. The lines have bled and softened but you can still see the winged shape of a cherub.

'Mondays and Wednesdays we have classes,' she says. 'Up to age eleven on Mondays and the older kids tomorrow. We don't have anyone over sixteen.'

I think about the missing girls again.

Toni plugs her phone into the speaker.

'So the girls compete?' I ask.

'Yeah, we compete. We've had a state-wide runner-up. Some excellent dancers come through those doors sometimes and leave even better.'

I make an approving sound in my throat. 'Must be a good teacher.'

She gives me a *don't-humour-me* look. 'I must be, huh.'

'In your dealings with Eshana, did she ever show signs of trouble at home?'

Now she looks right at me. Her eyeliner is thick and dark. She's in her forties and was probably a dancer once, but it's a little hard to imagine her floating around the room nowadays.

'No,' she says. 'Nothing like that. Not that she'd show it. She was – she *is* a private person about her home life. She mentioned once she had trouble sleeping but all I can say is she must love watching the girls dance, because it's a chore and she wasn't getting paid. She could have gone along with the mothers up to Gerald's for a drink instead, but she always wanted to stay and help. I find that nice, endearing even. I don't know if everyone saw it that way.'

Someone comes through the door. A woman with her daughter. The kids are arriving. I'm thinking about Eshana's trouble sleeping. Maybe she was so over tired she really did fall asleep at the wheel?

'She was drinking the night of the crash,' I say. 'Did you know her to be much of a drinker?'

She smiles now. 'Why don't you talk to Larissa about that? She's here for the older group.'

'I'll come back Wednesday. One last question.'

'Yeah? Make it quick.'

I swallow. I know this isn't my case but I've got to trust my instincts.

'Did, ah, did Kiara King or Maddison Stubbs ever come here? Or have anything to do with Eshana Stiles?'

There's an intensity about her gaze for a moment, then she lets out a full-throated smoker's cackle. 'I said make it quick. That one might take a while.'

'Give me the *Cliffs Notes* version.'

'The what's-it now?'

'Give me just the highlights of the story, if you can?'

'Look, it's not my place to go repeating rumours or lies. Larissa probably knows more about it than me. Just, one day, out of the blue, Eshana Stiles asked me about some girl who came to two or three classes a few years ago. It didn't mean a thing to me at the time – she just wanted to know why the girl stopped coming to class. I told her the girl's mom was sick and they couldn't afford the lessons.'

'She was asking about Kiara King?' I say.

'That's right. Then a month or two later, that girl goes missing.' She turns towards the kids waiting in the hall. 'Now if you don't mind, I have a class to teach.'

I leave, scooting past the parents lingering outside. They're all close to my age, so I don't make eye contact in case anyone recognises me.

Back at the car, I think about what I've discovered. Eshana asked about Kiara King. Tenuous as it is, I've found something linking them.

•

On my way to the hospital, I have to drive past Fenton Park. If I turn down the side road there and follow it long enough, I'll reach Stillhouse Road. And if I turn there, I'll pass my old house and it'll all come back.

Mom was depressed after Dad died, silent and weeping most of the time, until she picked herself up, made new friends and started to drink. On Fridays, she'd make me dinner, put the TV on, then go out and get back around midnight. I was always awake when her key scratched in the door, but I'd keep my eyes closed and let her kiss my forehead and wake me to go to bed. Doesn't matter how much time passes, I'll always associate the sweet smell of bourbon and coke with that old three-seater couch.

Looking back, I really don't blame her for going out and leaving me at home. A single woman, with little income, raising a son on her own in a rough part of town. You couldn't tell me at the time though. I resented the loneliness and began going out with my own friends, making trouble in the neighbourhood. The usual cliches associated with boredom in the nineties – throwing stones at passing trains, smoking weed stolen from someone's parents' stash, listening to pirated CDs of Korn, Slipknot, whatever.

One night, Mom got home extra late and she wasn't alone. Two voices outside the door, stage whispering, and the muffled laughter of giddy teenagers. After some time scratching around, Mom got the key in the lock and two people passed me by on the couch. Soon after came the knocking sounds from her room, then sometime later I heard the front door open. I lifted one eyelid to see the back of a tall red-headed man in a blue flannel. Then the door closed.

Mom came back out to the couch and I had to pretend to be asleep again but I'm sure she could see my cheeks burning with shame and a hint of rage. I managed to hide the tears, but she must have known. It's naïve to think she wouldn't move on from dad eventually.

A few weeks later, Dennis started coming to the house just to hang out. He'd bring a pack of Mondo, always grape flavour, and I'd drink his bribe and let him sit in Dad's spot on the couch and put the football on the TV, even though we were a hockey house.

Dennis took me to Fenton Park one afternoon to throw a football. It only happened once, early on when he was still making an effort. I must have been eleven or twelve. I'd crashed into puberty like the side of a brick outhouse, which meant I was big for my age and racked with acne. People were always mistaking me as an older kid. But Dennis still dwarfed me, and would do so for another few years. He liked to stand just far enough away that I could barely get the football to him. I don't know if it was to push me to become better, or to make him feel stronger. It was easy for him to launch the football right over my head with his long arms and huge hands.

Dennis and Mom were off and on for a few years. At first, when they quarrelled, I would sit in my room with the door closed, a pillow wrapped over my face and pressed to my ears. The arguing would grow louder, and I would squeeze tighter.

The first time Dennis hit her was a Friday night at around 1 am. I heard it – the unmistakeable meaty thump of a fist hitting flesh. It seemed to shake the foundations of the house.

Mom's howls probably woke the entire neighbourhood. We lived in the *good* part of Manson, near where my grandparents had lived, and the sounds of fighting weren't as common around there.

I rushed out into the hallway. I was fourteen, tall and strong for my age, but nothing compared to Dennis. We came face to face in the doorway to the kitchen and suddenly I was frozen, my feet turned to concrete.

Neither of us spoke. Dennis just grabbed his coat from the couch and left.

I went to Mom. She was mumbling like a baby, and her tears shined on her face in the light from the street. Her yellow sundress was torn and blood-spotted.

She hugged me close, squeezing me as if she was holding me together, when it was her who needed it most. I couldn't do anything to stop Dennis hurting her; I couldn't change a thing. So I just let Mom grip me against her and tell me it was okay.

But I knew things would get worse before they got better.

Then there was that Friday night two years later. They didn't go out that night. They didn't have the money, I guess. They sat in the kitchen with the radio up loud and they drank.

The anger started when Dennis spoke about Dad.

'Maybe there was no car. Maybe he just went out there and shot himself so he didn't have to deal with you.'

Hearing my mother's fake chuckle was even worse than his words. It was the type of strained laugh people use to mask their anger.

'Maybe his buddies in the police covered it all up,' Dennis added. 'Who knows?'

And things escalated from there; a pot boiling.

'What do you think, boy?' Dennis asked when I entered the room. I was sixteen by then, and as close to being a man as anyone else in my class.

'What?' I said.

'Don't,' Mom hissed.

I could see the cords in her throat. She was drunk and growing fierce. I knew trouble was only a few words away.

'He's a man now,' Dennis said. 'He can talk about this.'

'Stop it,' Mom said.

'Does he know you let me wear his medal? You should have more respect for your dead husband than that.'

I was getting something out of the fridge, but I couldn't move when I heard that. The police gave Mom and me that medal in honour of my father after he died. It was a precious thing; something I still have now. The idea of Dad's medal around that man's neck made me instantly sweat. I could feel the rage rising inside. Mom was even angrier.

When the police arrived sometime after midnight, they took one look at Mom and knew it was self-defence.

At the hospital, Dennis fell into a coma. He was pronounced dead three days later when his life support was switched off.

Mom was charged with manslaughter. It was easy enough for everyone to see why a woman like her would do it, at the end of her tether after being brutalised by an insecure man with anger issues. She spent twelve months in prison, with the second twelve months suspended. It could have been a lot worse for her. In most circumstances, that would have been murder.

I learnt then what the police will do to protect their own.

ESHANA
BEFORE

IT'S BEEN A month since that day I followed Oli and although my suspicions have allayed, they haven't disappeared entirely. The pizza, the hairclip. Was it really a cleaner who came to the house that day?

In the afternoon, I'm on the phone to my old college friend, Becky, when a call comes through from Oli's sister, Clare.

'Sorry, Becky, I better take this,' I say and head back to my study.

'Shanie,' Clare says, using the nickname she gave me, which I still cringe at. It's not that it's patronising, it's just the sound of it I hate. 'How are you, darling?'

'I'm well. And you?'

'Oh, you know, the same old. I dumped Eddie last week – he was a bit too attached.' She gives a flighty little laugh.

I don't mind Clare, despite her obvious self-consciousness. Some people just know exactly where they fit in the world; they follow the path that seems cut for them. She never left the city, unlike Oli. She stays close with their mother and has all her same friends from high school and college. She landed a role in real estate years ago and is now the director of the agency. Since her divorce, she has been very active on the dating scene.

'Back on the market then?' I tease. 'Who's next at the front of the queue?'

'I might stay single for a while,' she says. 'Men are all so sentimental in this city. They get attached and want to bend me to a shape that fits around them. I'm done with dating.'

'Who knows, the next one might be *the one*.'

'There's no such thing as *the one*, Shanie. I hate to break it to you.' I don't know how to respond but thankfully she continues. 'I mean, there's love, but there could be loads of suitable partners out there for me. Not necessarily just one. Besides, that's enormously depressing to think I have to find a needle in a haystack.'

'Well, I did,' I say.

A pregnant pause. Who will fill it?

I break first. 'So what else is new?'

'Not much, really. Mom's the same; she's always asking when you guys will visit. Henry has officially retired. He took his golden handshake and they spend most of their time up on the coast these days.'

It's been at least eighteen months since Oli saw his mother, and probably longer since he's seen Clare. They're only eighty miles away but whenever they offer to visit Oli says we're too busy.

He told me shortly before our wedding that there are things about his family he hates. They were all really close with his ex, and naturally nobody liked me much at all at first. Sometimes I wonder if that's ever changed. His mother and her husband left our wedding sometime between the ceremony and the reception. Their seats at the table remained empty, as glaring as a missing tooth. Oli never mentioned it and neither did I. But I didn't forget it.

He'd introduced me to them at a restaurant in the city. We stayed at a hotel, despite the fact there was room at his family home. The first thing I noticed when we arrived was the formality. Not the warm family reception you would expect. Then his mother said, 'So this is the new Annabel,' and I felt a rush of vertigo, like the entire room was spinning.

Oli simply said, 'That's not funny, Mom,' and I instantly understood why we weren't staying at his family home. He resented her and I could see why. She was mean.

That more or less set the tone for the evening. I floated on the surface of the conversation, aware of the strong undercurrents but never drawn into them. Clare was nicer to me than her mother was, but still mean to her brother. *Sibling rivalry*, I thought, but there was more to it than that.

After the dinner, I asked Oli, 'So they liked Annabel?'

'I'm so sorry,' he said. 'This is why I didn't want you to meet them.'

And then he'd told me the full story. The marriage was on its deathbed before I came along, but when he'd met me, that was when Oli pulled the trigger on it officially. But Annabel's parents were family friends, so all they saw was Oli breaking Annabel's heart, and they weren't impressed.

'So,' Clare says now, 'how is my brother? Still working like a madman?'

'He has been working late a lot,' I say.

'Has he now?' There's a teasing note in her voice. 'I've never understood that. Why would he still work? Why not just stay at home and write? Or go on endless holidays?'

Oli made his own money, which is also a point of contention with his family. It means he doesn't have to rely on them anymore, and part of me thinks that frustrates them. He has more than them now and can do whatever he wants without their approval.

'You know what he's like,' I say. 'Teaching and writing is his life.'

She sighs. 'Yeah. And how are *you*? How is work?'

'It's good. Nothing new to report.'

At that moment, the front door opens and Oli comes in. I turn to him with a smile, but he doesn't reciprocate. I see an angry bruise below his eye and a scratch on his forearm.

'Clare, can I call you back? Your brother's just stepped in the door.'

'Sure thing, darling. Speak soon.'

Oli's frowning at me. I feel a smack of heat at the base of my throat.

'You were talking to my sister.' He says it like an accusation.

'Yeah,' I say casually, following him into the kitchen from the entrance way. 'She was just checking in to see how we are. What have you done to your face?'

'Squash,' he says, tossing his keys on the bench.

When he gets closer, I see under the kitchen lights that the bruise is black and it pinches the corner of his eye closed.

'And your arm?'

'Erikson got a little too competitive.'

He drops his gym bag and work satchel, marches to the fridge, pulls out a cider and has twisted the cap off before the fridge door has closed. He chugs a third of it in one go.

'One of those days?' I say.

He looks at me without taking the bottle away from his mouth. 'So what did you tell Clare?'

'What do you mean?'

'You know I don't like you speaking with them.'

'I know,' I say. And he has good reason, but with my mom now gone, I feel like he'll regret it eventually if he doesn't reconcile with his family.

He drains the cider, gets another, then goes and falls on the couch. I can feel the frustration radiating off him. He's been drinking a lot more lately too.

'You had an early start again,' I say. 'Did you drop money off for Kiara?'

'No. I just had work to do. Did Clare have anything else to say or was she just mining gossip?' he asks.

'Just the usual. I don't think your sister is the bad guy here. Maybe you should visit her, or your mom, soon.'

'That isn't happening,' he says.

'She broke up with the guy she was seeing,' I tell him.

He pulls out his phone. 'Well, that's not surprising. She likes to lecture others on love but she's hardly an expert.'

'You're in a mood, Oli. Do you want me to run you a bath or make dinner?'

'Run me a bath? I'm not a child, Eshana.'

I squeeze my molars together. He's just had a bad day. No need to respond in kind.

'Well, what about dinner?' I try to keep my voice light.

'Yeah, takeaway?'

'I'll cook,' I say.

I go to the cupboard. My hand hovers over his gluten-free pasta, but instead I reach further. There's another packet right at the back that I accidentally bought months ago.

I cook, and we sit down across from each other at the round dining table. Oli scoops up a mouthful, and places it his mouth. I do the same but he doesn't swallow. I feel his eyes on me. I glance up as he spits it back out, then studies the plate closely.

'Where's the packet?' he asks.

'Sorry?'

'The packet? For the pasta. This doesn't taste like gluten-free.'

'Oh,' I say. 'It's in the bin. It was just one from the cupboard.'

He gets up from the dining table and strides from the room. When he returns he has the packet. He tosses it on the table.

'It's not gluten-free, Eshana. Where does it say gluten-free on the packet?'

'Oh my god, Oli. I'm so sorry. Did you get any down?'

'I ate enough for a reaction, I think. It could have been a lot worse.'

'What can we do?'

He looks down at the plate with contempt. I expect anger but it doesn't come. His voice is quiet.

'I'll be sick.' He sighs. 'I'll just have to drink lots of water and ride it out. Maybe I'll sleep in one of the guest rooms.'

'Oh, I'm such an idiot. I should have double-checked. But there's no need to sleep in another room, I can look after you.'

'You don't want me in bed beside you tonight,' he says. 'You have enough trouble sleeping as it is. I'll probably be up and down through the night.' Then he takes his plate to the kitchen and I hear him scraping it clean into the bin.

REID
NOW

'HOW DO YOU know her?' the young receptionist at the front desk asks.

I should have been expecting this, but I've been off my game since the run-in with Sticks. All the way to the hospital, whenever I checked the passenger-side wing mirror I was reminded of his warning. It wasn't until I was out of the Manson–Ethelton district and into the clean open air that I felt relaxed.

'She's my cousin,' I say. 'I just flew in last night – it's the first chance I had to get here.' I know she's in the ICU, and they might only be letting family through.

I stopped to buy flowers on the way and I lift them up a little, as if this confirms I know Eshana. I didn't buy them just for this reason; I bought them because it's the right thing to do.

'Where did you fly in from?' she asks, touching the screen in front of her, typing something in.

'Seattle. Landed, then drove up from the city.'

She looks up. 'She's in the intensive-care unit. Follow this hall around to your right, then take the elevator up to the third floor. Then through the doors and she's in room 301. Want me to repeat that?'

'Room 301. I think I'll manage. Thanks.'

She turns back to her computer.

Visiting hours at Pottsville General Hospital end at 8 pm so I have plenty of time. My shoes squelch on the linoleum floor as I stride along the corridor. The elevator gears hum like the filter in a fish tank.

As I enter the ward, I wonder if I'm the only one visiting Eshana Stiles today. If I bump into her family or friends while I'm here, the prepared backstory should suffice: I'm an old chum from college who read about the crash on the news.

I stroll by the nurses' station, staring straight ahead. I reach room 301 and find Eshana's name on the door chart. I gently press the door open.

She looks very thin beneath the sheet, but bodies change when they're kept still, even if it's been just a couple days. Atrophy sets in; nutrients are pumped directly into the stomach. Her right arm, in a cast, sits atop the sheet. Her face is pale, her eyes sunken. She's intubated, an apparatus is helping her breath and a peg is attached to the index finger of her left hand. Monitors hover like angels watching over her.

Well, she's not faking it, that's for sure.

The typical hospital cards sit beside the bed and a narrow glass vase is filled with carnations. I lay my flowers down on the bedside table and take a couple of quick photos of her on my phone. I don't feel great about it but it's part of the job – keeping records of everything gives me reference points to come back to and potential evidence if required.

Nothing at all stands out here, and I didn't expect it to. Her injuries are consistent with the crash. Head trauma, broken arm, cracked nose. Substantial bruising. If she does wake up, she's looking at millions of dollars in insurance payouts. *If* she wakes up. And if she doesn't and she's kept on life support for years, the bill for Crown will be even higher.

I read somewhere that the chances of waking up from a coma go down with every day that passes, especially in the first month. Patients who wake up usually do so between two to four weeks. But this is different. The doctors put her in a coma. Eshana can't have planned this; she almost died. So if it's an accident, if she was under the alcohol limit, if the car was in working condition, then from where I'm standing there's really no basis to deny any claims.

I check her charts. It's dense medical jargon but I take a photo anyway.

Then I read through the cards. A couple from friends, wishing her well. Toni's dance moms have all signed a big card.

The door swings open. 'Can I help you?' someone says.

I freeze, then turn slowly to the nurse who has entered the room.

'Hi,' I say, lowering my voice, swinging for deep sadness while I slip my phone back into my pocket. *Did she see me take the pictures?* 'Just visiting.'

'Relative?' she asks.

'Cousin.'

She checks the monitors and makes some notes on the charts at the foot of the bed.

'I'm sorry,' she says. I can't tell if she's just affecting sadness but it's convincing.

'How is she looking?' I ask. 'I just hope she pulls through.'

'She's doing well, all things considered.'

As she goes to leave, I say, 'Can I ask you something?'

She turns back at the door. 'Sure.'

'I was hoping to catch Eshana's mother-in-law. Do you know if she's visited?'

'There's been a blonde woman coming every day, but she seems young,' she says.

'Right.' I make a mental note. I wonder if this could be the woman at the house? Oliver has a sister too. 'What time did she come today?'

She glances down at her watch. 'I guess it was around lunchtime. She probably left at one.'

'Thanks. Hopefully I'll catch her tomorrow then.'

After the nurse has gone, I notice something about Eshana's left hand. It probably means nothing, it's probably just something that happened when she was having her MRI, but I can't help noticing that where her wedding band should be there's no ring.

•

Later, after I've stopped in at the motel and sent my notes off to Sarah at Crown, I head back out. It's 10.14 pm. By the time I get to the restaurant, The Pearl, it should be about the same time Oliver and Eshana Stiles left the night of the crash.

I drive through Manson, heading towards Ethelton.

The bridge hums below my car. Starting from the restaurant, I recreate the Stileses' drive home. No traffic, but it is a Monday; they were out on a Wednesday. It was also raining that night.

There are a few sets of lights on the drive. I come up beside the town hall and continue on toward the Boulevard. I follow the curve of the road towards the cafe. The streets are empty in the heart of Ethelton. A light fog has settled in, making ghostly orbs of the streetlights.

As I get close to the cafe, I check the time: it's barely ten minutes' drive without any traffic and I kept close to the speed limit the entire way.

Slowly approaching now, I realise the road isn't straight leading up to the lights. The car would veer off the other side of the road if I stopped steering, even for a few seconds. The sleep theory doesn't make sense, especially when you consider the confrontation that happened at the restaurant just before they left. Adrenaline is about ten times better than caffeine at keeping you awake.

So what else? The way the vehicle hit and the angle of the approach means the car must have turned late, less than twenty yards before the intersection. A fight in the car? A raccoon or even a deer rushing onto the road? Or maybe Oliver grabbed the wheel?

Suicide is possible, but nothing in Eshana Stiles's personal life points at that outcome, other than some antidepressants in the bathroom. Half this country is on the same class of drugs so it's not a strong indicator of suicide.

As I come up beside the cafe at the lights, I see someone on the corner. My senses are firing. I don't turn to look, but keep them in my periphery, focusing on their movement. When the lights change, I continue on, circle the block and come back around, my headlights off. I pull over and kill the engine.

The person is squatting down near the crash site. A black hoodie hides their face. *What are they doing?*

They rise from the sidewalk, go to the memorial flowers at the base of the fallen power pole, swivel their head left then right, and stomp down hard on the flowers. The figure bends at the waist, as if to spit on the ground, then marches off.

I wait a moment before starting the car and driving towards the intersection. I stop at the red light and watch the hooded figure walking towards a Jeep parked a little further along. They climb in and set off towards me as the light goes green. It's white, a Wrangler, but the glare of the headlights keeps me from seeing the person behind the wheel.

The Jeep flies past me. I go through the lights and swing the car around to follow. This is a lead I can't lose.

The light goes amber, but I press the car on, shifting through the gears, needing to see who felt compelled to deface the memorial. I give it a lot of gas, but the Jeep has disappeared around the bend and this old Camry hasn't got the guts to keep up. I press the accelerator to the floor but still I can't see any tail-lights. They've turned off or parked up.

It's not worth getting pulled over.

I slow down and mute the radio to focus on the road ahead. I find one empty straight after another, before giving up and turning back towards Manson. It was probably just a disgruntled local, but you never know.

On my way back, I stop at a gas station. The supermarket is closed so this is my only option to get what I need.

The girl behind the counter takes a piece of gum from her mouth and drops it in a bin under the counter as I walk by her.

'Evening,' she says.

'Hi.' I find some overpriced toothpaste in an aisle.

'We're closing in five, just so you know.'

I circle the island of shelves at the centre of the store. 'Where are the painkillers hiding?'

'They're back here by the cigarettes. Mr Horner moved them. Kids have been stealing them.'

'*Stealing* them?' I ask, approaching the counter.

'Yeah, that's what he said. I caught one of them once.' A self-conscious smile climbs up her face. I notice she has a wine-stain birthmark on her neck. 'They take them for fun,' she adds.

They're not going to get a buzz from paracetamol. I put the tooth-paste on the counter. She reaches under the Perspex divider and scans it.

Eyeing a pack of Advil, I shoot it with my finger. 'Advil extra strength, please. And you can be dead sure I'm not taking them for fun.'

The girl drops her gaze, her smile slipping. 'No, I didn't—'

I take pity on her. 'Tell me, is there a drugstore on this side of town?' I could just google it. I'm being friendly.

'It won't be open now,' she says.

'I know that.'

'Hayes Drugstore is near the primary school on the corner. Otherwise, Ethelton has a drugstore about twenty minutes away. They won't be open either.'

'Thanks,' I say. 'You at Manson High or over in Ethelton?'

She looks up again, reading me. 'Manson High. You from round here?'

'No. But I was a while ago. Manson High myself, actually.'

I place the cash on the counter and she reaches under the divider and counts it.

'Is Mrs Belfour still there?' I say.

'I had her for English last year.'

I laugh. 'She must be about seventy by now.'

'Probably,' she says with a smile and hands over my change.

'Take care,' I say.

Outside, moths beat about the lone fluorescent streetlight and knock against the glass shopfront.

There's another car beside mine; I notice a woman in her fifties resting a book on the steering wheel. She's sitting too stiffly, like she wants to look over at me but can't.

As my gears crunch into reverse, I see the girl in the gas station place a fresh piece of chewing gum in her mouth. She picks up a mobile phone, starts scrolling.

The woman in the car is looking into the store now. She raises her wrist and taps it with her index finger.

The girl waves back, her fingers splayed as if to say, *Five minutes*.

ESHANA
BEFORE

AT THE CLINIC, I sit in a chair, squeezing the ball in my hand and watching the bag fill with my blood. The nurses know me by name now. My mom was O negative and I am too, which means my blood is compatible with all others but I can only receive donor blood from other O negatives.

It's quiet here today and the nurses are chatting while I fill the bag with blood.

'The exact same thing happened to Amanda Marley,' one of them says. 'A poor girl in a bad neighbourhood disappears, then turns up out of town dead.'

'What?' I say.

'Oh, just in the news today. A girl from Manson has been reported missing.'

I feel a pressure in my stomach.

'How long ago?' I ask.

'What?'

'When did she disappear?'

'I think the news said last night. Probably a runaway,' the nurse says.

'What's her name?'

'I can't remember exactly. She's a Manson girl.'

'Are you okay, honey?' the other nurse says to me. 'You're a little blue. You're almost finished, let me get you some water and a snack.'

'I'll be okay,' I say. 'I'm going to a cafe from here.'

She hands me a bottle of water. 'At least have a drink.'

As I sip, she removes the needle. I wait for ten minutes before walking back to my car, then wait five more minutes to let the mild nausea clear before turning on the ignition.

I call Larissa as I drive. 'Sorry, I'm running a few minutes late. Had a moment at the blood clinic.'

'Are you sure you're okay? We can always raincheck on lunch.'

'No, I need to eat and we haven't caught up properly in a while. I won't be long.'

•

It's quiet inside the cafe and the waiter comes over straight away to take our orders.

'Afternoon, ladies. Coffees?'

'Cappuccino, please, two sugars,' I say.

'I'll take the same with one sugar,' Larissa adds.

I spy a newspaper on the neighbouring table and reach over to get it. The disappearance is on the front page. When I see the photograph, my blood stops pumping through my veins. It's a photo of Kiara in the paper. She's the missing girl.

I feel such an intense heat in my cheeks that I'm convinced for a second I will cry.

'Excuse me,' I say to Larissa.

I head to the bathroom and hold myself up over the basin, staring into the mirror, trying to settle my breath.

It doesn't mean anything, I tell myself. I know Oli, I know his heart. He wouldn't hurt someone. It's not in him. And Kiara hasn't necessarily been hurt at all. She might be a runaway, like the nurse said. He was at home last night anyway. Another voice in my head. *He wasn't beside you, how can you be sure he didn't sneak out?* He was sick, I remind myself.

'Okay,' I say softly. 'Okay. You're fine.'

I drag my thumb over each of the bags under my eyes, exhale, then head back out to the cafe.

'Sorry,' I say, sitting down with a smile.

'What is it?' Larissa says. 'Has something happened?'

'No,' I say. 'I'm still a little woozy from giving blood.'

She leans over the table towards me. 'You would tell me if there was anything wrong, wouldn't you? If you had . . .' She pauses, shaking her head a little as if she's not sure what she's saying. 'If you had issues at home maybe?'

I look her in the eye, then let my gaze roam over her face and up to the big sunglasses in her beautiful blonde bob. 'Of course. And we're fine at home. That's definitely not it.'

Larissa is the closest I have to a real friend in this town. I tried to fit in, to meet people, but I've always felt judged, or like people are judging Oli. Sometimes I think we're socially repellent, despite my husband's charisma.

'Okay,' Larissa says. 'Well, you know the story of Nic Wojcik, right?'

The name is familiar, but I don't know why. 'What did he do?'

'He grew up rich and thought he could do what he wanted. He got into drugs and started dating a girl from Manson, Amanda Marley. It's the same old story – lots of booze and dope, and he got abusive. One day, they had a fight, she broke up with him, and he dragged her to his car and took her up to his family's holiday home in the mountains.' She exhales. 'Anyway, the police found her at the house, she's got signs of abuse, but the kid gets off. She doesn't want to get back with him so he does it again a few weeks later.

Only this time, when they find her . . .' She pauses. 'Well, she was dead. He choked her.'

I feel a chill and can barely swallow. 'That's awful.'

'He's dead now too, thank god. It's a horrible story, but that's why the town gets on edge when a girl goes missing.'

'The police couldn't arrest him the first time?' I ask.

She rolls her eyes. 'That's a whole other story. The police in this town aren't the sharpest tools in the shed. Here's hoping you or I never need them.' She flaps her hand at her face as if fanning herself.

'How did he die?' I ask. 'The Wojcik guy?'

'The police shot him. He'd been holed up out there for a few days with the girl's body. The journalists had a field day as you can imagine. The police messed up the investigation the first time, that's why he was still free.'

'Well, it's different this time,' I say. 'Wojcik is dead and the girl's probably just run away.'

'You know how people like to talk, Eshana. I just hope she's out there somewhere safe. I hope it's not all happening again.'

After lunch with Larissa, I head to the town hall for dance class.

Oli, I think, my chest filling with an uneasy guilt. *Could you be involved in this? Could I have stopped it?*

REID

NOW

THE CAFE IS packed. I suppose I had the same plan as everyone else there: I saw the news about the vandalism of the memorial and decided to get a closer look. Someone has sprayed *CROOK* just beside the flowers. I'd missed it in the dark the night before and only saw it when I opened the website for the *Ethelton Herald* this morning. It's clear someone didn't like Oliver Stiles very much. It must have been the hooded figure in the Jeep.

At the cafe, with all the buzz around me, I feel exposed. I find a seat and open my laptop.

At the bottom of the news story is a call to action. *Phone the Manson Police if you noticed anyone acting suspiciously last night on the corner of the Boulevard and Main.*

I doubt the PD will receive many calls, and even if they do, I doubt there'll be much in the way of an investigation. In the end, it's just graffiti.

What does it mean for me though? Whoever it was I saw last night may hold the key to the investigation.

I go through the facts of the case again, poking at the soft spots like irritating a bruise. A woman falls asleep at the wheel of her car; no, not a *fact*, a possibility. A woman crashes her car, killing her husband and putting herself in hospital. The point of contact was slightly on her husband's side. Now someone has gone to the site of the crash and defaced the memorial, calling him a crook. An assertion that isn't reflected in his criminal history.

Could the car's brakes have been tampered with? Unlikely but possible. The police don't believe a crime was committed, so they must have assessed the working order of the car. If they suspect Eshana drove into the pole on purpose, would that change things? Would they have investigated more?

I'll call around the junkyards again today. Hopefully the car hasn't already been scrapped.

I feel like the clues are disappearing the more time that passes.

Out on the street, someone is setting up cones to divert traffic. Parked up near the police tape is a truck with the words *Graffiti Busters* on the side. A portly man stands with his hands on his hips, looking down at the painted word. He speaks with a police officer, then pulls a face mask on, unreels a hose from the truck and starts spraying the sidewalk.

The waiter from my previous visit is serving a table nearby. Someone else, an older woman, is helping out too today.

'Back again,' the waiter says, catching sight of me. 'Eating in or just coffee?'

'I'll have a bite too,' I say. 'Busy?'

He rolls his eyes.

'You should be happy – good for business.'

'Oh, my boss will be happy,' he says, with a smile. I wonder if he realises how sexy that smile is. 'It's like they're expecting some action out there.' He nods at the people at the outside tables.

'The action was last night apparently,' I say.

A woman hails him from her seat near the entrance. 'I'll get you a menu,' he tells me and starts towards her.

I drag my laptop closer, lower my cap and get to work. I need to be at the hospital in the middle of the day to figure out who is visiting Eshana, but then again it's out of town and I have so much investigating to do here. However, the hospital visitor might be the beneficiary of any life insurance policy. Depending on the payout, would it be enough motivation to tamper with the car?

I also need to speak to Oliver's ex-wife, Annabel. I wonder if there is still bad blood between them.

I go back to the initial reports of Oliver Stiles's death and see that the coverage was deeply sympathetic, as you would expect. I read the comments section: all express sadness, with one suggesting the speed limit should be lower along the Boulevard. Any negative comments would probably have been removed by the moderators.

After my coffee and omelette, I notice the cafe's quietened down. The waiter stands just inside the door, leaning against the frame and watching the world outside.

I look past him to where the graffiti removalist is squatting to review his morning's work. Across the road at the memorial, there's another cop, not a regular one. He's got greying hair, a heavy, serious brow and thick hair-covered forearms. I'd recognise him anywhere even after a decade. *Stubbs.* He might have walked down from his home. Why is the chief of police here for a crime like this, especially given the situation with his daughter? No one would blame him for taking time off. Then again, if he is on leave, he'll still be investigating his daughter's disappearance. If Stubbs is anything like he was when I was on the force, he'll be out there searching day and night.

When the waiter comes over to collect my plate and top up my coffee, I ask, 'Any updates on all that? Must be important with the police here.'

'Someone said they've found footprints. I see about fifty people walk along here every morning, so I don't know what use footprints are.'

'Is it a big deal? We're talking about upsetting public decency – that's the crime, right? A bit of graffiti strikes me as low priority given the situation with the missing girl.'

He gives me an odd look. 'Why do you know so much about the police?'

'Watch a lot of cop shows.'

He smiles. 'Sure thing.'

There's something in that smile, something warm and flirty. I believe it for a split second before reminding myself I'm on the wrong side of forty, greying and not in the best shape. *Whatever you are seeing in him, it's what you want to see*, I tell myself.

'Feels like this town is going to shit,' the waiter adds.

'I'm sure it's always felt that way,' I say.

His tongue rolls around beneath his top lip, and I can't read his expression. Is he offended or just trying to figure me out?

'I just mean, most people feel like things are always getting worse,' I say. 'Even when they're just the same. Young women have been targeted by men forever, and people have died in car crashes since we decided vehicles were a better mode of transport than horses.'

I smile, swinging for humour, but I miss.

'Maybe you're right,' he says and goes to serve other customers.

I turn back to my laptop and build the links again in my mind: the school uniform; Eshana asking Toni about Kiara; the crash and the disappearances of the two girls.

I'll have to head up to Sandown College this afternoon too. And I need to work out who owns that white Jeep I saw last night.

I look back at Chief Stubbs on the corner. He's talking to another cop now, his hands on his hips. He's still as tall and strong as an NFL linebacker, but it looks like his jaw's softened a little over the last decade.

Stubbs starts across the road towards the cafe. I cast about for an alternate exit but there isn't one.

He comes in, his big frame jostling between chairs and diners. I rest my face against my hand and look away out the window. *Ignore him,* I tell myself. *He can't recognise you from there.*

He gets to the counter and I hear his voice as he orders two coffees.

When I turn back, it's to find him staring at me with those same scrupulous, canny grey eyes. It feels like I'm looking at a bull ready to charge. A tired, run-down bull, but a bull nonetheless.

But then something miraculous happens. His eyes move on to something else. He doesn't recognise me with the hat, the glasses, the stubble. He must know I'm in town. Sticks would have told them all.

He turns back to the counter and picks up the coffees. Then he heads back out to the street and is gone.

•

When I get to the hospital, a nurse advises me the daily visitor, whoever she is, has been and gone. I've wasted almost an hour driving out there and back. Next I head to the college. The Sandown campus is on the other side of the river, twenty minutes north of Manson. When I was growing up, it was one of those places that had a sort of esteem about it. Everyone just called it 'the college', and no one I knew had anything to do with the place. It might as well have been on the other side of the planet.

The first time I went there was when I was a cop: we often had call-outs to the campus and the student accommodation nearby – usually for parties that had swollen beyond the seams of the dorm rooms and spilled into the streets, too big for the campus security to handle. There was a sizeable file on sexual assault accusations too, but almost no convictions. I'd like to think things have changed in the past decade.

Heading in that direction is a different experience altogether now. First, I pass Bakers Creek vineyard, then further out of town there's a small roadside church and an old-timey bed and breakfast that would make the perfect setting for a horror film. When I turn off the main road towards the college, it emerges like a temple on a hill, looking over the town. Residential streets give way to the open land surrounding the college as a sort of moat to keep the world outside.

I park against the curb and decide to walk in through the front gates instead of parking on campus. Turning up in a police uniform meant every door would open for me. Now I'll have to be slightly more strategic. I could put on a hard hat and a fluoro vest, as if I'm a worker checking out smoke alarms or undertaking general maintenance, but that's just as likely to attract attention as deflect it.

What's the worst that could happen? I tell them the truth and they ask me to leave.

The campus is a sort of mini metropolis, much more bustling than anywhere else in the twin towns, with coffee shops, a book-store and various types of accommodation all within the broader boundaries of the college.

Students move about between the buildings with the industrial efficiency of a hive, some riding scooters and skateboards, most wearing hoodies, with bags and satchels slung low. It won't be long before the Christmas break arrives.

With the same sense of purpose as some of the students around me, I stride across the vast open space toward the arts department. I could be a mature-aged student. Or a teaching assistant.

Once inside, I flick my gaze towards the security guard near the door, before continuing deeper into the building. One of the rooms sucks up most of the students in the hallway but I continue on, trying doors and finding them all locked. I don't see Oliver Stiles's name on any of them anyway.

I emerge from the building near a gym and a series of basketball courts. Someone comes out of the gym and I grab the door and slip inside. I look around at table-tennis tables, squash courts, basketball courts. Outside, through the glass, I can see tennis courts too. There's a wall of lockers. And a weights room where people are working out.

I leave and go back into the main building, eyeing all those dark wooden doors as I pass. A guy wearing slacks, a knit and glasses looks friendly enough so I stop him by raising my hand.

'Hi,' I say. 'I don't know if I'm in the right spot – I'm trying to find the creative-writing department.'

He clears his throat. 'There's not a department per se, but you're more or less in the right spot. Are you looking for your class?'

'Are the offices for the tutors and lecturers around here?'

'No,' he says, his brow lowering. 'End of the corridor and turn right, then you'll find the arts faculty offices on both the ground floor and upstairs.'

'Thanks,' I say, going to leave, but he stops me with his voice.

'Who in particular are you hoping to see?'

Shit. I should have prepared for this. I turn back slowly. 'Oh, no one, I'm just meeting my partner. He's been chatting with one of his tutors.'

His expression doesn't change when he says, 'Well, good luck finding them.'

I can feel his eyes on me as I go. I try to walk slowly, keeping the internal tension from reaching my limbs.

Following his directions, I come to another series of doors, only these don't have room numbers, just names. Names with titles after them.

There's nothing on the ground floor so I go upstairs.

A woman passes and gives me a warm smile. I nod in return. Then I see his name on a black tile: *Oliver Stiles MFA.*

I glance around. A couple come up the stairs and walk past me. When they've gone, I try the door. Unsurprisingly, it's locked. I could come back at night, but that would be more suspicious. Security would have fewer people to focus on. I have to be quick.

I reach into my back pocket for my lockpicking kit. My heart is already racing, thinking about the consequences of getting caught. If I'm lucky, the college will deal with me themselves, kick me out with a warning. If I'm unlucky, they'll call the Manson PD.

I look at the lock: it's precisely what I was expecting. I try the bump key first. A quick no-fuss entry is what I want. It slides in; I bump and turn. It doesn't go the first time. I don't want it to be too loud – I can hear footsteps on the stairs. I try once more; this time the cylinder turns. I pull the handle down just as someone reaches the top of the stairs. I slip inside, closing the door silently behind me.

From photos I've seen, Oliver Stiles was kind of hot, with nice arms and sharp green eyes. Not my type, but it's clear he looked after himself. He wasn't your typical academic in the looks department, but apparently he was when it came to the chaotic nature of his workspace. The desk is cluttered with papers, pens, Post-it notes.

The view through the blinds is over the expanse in the middle of the buildings, where I see more students. Some sitting on the grass in the sun; others moving about silently.

Time to get to work.

The bookshelf is full, and I've only heard of a few of the titles. I sit down at the desk and scan through everything before me, trying not to change the order of the papers too much. It looks like he was in the process of marking essays.

I gently slide out the desk drawers. Pens and stationery in the top drawer. More of the same in the next one. In the bottom drawer I see a book, and beneath it are stacks of notes. I scan through a few layers and realise they're all from his classes, like the papers on his desk.

Then I see something else. A couple of small bright-green thumb drives with *Ethelton College* on the side. I shove them in my pocket.

I turn the computer on, but when I'm prompted to enter a password, I realise I can't get any further.

I check the in and out mail stacks. The out stack is empty. Atop the in stack is a bank statement addressed to Oliver Stiles. Odd that he'd have it sent here. Especially when he's received one at his house too.

I search a filing cabinet in the corner and find a file full of bank statements, all addressed to him at the office. A couple of years' worth.

The office door swings open. My heart freezes.

A young woman is standing there, looking just as shocked as me.

'You're not supposed to be in here,' she squeezes out. 'Who are you?'

'Me?' I say, stepping slowly towards her. She shrinks back. 'I'm . . . ah, just leaving actually.'

She turns to let me pass, scared I suppose that I will just charge into her if she doesn't. I fold the file of bank statements and shove it down the back of my jeans.

As soon as I'm out of sight, I strip out of the bomber jacket I'm wearing and shove it in a bin. I take off the red cap and drop it behind a seat.

I'm moving quickly now. She'll definitely call security, describe me; then they'll probably check CCTV footage. Share it with the police. It's all racing through my mind as I pace towards the exit.

Right at the door, the security guard swings a hand out, blocking my way. I turn, scanning for another exit.

'Hey,' he says, and I see he's pointing at the ground behind me. 'Dropped something.'

I turn back and see the file on the ground with the statements spilled out. I stoop, push them all back inside and clutch the file to my chest.

'Thanks,' I say as I pass the guard.

When I get outside, far enough away from the doors, I begin to run, a light jog at first, then a little faster. I get to my car, drop into the driver's seat and floor it back to Manson with an arm full of bank statements and two green thumb drives.

ESHANA
BEFORE

TONI SENDS ME to work with a knot of dancers while she takes the rest.

I don't know what attracted me to volunteering at the school. I get the sense the dance moms think I'm odd. Most of them grew up around here and have known each other forever. Larissa's the only one who took to me; she moved out here with her husband just a few years before us. It's different for her though – her daughter goes to school with the other kids. She's known them for much longer. I do what I can and block out the backhanded compliments and those looks they seem to think I miss.

Towards the end of class, the mothers gather near the entrance and I hear them talking about the missing girl. Toni doesn't like them waiting in the hall, but we've run a few minutes over time and it's raining outside.

I try to just focus on the task at hand, but I think I hear the name Kiara King. Everyone knows it's her.

•

When I get home, Oli's waiting for me in the living room, staring out the window. Classical music comes from the speakers in the ceiling. He has a glass of something strong in his hand and a small book of short stories open face down on the couch.

'Eshana.' He says it like a sigh. 'How was your day?'

The lack of buoyancy in his voice makes it sound like he's reading a script for a conversation.

'It was fine,' I say. 'I gave blood this morning. Then had lunch with Larissa.' I swallow. 'Did you see the news today?'

He looks up at the ceiling as if watching the music coming through the speakers. *Chopin*, I think. One of those flighty waltzes.

'About Kiara? I saw it. I was going to call you. I've been worried sick all day. Apparently, she's run away.'

I just nod. He speaks again.

'I'll call the police in the morning and tell them what I know.'

'And what is that?'

He looks at me again. 'I know she was afraid of her brother. He's a drug user – he'd make up stories about her and would steal things. That's why he was kicked out. She once told me she wanted to run away.'

'She told you that?' I say.

'She did. She chats to me on our drives out to her grandmother's place.'

'Well, maybe you should call the police then. But there's no need to wait until the morning, is there? Her family will be worried sick. Your information could help find her.'

This seems to surprise him. He takes another sip from his drink. 'I suppose it could.' Then, 'No, it's already late.'

'But why—'

He slams his glass down on the coffee table and looks me in the eye. 'Eshana, I said I'll call in the morning.'

'Please,' I say. 'The family will be going through hell.' I hold out my phone, but he looks away. 'Just call them, Oli. They'll understand.'

He exhales and eyes the phone in my hand. 'Cops don't like people like me – you realise that? From the city, with money, an academic. I'm sure they'll think I had something to do with it, but I was at home all night with you. Wasn't I?'

I nod. But I can't be certain. How can I? He was in the spare room, and for once I actually slept well. I could hear him heaving at one point in the night, and I went to help him. But from about midnight until five or six in the morning I managed to sleep. I realise he's still watching me, waiting for a stronger affirmation.

'Yeah,' I say. 'I remember.'

He reaches out and takes the phone, he searches for the number for the Manson PD and makes the call.

The cops arrive late, after we've eaten, not that either of us can stomach much. It was obvious Oli was just moving the food around his plate with his fork. He might still be sick; it takes a while for the inflammation to go down. Or maybe he's nervous about this visit from the police. What if he really does have something to hide?

He shows the two cops through to the sitting room with the open fire. It's just coals now. It's warm enough though, despite the wind beginning to howl through the trees.

'We won't keep you longer than we need to,' one of the cops says as they take seats on the chesterfield. Oli sits in the armchair.

I want to listen, but I don't want to impose. 'I'll just be through here,' I tell them, walking into the kitchen.

As soon as I've closed the door, I rush around to the other door into the sitting room, leaning with my ear pressed to the wood.

It is all routine to begin with: Oli's name, how he knows Kiara, when was the last time he spoke to her.

'The moment I heard it was her, I knew I needed to call you,' he lies. 'I needed to speak to you tonight.'

'And why is that?'

'Because I'd been paying for her mother's treatments. She's unwell, cancer, and they're not in the best financial position. Kiara is a very clever young woman, and I didn't want her to lose her mom to an illness that can be helped with treatment.'

'So you just paid her and expected nothing in return?'

'That's precisely how charity works, officer.' I can hear the note of annoyance in Oli's voice. 'My wife and I are very fortunate to have some measure of economic security and we give to a number of charities. I'm happy to share further details on how much we give. And that's what it was with Kiara's mom. I just wanted to do something to help.'

'And you spoke to Kiara regularly?'

'Yeah, I guess I'd call it mentoring. We chatted. That's why I called you. She was afraid of her brother. She couldn't keep cash in the house in case he turned up.'

'Kiara feared her brother?'

'Oh yes. He's a drug addict, a thief, a compulsive liar. He used to follow her and intimidate her. She mentioned to me that she wanted to run away, but she was staying for her mom.'

'Kiara told you she would run away?'

'Yes, a number of times.'

'Have you got any communication you can share – messages, emails, anything like that?' the cop asks.

Something comes to me; something I heard somewhere. *Cops always know who's guilty, but they can't do anything unless the evidence is there.*

'No,' Oli says. 'It was just on the phone or in person that we spoke. I might have the occasional text message, I'll go back and check. I think the brother could have had a violent streak at times too.'

'So Kiara told you she wanted to run away, but she also wanted to support her mother. Did she mention where she might go?'

'No. She was a good writer though, and she did say she had dreams of screenwriting. So my guess would be LA. Or maybe Vancouver – they've got a good film scene up there. I'm speculating; she never gave me a destination.'

'Was there anything else she told you that might help?'

'Nothing else really springs to mind,' Oli says. 'But you can be sure if I remember anything else I'll be in touch.'

After they've left, we get ready for bed in near silence. I can read my husband; I know when he's carrying a burden.

'I hope she turns up,' I say when we're in bed. I reach out and place my hand on his chest, but he removes it.

'Sorry,' he says. 'I just don't feel like being touched.'

'Oli . . . you would tell me if there was more to this story?'

He sucks his lips, stares up at the ceiling. 'There's not. I told you and the police everything. As far as I know, she ran away. If you tell the world you're doing something good, then you're just virtue signalling. But if you do it privately, people think you *must* have something to hide.'

'But Kiara's missing, Oli. That's why I'm asking. I don't care what happened, you just need to help if you can. Her mom must be so worried'

'Her mom didn't care about her, Eshana. Yes, she's sick, but she didn't care, really.'

Didn't. Not *doesn't.*

'All her kids are running around looking after themselves,' he continues. 'That's just how it is. Wherever Kiara ran away to, I'm sure it will be less burdensome and at least she'll have a chance at a good life.'

I take my melatonin, and play a podcast via my headphones. I don't fall asleep though. I lie there for some hours thinking about Kiara King.

REID
NOW

At the motel, I check the thumb drives and find them both empty. What was I expecting, a confession? Next I read through the bank statements. There's got to be a reason they were sent to Oliver's office and not his home. It might be innocent. Maybe he bought his wife gifts from this account and didn't want her to see the cost. Or this account could be for his work expenses. Then again, it could be something else.

It's a cheque account that floats between twenty and thirty thousand dollars. It's all pretty standard: dry-cleaning, groceries, Netflix. Nothing over a few thousand transferred in or out.

I continue on down the list. There's a payment of nine hundred dollars to American Airlines made just a week before the crash. That's interesting. I take a photo and upload it.

I methodically work through all of the bank statements, losing faith that I'll find anything else. Then something sticks out. Five months ago, Oliver withdrew five thousand dollars in cash. Then again, a month earlier. I go back further and find more regular withdrawals: five thousand dollars, the same day every month.

And there's another regular payment that started almost a year ago: ninety-nine dollars and ninety-nine cents to SBFU Holdings. A one-hundred-dollar subscription.

I search SBFU Holdings and excitement swells in my chest. I could almost laugh. This is it – I've found it.

Sugar Babies For You – Connecting beautiful young women with sugar daddies.

It's a service used mostly by wealthy men to find young, often vulnerable women. No, maybe not *all* vulnerable. Some may just need money, or need the thrill of being wined and dined. It's a different form of sex work: companionship without the strings. The arrangement is simple: wealthy men provide financial support for younger women. They take them out, buy them things, or just have them on the payroll. In exchange, the men get company, photos and videos, and often sex too. Powerful men have always done this in one form or another, but websites like SBFU give them easier access to many more willing participants.

I wonder how much this sort of thing costs. I suspect the monthly subscription keeps a profile active. Could that be where the five thousand dollars goes every month? Did Oliver Stiles have a sugar baby and was he paying her cash?

The flights booked via the cheque account might be for her as well. Assuming that's what he purchased from American Airlines a few days before the crash.

•

In the car park, I go to Sugarbabies4u.com and start an account. It's simple enough. I lift a photo from a random Facebook page, change the colour and mirror the picture so it won't show up in a reverse image search. I make up a name, and when the website asks me to enter my net worth, I click the button for $5–10 million, increasing my net worth by at least ten fold. I add a value of what

I'm looking to spend on my sugar baby. It's entirely transactional: everything is based on a price, everything is measured in dollars.

Soon enough, I'm prompted to add a credit card to my account and either pay the monthly subscription or buy 'credits' to start interacting. That's not why I'm here. I close the prompt and start searching. There are so many photos, so many profiles, so many young women looking to meet someone who can help pay their bills, or tuition, or anything. This is a function, not a bug, of capitalism – literally selling yourself to pay for essentials.

I narrow the search down by setting the age at 18–21. It doesn't go any lower than eighteen, but judging by some of the profile photos I'd say there are under-eighteens on here. Then I shorten the radius to ten miles. The field narrows right down to sixteen sugar babies. I scroll through them slowly, checking every profile photo for a recognisable face.

I go out further. At thirty miles – as soon as the college campus is included in the search criteria – there are dozens of profiles. It occurs to me now that if Oliver Stiles was using this website, he could have encountered young women who work or study where he worked. What are the ethical implications of that?

I don't see Kiara anywhere on the website, but of course she could have taken the profile down. I reverse the process, this time setting up an account as a young woman and checking which men are on here. Unsurprisingly, there are many more profiles for men but far fewer have profile photos, although their net worth is listed, along with what they're looking for. I don't see any profiles that match Oliver's persona.

The lead runs cold, but it's all revealing a bigger picture of marital issues.

I wonder if he did the same thing to his ex? Maybe that's the source of the animosity and why their divorce ended up in the courts. I find the ex-wife's interior design business details online – there's a phone number listed. I call it. It's almost five o'clock and I don't expect an answer but then a voice comes down the line.

'Stiles Interiors, Jasmine speaking.'

'Hi,' I say. 'I was hoping to speak to Annabel.'

'Sure, can I ask who's calling?'

'My name is Vince Reid, and I'm investigating the death of her ex-husband.' It's the nuclear option, but it's a good way to bypass the gatekeeper.

'Oh, right. I'll put you through now.'

A moment later, Annabel is on the line.

'Hello,' she says.

'Annabel, I'm just calling to speak with you about your ex-husband Oliver.'

It only occurs to me now that she might not be aware that Oliver is dead. That is until she speaks.

'Oh sure,' she says. 'It's so tragic what happened.'

'It is.'

'So what can I do to help?'

'I just have one or two questions.'

A pause. 'Why is there an investigation if it was an accident?'

'Just a procedural matter,' I say. *Could she be the one who vandalised the memorial?* 'I'm actually calling to ask where you were last night at around ten pm?'

Another pause.

'What is this about?'

'Please just answer the question.'

She clicks her tongue. 'Last night at ten pm I was home in bed with my partner.'

'You were at home all night?'

'Yes, can you just tell me why? What happened?'

'And what sort of vehicle do you drive?'

'Vehicle? I'm not answering any more questions until you tell me why you're asking this.'

'I'm just hoping to exclude you as a suspect in an investigation into some vandalism that occurred to a memorial at the crash site last night.'

'Me? Why would I vandalise the crash site? I haven't seen Oli in years.'

'Was it a messy break-up? I'm surprised he moved on so quickly. Married again a couple of years later.'

She laughs. 'Everything with that man was messy. We were separated long before we divorced. But to answer your question: *no,* it was amicable. We let our lawyers settle things. We moved on.'

'What about the night of the crash? Your whereabouts can be accounted for?'

'What are you suggesting? That I was somehow involved in the accident?'

'No, I didn't say that.'

She makes an irritated noise. 'I don't have time for this. I haven't had anything to do with Oli, or the crash, or the vandalism, okay? And for the record, I drive a Mercedes-Benz GLS.'

Then the line cuts out. I go back to her Facebook profile and scroll through all her public images. Sure enough, a photo from two years ago shows her standing in front of a new Mercedes-Benz.

Picked up my new ride today.

As far as the vandalism goes, I can strike a line through Annabel's name.

I open the local news site. There's an update on Maddison Stubbs's disappearance: they've found some of the jewellery taken from the house. There's a map showing where the items were found, not too far from town, probably a ten-minute walk from the cafe.

A sock was found in a derelict shed on a rural property, along with a mattress and a few strands of hair. The jewellery was found somewhere between the shed and a nearby road.

Police searched the area yesterday, the report says, which must be why Sticks and his colleague were called away in such a hurry.

ESHANA
BEFORE

THE POLICE COME again the following afternoon. Oli doesn't have any classes on Friday afternoons so he works from his office at home.

I answer when the call comes in from the gate and buzz to let them through.

The knock at the front door is hard, despite the fact I knew they were coming up the driveway.

'Oli,' I call, rushing towards his study. 'The police are here.'

'Just tell them I'm out.'

I look at him, but he doesn't turn away from his computer. 'I've let them through the gate.'

He makes an irritated noise in his throat. 'I've got so much marking to do. I don't have time to go through it all again.'

'They know you're here.'

He swivels back on his chair, cuffs the sleeves of his shirt one at a time. 'I'll be right out.'

I greet the officers at the door. They're not the same cops that came out last night. There's one in uniform, and another big man in a loose-fitting shirt and pants. He could almost be a bank manager, but is clearly a cop from the gun strapped to his hip.

'Good morning, Mrs Stiles. We're hoping to speak to Mr Stiles if he's about.'

'I'll just get him,' I say.

Oli strides towards the door. 'Who is it? I'm very busy this morning.'

It's a pantomime to show he hasn't got time for this. He eyes the police and says, 'Oh, hi. What's this about?'

The big man in the slacks and shirt clears his throat. 'You gave a statement yesterday about the Kiara King missing persons case. We just want to clarify a few things.'

'Right, well, you couldn't have just called me? I've got a lot on my plate with work.'

He's bristlier this time. He didn't sleep much either last night.

'We were hoping you might accompany us to the station,' the big man says. 'We can complete your statement there.'

Oli's frown deepens. 'I'd prefer to go over it again here. Like I said, I'm busy. The last thing I need is to drive to Manson with you two.'

The man eyes me, then moves his gaze back to Oli. 'We *can* talk about it here. But I think it would be best for *everyone* if you came into the station. Like I said, we can just clarify a few things that might help us progress the search.'

I'm missing something. A second conversation is happening before me, one I can't quite hear.

Oli looks at me, forces a smile and rolls his eyes. 'Okay, if you insist. I can't be gone for long though.'

'We won't keep you any longer than we need,' the big man says.

Then they're all gone and I'm alone in the house. Oli takes his car, following the police out. Is there something they want to ask him about me? Or is it something they can't ask in front of me?

That day, weeks ago now, when I followed Oli, I was so certain he was having an affair or perhaps paying for sex. So, what changed? Oli talked me out of it. He made me feel foolish for even questioning him, but now the young woman he was meeting has disappeared.

I know there are other reasons the police might want him at the station: to show him evidence, ask him if he can help identify someone on CCTV, that sort of thing. But they did say they 'could' do it here, so it can't be that. Maybe they want to get him on their turf for more effective interrogation. Or so they can record him and have someone assess his body language. My mind flies through the possibilities.

The only people who could know Oli better than me are his family. Oli's always insisted his sister is a pathological liar and his mother is a narcissist, but Clare's always been okay to me. I have to look past what Oli has said and consider what Clare might be able to shed light on.

'Eshana,' she says when she answers. 'Hi.'

'Hi, Clare.' There's a pause.

'So,' she says. 'What's Oli up to?'

'He's, ah, busy.'

'That sounds right. Is he there?'

'No.'

'I didn't think so – I'm sure he doesn't like us chatting. He's not been my biggest fan lately.'

'No, you know what he's like,' I say. 'It's just a grudge.'

'It's a little more than that. I take it this isn't a casual call, Eshana? Where is he?'

I exhale. 'He's at the police station.'

'The police station? Has something happened?'

Oli will be mad if he finds out I've been talking about him.

'No, he's just helping with an investigation. A young woman has gone missing and Oli was helping her.'

Clare's silence comes down like a gentle rain, itching my skin.

I feel compelled to add, 'She was a student through the high-school program at the college.'

'Right. Well, hopefully she turns up. Something else is on your mind?'

'Oli and I don't really talk about his finances,' I say. 'I know he made a lot of money, but I don't know how much. He's always insisted that I don't need to worry and it's in a trust.'

Clare scoffs. 'He did make a lot of money. I guess he hasn't told you how?'

I feel a contradictory urge to defend him. 'No, he has.'

'Oh, he has. What did he say?'

'He told me he got lucky. He put it into cryptocurrencies off a recommendation from his friend.'

'Well, maybe he's more honest than I give him credit for. You probably don't realise this, Eshana, but my brother can be quite selfish. Always has been. Wouldn't share as a kid, always hoarded his toys and treats even though I was younger. I know he does all this charity stuff now, but it's just for the recognition. I don't think that's really him.'

Again, that almost violent urge to defend Oli comes over me. I want to tell her about Kiara, how he was helping her and her family without wanting any attention or gratitude for it. It's not just about the kudos and backslapping. Oli believes in altruism; he always has. He rants about the responsibility of the rich and the evils of accruing excessive wealth. I know he would have gone to the ends of the earth to help my mom.

'I don't understand,' I say. 'Is there something wrong with how he made his money? He's a good person, Clare.'

'Look, I don't want him to hate us any more than he does so I'm not going to try to convince you of anything. There's nothing wrong with how he made his money, but did he ever tell you where he got the money to invest?'

'He said it was an inheritance, from your father.'

'It was. I was sixteen and Oli was twenty-two when Dad died. Oli accessed the trust that Dad left for him and me, and he invested my money too, without telling me or Mom.'

'He didn't pay you back?'

She scoffs. 'He put the money back in, alright. Just my share of the original inheritance a couple of years later, while he made millions of dollars.'

'But—'

'*But* nothing, Eshana. He took a big, big risk. If he had lost my money, would he have paid it back? He risked both of our futures. That was my college fund, maybe enough for a deposit on a house, and he took my money and gambled it. If you don't think I was entitled to my share of the profits, or at least some of the profits, then I guess we have a very different view on it.'

'If you believe he did the wrong thing, can't you sue him?' I ask.

'I did. Years ago, when I first discovered what he'd done. My lawyer cost about ten thousand dollars all up. Oli's probably cost five times that. In America, *fair* is a word only rich people believe in. Hell, even I believed the legal system was fair until all this happened.' I hear her sigh and draw another breath. 'Everyone knows what is right and what is wrong, and what my brother did was wrong. Since then, he's blocked us out of his life completely.'

'He didn't give you back anything extra?' I ask.

I hear her exhale. 'He paid my college tuition, which I thought odd at the time – I wasn't going to say no. That meant I had Dad's money to put towards a house. And Oli added the interest we lost from the account when he put the money back in. He didn't give Mom a cent.'

'When did this all happen?'

'I guess around ten years ago. We knew he'd made a lot of money when we saw Annabel's engagement ring. It was before they were married. She didn't get a cent either.'

'She got the house.'

'They both put in for that place,' she says, ignoring the fact Oli still gave up his half.

After the call, things are no clearer in my head. I suppose what Oli did with the trust money was wrong, but only in a theoretical sense. The end result is the same. Clare, a divorcee herself, seems to have a good job and enough money. She still had the money her father left her after Oli made his millions. If she didn't know what happened, she wouldn't care. And if Oli had lost her money, I know he would have done the right thing and paid her back.

•

Oli returns a little while later. He doesn't talk much about what happened at the police station, just says they wanted to run through everything about the brother again.

'I think we should keep giving her money,' I say. 'Kiara's mother. I think it's the right thing to do.'

He nods. 'If that's what you really want to do. But the treatment has worked, Eshana. The tumours have shrunk. So it's not quite the same anymore.'

Why does it feel like giving the King family money will assuage the guilt? Why do I feel guilt in the first place?

REID
NOW

I'VE MAPPED A route to cover all the junkyards in the area. It's almost four, but if I race I can knock them off tonight.

No luck at the first place, close to town. The second one is a little further out, but again he's not got the car.

I continue on to the third. I don't know why none of them could answer their phones – it's not as though any of them are run off their feet when I turn up. Another swing and a miss at the third stop.

I'm losing hope on the drive to the final wreckers. It is ten minutes out of Manson. As the road takes me into open country, I find my mind going back to a statistic I read soon after I left the police force. In 1900, sixty per cent of the American workforce was in agriculture. Now it's three per cent. First the workers moved to manufacturing jobs, then when machines squeezed that workforce they moved into services, and now the squeeze is on there. Each time it happens, the skill set rises upwards, which means the jobs of the future aren't going to be for the farmers or the labourers. They're going to be increasingly for those with higher education and higher skills, primed for the tech age.

That's why I moved into private surveillance. I assumed there'd be at least another twenty or thirty years in it before people like me become redundant, and I had the skill set already. But so much of it happens online now that some of the old-timers get left behind. Instead of reading people's mail or breaking into a mark's home or placing a tracking device on their vehicle, some PIs will hack phones, or catfish a mark to get a confession online, or install keystroke trackers on their personal devices to steal passwords. I've even heard of some who have hacked cameras on laptops to record incriminating footage. What next? Stalking marks in the metaverse? It's not all about digital surveillance yet though. Sometimes private detectives need to get their hands dirty, they need to get in the trenches.

I see the sign from the road, *Cooper & Sons*, and turn onto a dirt track that leads towards a shed and a house behind it. The paddocks are full of cars in varying states of ruin. Some without doors, or windshields. Some partially crushed from an accident.

I wheel around beside the shed and see a tattered old Trump flag.

A rottweiler barks and leaps up the side of the Camry as I park. Its nails squeal on the paint and I wince.

An old man wearing a red flannel shirt tucked into blue jeans comes striding over. The white stubble on his chin wobbles as he waves a hand at the dog. 'Go on,' he says.

The dog steps back, barks once or twice more, unsure of itself. 'Go on I said!'

As the man gets close, the dog skirts away. I open the car door. 'Sorry about him,' he says.

'It's fine.' I eye the scratch marks. 'It'll buff right out.'

'How can I help you?'

'Well, I'm actually looking for a car. A wreck from a recent crash in Ethelton.'

He squints, assessing me. 'You're the guy who left the message?'

'Yeah, that's right.'

'Why you interested in *that* car? Ain't worth anything more than scrap metal.'

'I'm investigating the crash.'

'Not a cop though, are you?'

'No, I'm helping the insurance assessors. Just want to rule out any issues with the vehicle.'

'Fifty bucks, right? That's what you said on the message. Just for a look?'

'Just for a look. Fifty cash. You've got the car?'

He nods. 'Been meaning to get back to you. I started to scrap it, but then got your message and thought I'd hold off.' He gives me a smile full of gaps. 'This way.'

The shed is a rusty old thing with a dust-covered concrete floor and junk everywhere. I see the car up on an old two-post hoist. It's almost torn in two down the middle and the airbags look like two deflated party balloons long after the music has stopped.

On the passenger's side of the shattered windshield is a hole, presumably where Oliver Stiles's body crashed through, even though it looks too small. He lost a lot of blood at the scene, but there's no blood visible on the car. I suppose the police would hose it down before sending it off.

They've cut the pillar and half the roof off to get Eshana out. The contact point must have been almost in the centre of the fender, just slightly on the passenger's side. It's hard to imagine how anyone survived this crash.

'What can you do with it?' I ask the old man.

'Strip it. Might get a couple hundred for the tyres, the rear panels and lights, the rear windshield. The scrap metal will make it worth my while. So what is it you're looking for?'

'I'm just checking that nothing went wrong with the vehicle,' I say.

I note that the car tyres aren't 225 Turanzas.

'Like what?'

'A faulty brake line maybe.'

The man chuckles. 'It'll be hard to see anything given the shape it's in. You'd think the cops would have picked that up, especially after someone died.'

Obviously this man has more faith in the Manson PD than I do.

'I know,' I say. 'But they've got a lot on their plate at the moment.'

He eyes me with open suspicion now. 'You got the cash?'

I hand him a fifty-dollar bill.

'Alright, she's all yours.'

With his help raising and lowering the vehicle, I finally acknowledge that it's impossible for me to tell if the brakes have been tampered with.

'Can't see a thing wrong with it myself,' he says. 'Other than being almost cut in two by a power pole. Maybe it really was just bad driving.' He laughs.

'Maybe.'

'Way I see it, if a car travels some way before the crash, can't be the brakes that cause the crash. If them brake lines are cut, you're not getting more than a hundred feet without noticing. Go on and drive for five minutes and tell me how many times you touch the brake. If the line's cut or damaged, it feels all spongy under your foot.'

'But what if it snapped while she was driving?'

'You could try, I suppose, set it up so it's hanging on by a thread. Or you could mess with the plates. Either way, you'd have to get pretty lucky with the timing for it to happen the way it did. Especially when someone could just reach for the handbrake.'

I look over to see the rottweiler's back leg raised against my rear wheel.

'He's partial to pissing on a good piece of rubber, that dog,' the man says with a chuckle. 'Don't mind him.'

'One last thing,' I say. 'Did you find anything in the car?'

'Like what?'

I shrug. 'Anything at all.'

'Nothing really. The service book in the glove box. Like I said, I've not started wrecking it yet.'

'The service book? Where is it?'

'You want the service book? What you going to do with that?'

'I'm just curious.'

'Right, I'll grab it for you. It's in the office.'

I follow him through. The service book is sitting on his desk and when he lifts it, I see something else underneath. A green thumb drive with a small key attached. Just like the ones I found in Oliver's office at Sandown.

'What's that?' I say, pointing, as the man holds the book out.

He cuts his eyes to me. 'Nothing. Just a USB thing.'

'Yours?'

'That's right.'

I cut to the chase. 'Do the police know you have Oliver Stiles's thumb drive?'

'It ain't his. Like I said, it's mine.'

'So you work at Sandown College?' I ask. He turns back to the thumb drive. 'Look, I know it's his, and I know that by law you have to return it to the police or the deceased's next of kin.'

He swings his gaze to me once more. 'You're a clever one, ain't ya? You can take it. It'll cost you another fifty.' That smile again. 'I read on the news he was an author, thought there might be a book on there, something I could sell. But there's nothing important. If you want a souvenir, it'll cost you.'

I exhale and reach for my wallet. There was nothing on the other drives, sure, but this one was in the car. Maybe he was actually using it. 'Here,' I say, holding out a bill.

He removes the key and hands over the drive.

'Both,' I say.

He shakes his head. 'Fifty for that too. Don't know what this key is for but it might be something good.'

'Hand it over,' I say. 'A deal is a deal.' I step a little closer but he's unfazed.

'Another fifty, I said.'

'I've got twenty left.'

'Twenty will do. Hand it over.'

I hold out the bill.

He puts the key in my hand and takes the twenty.

Back in the car, I examine the key. It has a number on it: *39*. It could be for a small lockbox, or a safe. I place it in the glove box and look at the thumb drive. It's exactly like the others.

I just hope this trip was worth the $120 I spent on it, but I won't find out until I get the thumb drive into my laptop.

•

Back at the motel, I take a long shower, as hot as the water gets in the mouldy bathroom. Then I open the service book and read through the records.

The last service was at Smith's Auto in Manson, but every service before that was at another mechanic's. Why the change? But what's really interesting is the car was picked up from Smith's Auto on the afternoon of the crash.

When I plug the thumb drive into my laptop, it seems Cooper was telling the truth. Nothing incriminating here. Not empty like the others, but just a note with a series of seemingly unrelated words:

child practice feeds shame never open despair stream path again sheet maple

Anagrams? Or some hidden message?

I take the first letter of each word and try to spell something out, then do the same with the second letter, and then the last letter.

I try to rearrange the words one at a time.

Or perhaps the number of letters in each word is significant? 5-8-5-5-5-4-7-6-4-5-5-5. It doesn't look like a bank account, or a phone number, or the coordinates of an address. It means nothing to me whatsoever.

I search the phrase online and again nothing comes up.

Bad poetry? Maybe. I put the thumb drive in my bag and zip it closed. I think about the key again. Could this phrase be linked to the key somehow?

Next I search social media platforms for information on Kiara King and Maddison Stubbs.

Most kids are everywhere online. Except for Maddison, who seems to be almost nowhere. A social media black hole, which is odd for someone who could otherwise be a sort of influencer with her girl-next-door looks and Colgate smile. I wonder if this is Chief Stubbs's doing. He would know what social media can do to the young mind, and all the dangers present in the cyberworld, particularly for attractive young women.

It's starting to get late and I haven't found anything of note on Kiara King; just the same old photos from the news reports on her Instagram. A few old videos on her TikTok. It's all reasonably private though. I search again, looking everywhere, but still find nothing new. I start looking through other local teenagers' social media, starting with anyone who attended Manson High and might have been in her year level.

Soon enough, on Facebook I see someone I recognise. She's younger, and her hair is shorter and dyed bright blue, but it's definitely her. The gas station clerk with the wine-stain birthmark on her neck. She's in a photo with Kiara, their faces pressed close together, cheeks drawn and lips puckered like a fish. I have a name: Angel. The caption is encouraging: *besties*. An affair with a married man might be the exact sort of thing Kiara would tell her 'bestie' about.

I go back to Oliver Stiles and search deeper. I try variations of his name in Google and find his employment history. He was teaching at a college in the city, Trinity, up until about seven years ago. No other notes about that but it was definitely a downgrade for him to go from Trinity to Sandown. Maybe he just wanted a change of lifestyle.

I search his name with *Trinity* across different search engines until something stands out. A blogpost from eight years ago with the title *I had an affair with my college professor*. I don't see Oliver's name in the result, but when I click on the post the first line grabs me and doesn't let go until I've read the entire thing.

It's anonymous, a sort of confessional. A young woman recounting her experience with a charming young English professor. It could be anyone and she doesn't name him, but I find Oliver's name in the comments section.

Was it Oliver Stiles?

The author responded: *It was a few years ago. I can't comment. Why do you ask?*

The response is just a link.

I click it and it takes me to a screenshot of a dating profile from Sugarbabies4u.com. There's a blurry photo of Oliver's face and all his statistics, and below are 'private' photos that have been unlocked for whoever took the screenshot. It's Oliver smiling at the camera. A series of selfies – the sort of thing that could end a career and a marriage.

Then again, he probably had plausible deniability. He could claim a phone hack for the photos; a convincing catfish. It's important to remind myself that no crime has been committed here. Being a shitty husband isn't a crime, even though it might be motive for a crime.

Outside, the sky cracks and rain comes down. Even on the bottom level of the motel, I can hear it drilling the roof. The storm rises, and for just a second, as the wind batters the windows, I think the building might tip over.

I close my laptop and get under the covers. I spend the next hour working through the bird's nest of the crash in my mind, while the rain continues to fall.

Finally, I pull my eye mask down. I can only doze off in absolute darkness and the streetlights from the road penetrate the room's thin curtains.

Sleep comes down like a hood over a canary's cage.

ESHANA
BEFORE

I'VE BEEN LIVING with this unexplained weight of guilt on my chest since the day I discovered Kiara is missing. It won't go away and I'm finding it harder than usual to sleep and hard to concentrate at work. If I speak with Kiara's mother and see for myself that she's better, maybe it will help. I've withdrawn money from my savings too.

Last time I visited Kiara's home, I had the door slammed in my face and didn't take in the surroundings so much. This time, the first things I notice are the large work boots at the door.

When I knock, I hear a woman call out.

The door opens a fraction and I see her, Kiara. Then I realise it's not Kiara but a small version of her with a freckled nose and gas-flame blue eyes.

'Yes?' she says.

'Hi. I was hoping to speak to your mother, if she's around?'

'Are you from the paper?' she asks. She must be eleven or twelve.

'No.'

'Mom doesn't want any visitors, sorry.'

She goes to close the door, but I get my sneaker in the doorframe. Something crunches in the side of my foot. The pain is intense.

'Ow,' I say, resisting the impulse to swear.

'Did that hurt?'

'Yes. A lot actually.'

'Who is it?' the woman calls.

'I don't know, she won't leave,' the girl calls back.

'Look, I've got some money for your mom,' I say. 'It's not as much as usual but it should help.'

'She says she's got money, Mom. Should I let her in?'

'She alone?'

The girl relays the question and looks past me to the street.

'It's just me,' I tell her.

She steps back and opens the door wider.

The house is reasonably well kept – I don't know what I was expecting. The carpet is threadbare and there are water spots on the wallpaper, but it's tidy and looks clean.

Kiara's sister leads me into a tiny kitchen, where a woman sits at the dining table watching a TV mounted to the wall. I'm surprised to see it and then wonder why. Do I just assume people in poorer neighbourhoods don't have any nice things?

'Hi,' I say.

The woman's eyes go a little wider when they settle on me. She has tight red curls and a sour mouth, and a tube runs from her nostril to an oxygen tank.

'What's this about, money?' she asks. 'You want to pay for an interview?'

'No. Like I told your daughter, I'm not a journalist. I'm married to Oliver Stiles.'

She shakes her head. 'Missy, that don't mean a thing to me. Am I supposed to know who Oliver Stiles is?'

'He's the man that was paying your daughter,' I say.

Her eyes narrow so they're almost closed. 'You better explain what the hell you're talking about.'

'For your treatment,' I add quickly. 'My husband was giving your daughter Kiara money for your treatment.'

There's a long pause and I realise I've made a terrible mistake. All I can think of is that everything Oli told me is a lie.

'That's Kiara's business,' the woman eventually says. 'I don't know what she did or didn't do with your husband. When she turns up, you can talk to her about that yourself.'

'Well, I thought I'd just check in,' I say. 'My husband said you don't need the money anymore.'

'The tumours have shrunk, if that's what you mean. But I still don't know what money you're talking about? We haven't *got* any money.'

'My husband was giving your daughter money for your pills, the treatment.'

'Well, that's kind of him,' she says with a laugh.

'So you're telling me you know nothing about the payments for your medication?' I ask.

'No, I don't. We saw the specialist, couldn't afford the treatment. Then Kiara does her fundraiser thing online and says strangers will pay for it – as if that will ever happen. Then my mom starts coming over with the medication. She says Kiara's got the money.'

'You weren't curious about how she could afford five thousand a month for your meds?'

Her expression changes, becomes stern. 'Over this side of the river, we don't ask questions. We just do what we have to do to get by. I don't know how Kiara was doing it, but she was. If your husband was involved in some way, then you have to talk to him or Kiara about that.'

I feel another presence in the house and turn to see the girl at the kitchen door. I remember what Oli said about Kiara's brother and remember the boots out the front that must belong to him.

'Is there anyone else home?' I ask, feeling a sudden and strong urge to get out.

'Just my girls,' the woman says.

'Your son?'

Now she stares me in the eye. 'He doesn't live here. Hasn't lived here for years. He's over on the other side of the river now.'

'So whose boots are those at the door?'

She shows me all of her teeth, the smile reaching her eyes. 'You see that, did you? The only pair of shoes out front and they're some big old dirty work boots. Made you think there was a man here, right? Those boots are my "beware of dog" sign. They tell anyone thinking of breaking in that a big man lives here, and he's home. We got our dog, Ham, out back but he's too old to do much these days.'

I'm still processing this when she speaks again.

'You see, we have to take care of ourselves over this side of the river. Only time cops turn up is after something has happened,' she says. She looks up at the clock and adds, 'That reminds me, that detective was supposed to be here ten minutes ago.'

I check the clock myself, see it's ten past three. It wouldn't be good for Oli if the police see me here.

'Thanks,' I say. 'I better go.'

'You said something about money,' the woman reminds me.

'Yeah.' I reach into my bag and pull out the sixteen hundred dollars bundled together in a rubber band.

Her eyes go wide. 'You feeling guilty about something?'

'Just trying to help,' I lie. 'I hope Kiara turns up soon.'

Then before the police arrive, I slip out of the front door and hurry to my car.

REID
NOW

I HEAD TO the cafe first to get a coffee and a bite to eat. There are cafes closer to the motel, but I'm drawn across town. Something feels *right* about sitting there at the site of the crash while I plan my day. Or maybe I'm just telling myself that. Maybe I drive over there every day to see the flirty waiter. There's not many eligible queer men in this part of the state, or there didn't seem to be when I lived here. There was Marco, but that didn't end particularly well for me. Marco leaked my chest-cam footage of us bringing in the dealer in the Amanda Marley case. Let's face it, if not for him, I'd probably still be a cop.

I joined the police force a couple years out of school. It was that or firefighting. I wanted a job where I could help people, I wanted to follow in my dad's footsteps.

The night he died, I woke to find Mom sitting on my bed in the dark in her dressing gown, trembling all over as tears rushed down her cheeks. She didn't want to wake me, she said. Maybe she thought if I kept sleeping, I'd never have to learn that my father was gone.

It happened after midnight. Dad was on patrol; he pulled over a suspected stolen vehicle. This was before cameras were mounted on cars and before stab vests were mandatory; before all the precautions they have these days. The road where he died is long and straight, and it was a cold night; a frost had turned the banks beside the road to concrete. I've spent hours out there at the spot, just thinking about him. Imagining his last hours.

Dad knew half the population of Manson, so when he approached the driver's door he probably expected to see one of the usual suspects. Maybe it *was* one of the usual suspects – who knows? They never got them in the end.

The funeral was at St Paul's Church in the centre of Manson. The heating was out, and it had snowed all morning but the church was so packed with mourners that it didn't seem so cold. It was closed casket. I've seen enough gunshot victims by now to know what a bullet fired at close range does to the human body, to the face and skull.

A couple years into the job, I realised there's nothing glamorous about police work, especially in Manson – no organised crime, cults or conmen – but it felt important, even the trivial things. The job was mostly filing reports; in small-town America, domestic abuse calls account for the majority, with a few drug disputes, and the catastrophic potential of overconfident teenagers and fast cars.

With my record and skill set, I thought I had a real chance at making detective. But every time a chance to climb the ladder came around, I was disappointed. There were promotions but never in the direction I so badly wanted. Maybe the higher-ups didn't like me, or maybe Mom and I cashed in all our goodwill years earlier when the PD helped out after Dennis died; the prison sentence could have been much longer. Or maybe I just wasn't as good as I thought I was. I guess that's why I work so hard now . . . to prove to myself that I'm good enough to crack cases.

The cafe is quiet. I take my usual seat in the corner and open out the newspaper. There's not a word about the crash anymore;

just a notice saying a public memorial service will be held for Oliver Stiles this coming Thursday at St Paul's Church, with a private funeral scheduled for a later date. His family has chosen to cremate his remains. Given Eshana is still unconscious, I wonder who made that decision. Just who is 'his family'?

'Back again,' the waiter says. 'Let me guess: omelette, black coffee?'

'That's right.'

'You've proven your point, you can stomach the bland omelette. Now you can try something else.'

'I don't want to change a winning formula,' I say.

He smiles. 'Apple pie to follow?'

'Apple pie at this time of the morning – what do you take me for?'

Another smile and I feel a warmth in my chest.

He leans back against the counter. 'I take you for the odd man who's been in every day this week to drink coffee and eat a' – his eyes flick towards the kitchen – 'mediocre omelette and still swears this is the best cafe in the state.'

'That about sums me up perfectly. But yeah, I'll have a slice of the apple too.'

He goes behind the counter and returns with a coffee. 'You slipped out yesterday without finishing your food.'

'Duty called.'

'Duty?' he asks, retreating towards the kitchen. 'Omelette, please,' he calls through the door.

An older couple come in and sit at a table near the window. The waiter carries a pair of menus over, takes their order, then returns to me.

'So what do you do for work that gives you so much leisure time to sit in cafes?' he asks.

'I'm retired.'

That gets a smile. 'Older than you look.'

'Salesman, actually,' I say.

'What do you sell?'

'Solar panels, believe it or not.'

It's my usual cover story. I don't want to lie to him, but telling the truth is a risk, especially in this town. I'm proud of my investigation work, but I know some people don't see it the way I do.

'Interesting,' he says.

'Not really, but it pays the bills.'

I sip the coffee. Instantly feel energised. I didn't get much sleep last night. There was some banging around in the motel in the wee hours, and a big storm was raging through the night. Not to mention the fact every time I woke up, I just had to make a note about another possible avenue to pursue in the investigation.

The waiter takes the couple their drinks.

'What about you?' I say when he comes near me again.

'I'm a waiter.'

'I know that, but do you do anything else?'

A bell sounds. 'That's your omelette.'

When he brings it over, I splash a little tabasco on it. Scoop a forkful into my mouth.

'Well?' he says.

'Best eggs I've ever tasted.'

A big smile. 'Oh, you could talk the shell off a walnut, couldn't you? I'm studying computer science actually. I thought it's time to do something with my life, maybe get out of this town.'

'Computer science? Clever then,' I say.

'Not really, but it's sensible. Computers aren't going away.'

'Unlike coal-fired power stations.'

'Hey now.' He brings his hands to his heart as if deeply offended. 'Can't make light of that around these parts. People are still hurting.'

I smile. 'Listen,' I begin. I feel awkward doing this but I like him, I like him a lot. And to quote my old hockey coach: *If you don't shoot, you don't score.* 'Say a guy wanted a drink in this town, where would you suggest he goes?'

His eyebrows rise. 'Where are you staying?'

'Comfort Inn.'

He frowns. 'Where's that?'

'Manson.'

'You're a long way from home, Dorothy.'

'Well, I like it over this side of the river,' I say. *Not to mention it's less likely I'll bump into someone I know.*

'Bars in Manson? Can't say I know many. Ye Olde Tavern is out that way, but you only go there if you want to get in a fight.'

I know the place from my days on the force. It's a working-class bar.

'There's The Lawn,' he goes on. I watch his lips as he speaks. 'That's mostly for students though, you may not fit in.'

'Ouch.'

'Out this way, you could try Gerald's.'

That's new. 'Gerald's, huh? Sounds a bit posh for me.'

'It's nice. Usually quiet with an older crowd.'

'What's your name?'

'Peyton,' he says, self-consciously eyeing the other customers.

'Vince,' I say. 'But most people just call me Reid.' I offer my hand. He takes it; his grip is firm and his palm warm.

'And would I ever see you there, Peyton?' I say. 'At Gerald's?'

He raises his finger. 'One second.' He goes to serve another customer.

Why did he choose that moment to go, leaving me hanging? I can't look over. I fork a blob of egg onto the toast and bite down. Too much salt, but otherwise just fine.

When Peyton comes back, he says, 'I go to Gerald's sometimes.'

'Would I see you there tonight?' I say, trying to hold his gaze. 'If for some reason I decided to go there at, say, seven pm?'

A telling hand slides up the back of his neck. Of course he's not interested. I'm far too old for him. All soft around the middle like some forgotten vegetable found at the bottom of a fridge.

'Umm,' he says. 'Well, I doubt it.'

Dagger meets heart. I try to keep the disappointment from my face.

The bell sounds again and Peyton's back in the kitchen, picking up a meal. Another group comes in and the place gets busy. I can hear them all talking about the missing girl, how there's a bunch of journalists in town. It reminds me that now is not the time to be pulling a move like this.

Peyton drops off my pie without comment. Ashamed, I quickly eat it and swallow the last of my coffee.

I catch Eshana's name as Peyton speaks to a woman who's just entered the cafe.

'She's awake,' the woman says. 'But no one can visit her yet. I've just been up there – she's still in shock.'

I stare down at the table, focusing on her words. *Eshana is awake.* I turn to look at her. *Shit.* I think I know that voice. It's the woman from the Stileses' house. She must be a relative or a friend. I turn away again, rest the side of my face in my palm.

'Well, that's good news she's awake,' Peyton says.

'We're just so relieved,' the woman says. 'Anyway, I'll take a cup of coffee, please.'

I can't stay in the cafe; what if she recognises me? She won't, I remind myself. I was wearing a balaclava.

When Peyton comes to top up my coffee, I cover the cup with my palm and say, 'No, thanks. I've had my fix. Just the cheque, please.'

The cheque appears on a tiny saucer. I lay a bill down and stand to get out of there.

'Aren't you going to take your receipt?' Peyton asks.

'It's fine.'

He picks it up from the plate and hands it towards me. 'I think you should take it.'

'Right,' I say, confused. I grab it and shove it in my pocket.

'Turn it over,' he says quietly.

I take the receipt out of my pocket and look at it again. Scribbled down the bottom are five words: *Shoot me a message later,* and a phone number.

I look up. Peyton is clearing my table. He sends me a wink so subtle and quick I might have imagined it, and I smile, nod and depart.

The smile stays on my face all the way back to the car, disappearing only when I see another note wedged in under my wiper.

Keep digging. You're getting closer.

I look around me. Who the hell knows what I'm here for? And what am I getting closer to?

I head off. The roads are still wet and littered with branches, debris, trash: flotsam from the storm that lashed the state through the night. At the lights, I see a shopping trolley tipped over on the sidewalk, and the signage for a clothing outlet has torn from the shopfront so it hangs down like bunting. At the motel, I place the note in my bag. Where have I been and who could have seen me? The cafe, the dance school, the gas station, the hospital, The Pearl restaurant.

Sticks pulled me over so it could be from anyone in the police force. But it's not a threat; this is something else.

I've received threats before; anyone in this line of work has – eventually you'll poke a sleeping bear. Sometimes it's legal threats, coming in the form of impenetrable legal parlance on a lawyer's letterhead. Other times it's an imperative scrawled on a piece of paper: *Leave town or else.* But I've never had anyone leave a note like this: *Keep digging.*

Whoever left this note mustn't know me very well. I don't need more encouragement; I'm going to get to the bottom of this, one way or another. I set out again, this time in the direction of Ethelton High. I can't wait until tomorrow's dance school to speak with Larissa and it's almost school drop-off time.

ESHANA

BEFORE

A FEW DAYS after Oli was taken to the police station, I open the newspaper and see the story.

POLICE INTERVIEW SUSPECT IN KIARA KING DISAPPEARANCE

Police have spoken with a person of interest at the heart of the Kiara King case. Police have not released a name but have acknowledged they are pursuing a number of active leads.

Seventeen-year-old King disappeared from her home sometime between 9 pm and 7 am on the evening of Wednesday 14th of November. Nothing was missing from the property apart from her sister's bicycle. Police are yet to determine if it was the missing girl herself who took it that evening.

The person of interest, believed to be someone close to Kiara King, is an older man in the Ethelton–Manson area. Police have confirmed the man has thus far cooperated with them. The nature of the relationship of this man and King is unknown, but it's believed they met online.

So that's it. Oli is *the* suspect. I wonder if anyone else has made the connection?

•

With everything I've had on my mind lately, it will be good to unwind tonight. The dance school's annual break-up involves a prize-giving ceremony for the girls, then a night out drinking cocktails, wine and gossiping with the moms. The last few years I've been invited along but always slipped away after the prize-giving. This time, I'm eager to join in. I've realised I rely too much on just one person for my fulfilment and happiness. I've always put Oli first, but sometimes it's important to put yourself first. Oli will understand.

Predictably, Sienna wins dancer of the year for the seniors, although her insufferable mother, Bree, gasps as if she didn't know it was inevitable. Sienna is a good kid; she placed in a category of the recent state-wide comp, the first of Toni's dancers to do so in years.

Renee takes out junior of the year, a decision that's slightly more controversial. I don't think Renee is the best dancer in the younger group, but she's compliant and obedient. More importantly, Toni hasn't fallen out with Renee's mom like she has a couple of the others.

The post-award festivities are at Mario's, which apparently is a favourite haunt of Bree and a couple of the other moms. Bree greets the owner, who, ironically, isn't Italian or called Mario. His name is Chris, and he sits us in prime position near the window on a long table already made up with plates.

Mario's offers bottomless bubbles between four and five on Fridays, but Bree insists Chris will keep the bubbles going for us until seven at least. Larissa and I are the only ones to opt for something different: I order a chardonnay and Larissa gets a beer.

I take the seat beside Larissa so I'm not marooned at the other end of the table with the cliquey moms. I get on well enough with some of them, but others not at all.

Despite the many vacant tables, I notice Chris turn away a group of students, then allow in a pair of couples who didn't have a booking. The clientele is clearly curated to create a pseudo-sophisticated atmosphere.

That it's supposed to get down to 40 degrees tonight hasn't stopped most of the moms from wearing dresses for the inevitable bar crawl later. Toni, in a body-hugging blue dress that's perhaps just a touch too tight for her figure, is the centre of attention, but after a glass and a half of bubbles, she departs. That's when the gossip commences. The moms at the other end of the table begin talking about who should have *really* won dancer of the year in the juniors. They talk loud enough for Renee's mother to hear and, unsurprisingly, she is the next to leave. Then the floodgates open.

'Toni has her favourites. She just *has* to please them and forget about the rest of us,' one of the moms says.

'Some of her favourites don't even have children!' another says.

There's a few bitchy little laughs at that.

I know it was Bree who said it, and I know most of the eyes at the table are on me to see how I react.

I turn to Larissa. 'So did you say you and Greg might be selling?'

She smiles at me, knowing I'm blocking the others out. 'We're not sure. We're getting an appraisal. Greg wants more space, but that just means more maintenance. The other option is to extend.'

The crowd begins to thin out, and the bubbles keep coming to our table well into the night. Chris also brings me and Larissa – the two who opted *not* to take the bottomless bubbles option – drinks much more frequently than the others.

We order food and soon there are only seven of us left. I decide that the moment Larissa calls it a night I'll leave too, but she's in it for the long haul it seems, downing beers like a frat boy with glazed eyes and a liquid smile. She's in jeans and has a long woollen coat over the back of her seat.

A round of shots comes to the table from Chris, some purple concoction.

'Nope,' Larissa says. 'I don't do shots.'

'Spoilsport,' one of the women says.

The last time I did shots it didn't end well, and that was at least ten years ago now. But, unlike Larissa, I don't have the backbone to refuse.

'I'll do hers too,' I say, and this gets the looks of approval I want.

We all clink glasses and throw them back. The first shot tastes sweet without much of a burn, then the second one goes down and the alcohol hits me pretty hard. I hear a 'woo!' from the drunk moms. They've warmed a little towards me.

Bree leans across the table and says loud enough so everyone can hear, 'We've all been talking about our husbands, but you never seem to talk about Oliver.'

Despite the fog of alcohol, I don't remember ever mentioning my husband's name to anyone at the dance school except Larissa.

Ignoring this, I say, 'Well, what do you want to know?'

Bree shrugs with a teasing smile. 'What does he do?'

'He's a professor at the college.'

Emboldened perhaps by this piece of information and no doubt the alcohol she's consumed, one of the other women says, 'Do you ever get jealous? He must meet lots of younger women in his classes.'

Sniggers all round, except for Larissa whose husband is also at the college.

'I don't get jealous,' I say.

'No?' Bree says. 'Me either. I don't get jealous; I just get even. Why do you think I'm wearing this?' She signals her cleavage – more laughter – and cuts her eyes towards the bar. 'Plenty of eligible bachelors here.'

'I think we should move on after these drinks,' Cherry says, and adds with a laugh, 'Chris is going to start charging us soon anyway.'

'You coming, Eshana?' Bree says.

'Yeah,' I say. 'Why not?'

It's not until I stand that I realise how drunk I am. It's a cold intermission between venues but fortunately it's a short walk in our heels.

The next bar is packed, mostly with people in their twenties, but somehow we manage to fit in. Bree commandeers half a table from a group of guys and begins openly flirting. Soon enough, the guys are sending drinks our way – beers and shots of whisky. I realise I've set the expectation that I'm drinking Larissa's shots. I think about throwing one over my shoulder, but it's too crowded and I'll never get away with it. I decide instead not to drink anything else.

One of the men notices. 'You know, it's rude to let a man keep ordering you drinks without touching them?' he says.

'Bit presumptuous buying drinks for us in the first place, don't you think? For your information, I have a husband.' My words all crash into each other as they come out of my mouth.

'A ring doesn't mean a thing,' he says, showing me his wedding finger.

The moms all laugh, but I feel slightly sick. The room throbs with the music and everything seems to be swirling. He comes a little closer now, but I turn away back to Larissa.

When the others don their coats and go out to the smoking area for a cigarette, I say to Larissa, 'I might head off. I'm really drunk.'

'We all are!' she says.

The table seems to shift away from me as I stand, and without the grip of Larissa's hand on my forearm I'd topple over.

'Whoa, come here,' she says, laughter in her voice. 'Sit down. Let's get you some water.'

'How did they know Oli's name?' I slur.

'What?' She moves her ear closer to my mouth.

'Bree and the others, they know who Oli is. Did you tell them?'

'Me?' She laughs. 'Bree asked me. She said, "Is Oliver Stiles Eshana's husband?" In that voice too.' She laughs again.

'Why did she want to know? Did you say anything else?'

The smile drains from her face. 'No,' she says, relaxing her grip on my arm as I lower myself onto the seat. 'I'm sorry, I didn't think it was so important.'

'He was the "person of interest",' I say, waving a hand. 'When that girl Kiara ran away. They cleared him. I told the police he was at home with me when she went missing.' I know I need to stop talking. 'Sometimes I think maybe he really did do something. Where there's smoke . . .'

'No, no, it's just rumours,' Larissa says. 'Ignore them.'

'Larissa,' I say, feeling my stomach turn. 'I might be sick.'

She grabs me again by the forearm and helps me towards the door. The world tips.

I see the dance moms coming in from the smoking area.

'What's wrong?' one of them says.

'Is she okay?'

Larissa says something I don't quite catch.

Outside, the cool air hits me and the ground rocks beneath my feet. We round the corner of the building into an alleyway, where I bend, hands on my knees. The vomit hits the concrete and splashes back onto the bare parts of my feet that aren't covered by my strappy shoes.

I feel Larissa's hands on my back, then hear her arguing with someone on the phone. I sit down, still nauseous, waiting for the next round of vomit.

I hear Larissa saying, 'Don't record her!' And look up at a bright camera light. I feel cold and scared.

'It's just the light on my phone! Is she okay?'

Someone puts a bottle of water in my hand and then a few moments later Oli is hauling me up off the ground and into the car.

Suddenly Bree is beside me.

'Hey Oliver,' Bree spits. 'What happened to Kiara?' She's drunk and her voice mean.

Oli says something back, low and harsh, and which I can't hear, then he's speeding off, narrowly missing Bree who is standing on the road.

I don't speak on the way home. The car makes me sway and I concentrate on not being sick. Oli sits beside me, his jaw tight, his hands on the wheel tighter still.

REID
NOW

I RECOGNISE LARISSA from her Facebook page when she arrives in her white minivan at the drop-off area outside Ethelton High.

The back door opens and a girl gets out. She's about thirteen or fourteen and starts toward the school gate. I quickly stride past all the other cars dropping off kids to where Larissa is parked. There's an uneasy feeling stirring inside. I hate being this exposed, and most of these people would be close to my age. Some of them might recognise me. Larissa's got a short blonde bob and wears sunglasses. Small-town chic.

I approach the passenger's window. Knock once with my knuckle. She looks confused for a second but drops the window a fraction.

'Hi?' She says it like a question. 'Do I know you?'

'No,' I say and flash my private investigator's badge.

'Right,' she says. I can easily imagine the words *I'm not talking without my lawyer* coming out of her mouth. But she surprises me with a smile, and lowers the window all the way down. 'I'm guessing this is about Eshana?' Her tone is light. It's possible I've misread her.

'I'm investigating a few things leading up to the car crash.'

'You're not a local cop,' she says.

It's a statement not a question but I answer all the same. 'No.' I fix her with my gaze. She still has one hand rested on the wheel like she might take off.

'Is there more to it than what was reported?' she asks.

I lean on the edge of the door. 'I'm just dotting t's and crossing i's.'

'Okay, well what do you want to know?'

She reaches out and shuts her engine off. Other cars are arriving, depositing school kids on the sidewalk and departing again. A teacher stands at the gate watching on.

'I want to know what they were like?'

She smiles now. 'Oliver and Eshana? Well, they're an odd couple.'

'Are?'

'Were. I keep forgetting he's really gone.' She bites her lips together so they disappear. 'I didn't really get to know Oliver well. We met, but . . .'

She trails off. Something tells me they didn't see eye to eye.

'After the dance school break-up a couple of months back, I don't think he liked me much,' she adds and smiles again. It hits her eyes this time. 'Long story.'

'Can you tell me more about that, the break-up?'

'I've got an appointment shortly.'

'Give me the short version,' I say.

'The short version – well, Eshana drank too much. The slightly longer version: we all had a little too much, but she really went overboard. I was looking after her outside the bar – she was sick, throwing up. I called Oliver from her phone to come get her and he was quite rude, told me to put her in an Uber. I was a little drunk, so I told him straight that he better come pick her up. I said guys were hitting on her, and she was too drunk. That made him hurry up. When he arrived, he blamed me for getting her drunk and we had a bit of an argument in the street. I haven't seen him since then.'

'Did he strike you as someone who could be abusive, or manipulating?' I ask. 'Anything like that?'

'It's always hard to tell. He could have been the type, but I don't really want to speculate about a man who's just lost his life.'

'What about Eshana? Did you think she was depressed or suicidal?' I ask.

'No! She had insomnia, I knew that, and was a little quirky, but I couldn't imagine her being suicidal. She sort of presents as this meek thing but she's strong really. She was just trying not to step on toes. Ethelton can be quite insular. Despite it all, she likes the town, I think. She even likes Manson. But Manson didn't like her apparently.'

'Oh, how so?'

She glances in the wing mirror, then turns back to me.

'Well, that night at the restaurant, someone started harassing them,' she says. 'Not just him, her as well.'

'There was an argument. I've seen the CCTV footage from the restaurant.'

'Not an argument. Just Cody Booth accosting them until someone intervened. He was drinking nearby, saw them from the street and went up to them.'

Cody Booth. I have a name. 'You know this guy, Cody Booth?'

'He's fixed my car once.'

'So you know where he works?' I ask.

'Yeah, he's over in Manson, at Smith's Auto. Bad reputation that boy.'

This gives me a moment of pause. Surely the police would have checked him out. They've got the footage from the restaurant and he works at Smith's Auto, where the car was last serviced . . . on the day of the crash.

I feel the itch, like I'm close to something important. I'm still processing this news when she speaks again.

'There was a run-in at a diner with some other redneck too,' Larissa continues. 'They thought Oliver did something.'

'And what exactly did they think Oliver did?'

She raises her eyebrows. 'Isn't that what you're looking into? I don't think they're linked by the way.'

'You don't think what are linked, Larissa? I need you to fill in some blanks for me.'

She glances towards the school gates, then lets out a long breath. 'Well, the rumour is that he was seeing someone else, someone younger.'

'Eshana knew this, I assume?'

'We're not supposed to linger here. Just drop off and go.'

'Just one or two more questions,' I say.

'Look, it was just a rumour I heard. I don't know if she knew about it or not.'

'And that's enough to make half the town hate you, having an affair?'

'The person he was supposedly cheating with . . . well, she was a teenager at the time.'

It can't be true, I think, *not in a town this small. The police would find out.* But this aligns with what I already know, the Sugar Babies website. The payments to Kiara.

We're both thinking it, I'm sure, but I don't want to influence her by saying the name first. 'Any idea who the girl is?'

She looks directly into my eyes, her face almost impassive. 'I heard it was Kiara King. So when she disappeared and Eshana was his alibi, that made people talk. Apparently someone saw him with Kiara. He used to pick her up from her house. They were doing something in his car. And I was with Eshana when she found out about Kiara's disappearance. She looked like she was going to be sick.'

'Any idea who saw Oliver and Kiara together?'

'No. That's how rumours work here – someone says something and it spreads like wildfire. I know Eshana was worried Oliver had had an affair. That's why she was drinking so much the night of the dance school break-up. I can't remember her exact words – we were both drunk – but I got the impression she thought he'd done something to Kiara.'

She draws a breath before continuing. 'So that's what everyone was asking when Maddison disappeared too, right before the crash. They were saying, "What did he do with Maddie?"'

Now her eyes go past me and I sense someone approaching.

'Come on,' the teacher says. 'Move it along please.'

'Time's up,' I say to Larissa. 'Thanks for your help.' Then I turn and walk toward where my car is parked further along the street. I watch as she drives away.

What did he do with Maddie? Larissa's words are still in my head. And the name Cody Booth – the guy who accosted Oliver Stiles at the restaurant the day Maddison Stubbs disappeared. Even if the cops aren't linking Maddison's disappearance with Kiara's, I am. In the car, I get online and search for him, Cody Booth.

He's got a public Instagram. In his profile picture, he's got a tiny puff of brown hair on the end of his chin, otherwise he's clean-shaven with short dark hair. He's got blue eyes and is good-looking in a Kevin Federline kind of way. Not that these kids would have any idea who Federline is. If it wasn't for the trashy magazines, I probably wouldn't either.

Once I've scrolled past the first dozen photos of Cody on his motorbike, drinking Jack Daniel's with a group of friends, and playing beer pong, there are photos of bongs and empty Whippit canisters. He's not shy about his drug use it seems. One image grabs me by the shirtfront. A beautiful blonde girl with Cody Booth standing behind her, his arms wrapped around her. It's Maddison Stubbs.

There's another photo with his arm around Maddison: *Six months with my baby girl*. A photo of her jumping into the dam: *Summer has arrived people*.

As much as Maddison managed to keep her life private, Cody Booth fortunately did not. And he works at the mechanics that serviced Oliver Stiles's car just before the crash, the day Maddie, presumably his ex, disappeared. The link is undeniable.

I continue scrolling through and every second photo seems to have her in it. I make a note of the dates. They start a year and a half ago, when Maddison was seventeen, and continue for close to a year. The Maddison images are bracketed by a photo of a car doing a burnout at one end and a photo of Cody giving the camera the finger at the other end. Both have the same hashtag: *#youngrichandsingle*.

This has to be something. My heart is pounding.

What did Chief Stubbs think of his daughter dating a man who openly posts images of bongs? It says something about Maddison too, I suppose – that she saw something in Cody Booth when evidently he's a parent's worst nightmare, especially if you've got a teenage daughter.

I think about it the entire drive to Smith's Auto. I park nearby and watch the garage.

Three things influence the price you pay at a mechanics. One: what's wrong with the car. Two: how much you *know* about the car. Three: how much the car is worth. Smith's Autos in particular looks like the sort of place that would see Oliver Stiles's nice shiny car and double the mark-up on parts and add a few extra hours of labour.

The garage sits one block back from the main drag of Manson, and the street is busy enough that I can survey the joint from my front seat without attracting any attention. The building is painted cinder block and stained concrete, and it looks cluttered and chaotic inside. There are three mechanics by my count, all wearing filthy blue overalls, and I recognise Cody Booth from his Instagram.

He's the youngest of the three, and he wears his overalls open at the waist, the arms tied around him like a belt. Despite the cold, he's wearing just a white tank top underneath. He's muscular and I can see a couple of tattoos, including one near the base of his neck. He's tall; he would have been an attractive prospect in high school for football and basketball. Until his late teens, that is, when – according to his Instagram – it was all parties and bongs, cars and motorbikes.

After half an hour, Cody emerges from the garage and climbs into a souped-up Honda Civic that, when he starts it, sounds like a waste disposal unit at full throttle. He has one of those stick-figure families on his back window, but it's just a stick-figure man behind a bent stick-figure woman with the caption: *Making my family.* Below it, a bumper sticker reads *Don't get too close, your daughter is probably in here.* No prizes for guessing how Chief Stubbs feels about that.

I start the Camry and follow him. He doesn't go far: around the corner and through the lights before he pulls in at the Dunkin' Donuts. I wait for him to go inside before parking in a spot two spaces down, a plan forming in my mind. I've got a toolkit in my trunk and enough automotive nous to tinker with my engine.

I pop the hood and quickly reach in to loosen off the vacuum hose. It'll make the idle inconsistent; it might even stall. I know it'll only take a mechanic two minutes to figure out, which I hope is enough time. Then I turn my baseball cap around, lower my pants an inch so they're baggy around my shoes, and stand with my hands on the edge of the engine bay, staring in.

'Car trouble?' a voice says behind me, right on cue.

I turn to see Cody Booth carrying a tray of coffees on top of a box of donuts. I experience the same satisfaction I used to get when I fished with Dad up in the hills . . . that feeling of a trout taking my bait.

'Ah, yeah,' I say. 'Got burnt by a dodgy mechanic, it's not been the same since.'

'What's it doing?' He comes closer, puts the coffees and donuts down on the trunk of his own car. He's even taller than I thought – six feet three – and lean and sinewy.

'It was fine until I got the oil changed. Now it's doing this.'

'What's this?'

'Stalling at the lights sometimes, or revving really high.'

'Could be a couple things,' he says. 'Our shop's around the corner. Bring it in and I'll take a look this afternoon. Could probably fix that wing mirror too.'

'Listen, if you can get me back on the road right now, I'll give you fifty bucks. I got to get moving.'

'How much they charge you for the oil change?'

'Hundred and sixty.'

'Crooks,' the kid says. 'We charge ninety and throw in a free tyre alignment.'

Crooks. The word that was left by the memorial.

'Well, you're a better sort than the last guy,' I say.

'Alright, let me see.' He bends over the hood.

As he surveys the engine, I look off down the road and say, 'Can't wait to get out of this place, to be honest.'

'Yeah?' he says. 'Where you from?'

'City. Nothing but crime up here.'

'Nothing wrong with the place,' Cody says, a hint of annoyance in his voice. 'Crime happens everywhere.'

'Maybe you're right, but I read in the paper about those missing girls,' I say. 'Two in six months. Hardly seems like a safe place to me.'

'Well, a lot more people get killed in the city than up here.'

'Were they killed then?' I say. 'I thought they were just missing.'

'I don't know much about it.' He's checking the fuel line now. 'They haven't found either of them. Can you turn the ignition?'

I start it, then come back out. It's idling high, revving up around three thousand, then drops right down.

'It's your gaskets or your hoses,' he says. 'I can have a look to see if there's a leak in the hose, or if it's just loose. Anything else, I won't be able to help you with here.'

He's too quick. I've not got enough time to get the conversation moving in the direction I want. I take a risk, pushing on with it.

'You reckon they'll catch the guy? Must be a local, right?'

He stops working his hands, glances back at me. 'The guy?'

'Whoever killed those girls.'

'Nobody killed any girls,' he says, letting the annoyance surface again. 'There is no *he* – I don't know what you're talking about. They ran away.'

'Well, that's not what I've heard.'

'Yeah? What have you heard?'

'That maybe there's a serial killer in this town and the police don't want to admit it. Only a matter of time before they find the girls' bodies. Probably one of their exes did it.'

He gives a short huff of laughter. 'That so? I don't think you've got the faintest idea what happens in this town.'

'Yeah? Well, what's the story then?'

He stares at my face, then says, 'Now turn her off.'

I walk to the driver's window, reach in and turn the key, before coming back to the front of the car.

He stands up, closes the hood. 'She's all fixed.'

I reach for my wallet, pull out a fifty-dollar bill.

Cody shakes his head with a wry smile. 'No, no, this one's on the house. A mechanic really did screw you over, huh?'

'I insist. Or let me get you a beer before I head out of town?'

'Here's a better idea,' he says, picking up his coffees and donuts. 'You stay the hell away from me. Tell him it's over. This has got to stop.'

'Tell who?'

'You know damn well who,' he says. 'Drive safe.'

Then he's back in his Honda Civic and roaring out of the car park, screaming through a light that's just gone red.

When I get in the car and turn the key, I'm not surprised that it doesn't start. When I open the hood, I see a clean cut through the vacuum line. Probably done with a box cutter.

'Shit!' I hammer one fist on the edge of the engine bay. 'Son of a bitch!'

I take my phone from my pocket, look up another mechanics. The closest one is on the other side of town so I dial for a tow. They can fix the car in the next day or two, they say.

If I take a bus to the city, I could be back in Manson by nightfall with the Challenger. It'll make me more visible but the police have me in a white Camry so maybe changing car isn't such a bad idea.

The tow truck comes twenty minutes later, loads up the Camry and drives off. I walk the mile back to the motel with my head down, headphones plugged into my ears and sunglasses on, but still feel like a fish in a tank. *Tell him it's over.* Who was Cody talking about?

Back at the motel, I phone for a taxi to take me to the bus depot. A Greyhound departs at 2 pm. I'll be in the city by four and back in Manson by six if it all goes to plan.

While I wait, I type up my notes for Crown – the information from the junkyard, the dance school, everything else – plus photos. I add a list of my expenses – the motel, food, gas – and press send.

Then I take the receipt from the cafe out of my pocket. As I punch the number into my phone, I imagine all the ways this could go, and very few of them end well. None really, if I'm honest, and yet I know I could do with the company.

Hey Peyton, Reid from the cafe here. I'd love to check
out that bar sometime.

A dissenting voice in my head reminds me: *Remember the last time you met a boy in this town?* Marco broke my heart and ruined my life.

ESHANA
BEFORE

HOLLY HAS HER legs crossed and her notebook propped on her knee.

'I still don't really know what happened,' I tell her.

'Are you saying that Oliver explained the situation, but you don't believe him?'

I shrug. 'I believe he was giving Kiara money for her mom, but I also feel like he knows more about her disappearance. And that night out with my friends from the dance school – he was different before then, but that seemed to make him worse. Like he doesn't really trust anyone at all.'

'Like the police?' Holly asks.

'Yeah, them, and just people in town.'

'Do you think the police have investigated Kiara's disappearance as best they can?'

'I guess I just assumed they did.'

'And you provided Oliver with an alibi because he was at home with you on the night of the disappearance?'

I nod. 'I did. He got in, he was in a mood. I made dinner and he became quite unwell. It had gluten in it. He slept in the spare room. He didn't want to keep me up.'

She makes a small sound. 'And the police spoke to your husband and cleared him of any wrongdoing at all?'

'Yeah,' I say. 'But I read online that a runaway doesn't attract the same level of investigation as an abduction. So maybe the police didn't look into it as deeply as they should have.'

'You think it was easier for the police to just say Kiara ran away?'

'I found an online message board where people try to solve disappearances,' I go on. 'Someone has built up a profile for Kiara on there and there's a discussion around why it's not a murder case because there's no body, no blood, no physical evidence at all. But they also say that she didn't do or say anything that suggested that she was planning to run away. And the timelines aren't exact because her mom didn't see her leave her room after six pm. She thought she heard her on the phone later but wasn't sure.'

'Eshana,' Holly says, 'do you believe it's possible that your husband was in some way involved in Kiara's disappearance even if the police don't? Even if he's told you he wasn't and there's no evidence?'

I know it sounds insane, I know it isn't logical, but I can't shake those lingering doubts.

'I just can't rule it out entirely,' I say. 'Sometimes I feel like I know him so well, then other times it's like I don't know him at all. He doesn't give up much of himself.'

'It sounds like it's a communication issue. Do you think it could be something you and Oliver need to unlock?'

'Maybe,' I say.

I could tell Holly that Kiara wanted to move away to become a screenwriter, according to what I overheard Oli telling the police. But the only actual fact I have to go on is that Oli was giving Kiara money, which he said was going towards her mother's medication.

'Do you think there are other issues in your marriage, Eshana? Things that you can't quite articulate?'

'Such as?'

'I don't know. The trust issues obviously come from the fact Oli was married when you met. I wonder if you feel like he respects you.'

It's a punch to the sternum. I stare right into her eyes, trying to find another way to interpret her words.

I exhale, look at the art on the wall. 'He respects me but sometimes I just feel like I don't have anything else in my life, you know?'

'He's the only thing keeping you here?'

'In this town? Yes. If anything happened, I don't know what I would do.'

'Do you ever feel like leaving him?' Holly asks.

'No, it's never crossed my mind. I know you probably think we're co-dependent, or I'm dependent on him. Maybe I am. I just have these insane moments where I realise I could be a completely different person if I hadn't taken his class and fallen in love with him. It makes me feel confused. I had my life planned out, this vision of where I was going and what I was going to do, and then it was all derailed. I could be somebody else entirely. I wouldn't be here.'

'Do you mean you wouldn't be here in my office?' she clarifies. 'In a therapist's office?'

'In this room, in this town. Who knows?'

She makes a thoughtful sound at the back of her throat. I know it's because we're going in a direction we've never been.

'Sometimes it depresses me to consider what that younger me would think if she saw me now,' I say. 'A part-time wage worker, part-time housewife, endlessly scrolling Instagram, perpetually paranoid my husband is having an affair. Not writing or dancing.' I give a laugh, but even I hear no joy in it. 'Sometimes I'll be driving the car and I wonder, what would happen if I just pressed the accelerator to the floor? Would anyone miss me?'

Holly stares at me, her eyes slightly narrowed. 'I think we need to unpack that, Eshana. Do you think you might be feeling depressed?'

'I'm not sure.'

Depressed. It's possible, I suppose. Now that the word is out there, floating around me, I recognise it.

'Well, I can write you a script for something to help you feel better. I want to ask you another question now though, and I need you to be completely honest with me, Eshana. Do you ever have suicidal thoughts?'

I stare at her, wondering if I should tell her the truth.

REID
NOW

THE CAMRY IS safe but it's no fun to drive. The Challenger is a completely different proposition. Ferrari red, an engine you can hear from five blocks away and, more importantly, *fast*. Those long straight roads back to Manson roll out before me.

As I'm nearing town, my phone vibrates in my pocket.

> I was waiting for you to message me.

My heart races in my chest and I read the message again. *Is that it? That's all he has to say?* Then I see the three dots appear.

> I changed my mind about tonight. 8 pm at Geralds?

Warmth spreads like an algal bloom through my body. I try to match his direct tone with my response.

> I'll see you there.

The Challenger has half a tank, but I stop at the gas station anyway to see if Kiara King's 'bestie', Angel, is behind the counter.

A news van with the satellite on its roof folded away pulls in beside me. Someone gets out of the driver's seat and starts fuelling up. I see a passenger in the front seat, staring down at her phone. What are they doing in town?

I fill up the Challenger, then go inside and grab a copy of *Star* magazine. Jennifer Aniston is on the cover. She's been on the cover of these magazines since I was a teenager.

'Just the gas?' Angel says.

'And the magazine.'

'These are all two for one,' she says, sliding her hand near the chocolate bars beside the counter.

'No, thanks. I don't need any more sugar today,' I say with a smile. 'I might grab a newspaper though.' I pick up the *Herald* and place it on top of the magazine.

She scans both. 'Twenty-eight ten with the gas,' she says.

I hand over thirty in bills. 'Can I ask you a question?'

'What is it?' I sense her discomfort.

'Did you know the girls?'

'What girls?' she says, staring down at the counter separating us.

'Kiara King? Maddison Stubbs?'

She looks out at the forecourt, as if hoping someone from the media van will come in. 'Umm, yeah. I went to school with Kiara.'

'Well, hopefully she turns up,' I say. 'I'm actually in town on an investigation.'

Her expression changes and she cranes her head a little closer. 'Like FBI or something?'

'A little like that, I suppose, yeah. I've heard a couple things but there's no real solid leads. Just some rumours about an older man.'

She stares down at the counter again. I bow my head a little to look into her eyes.

'Does the name Oliver Stiles mean anything to you?'

Her eyes flick up to meet mine. She shakes her head.

It's time to take a risk.

'Look, I know who you are,' I say. 'I know that you gave a statement to the police. You told them that Kiara was planning on running away and also that she was on the Sugar Babies For You website.'

'She just wanted to go to California one day,' she says, defensively. 'She wanted to help her mom and get out of here.'

Bingo.

'She was seeing Oliver Stiles, right? A married man.'

She shakes her head and her hair falls down across her cheeks. She sweeps it back. 'No one was supposed to know. She just needed money. That's why she was doing it.'

'Doing what?'

'The stuff with the websites.'

I hear someone enter behind me. 'Did she meet anyone else?' I ask more quietly.

She shakes her head again. 'Not that I know of. She said no one else had any money. He was rich.'

I have to play this just right – act like I know more than I do. 'What about the other guys she was seeing?'

She looks guilty. 'She wasn't seeing other guys,' she says. 'She didn't have a boyfriend or anything.'

A girl from a poor neighbourhood selling herself to pay the bills. It's such a damn cliché.

'You were good friends then?' I ask.

'We were best friends. She's a little older than me, so maybe like sisters. Then one day she just stopped coming around – she was always thinking about something else.'

The door opens again and someone else comes in.

Angel holds out my receipt.

'I'll grab your number in case my colleagues have any follow-up questions,' I say.

She's hesitant.

'Unless you want someone to visit you at home to talk about it?'

'No, here.' She takes back the receipt I'm holding out and writes her number down across the top of it.

'Will I get in trouble?' she asks.

'For what?'

'For not telling the police that she was meeting him?'

'No. So long as you tell the truth now.'

I turn around and see a cop perusing the snacks. *Shit*. Did he overhear me?

He looks over, a moment of eye contact. I don't recognise him, but I wonder if he recognises me.

●

Back at the motel, I have forty minutes before I have to leave for the bar. I map out each of the players: Oliver and Eshana Stiles, the two missing girls, Chief Stubbs, Cody Booth, Larissa. I write down what I know about how they're all connected, hoping something else will unlock.

One thing I do understand is how undercooked the investigation into Kiara's disappearance was. The police treated it as a runaway. Kiara's mother told them that her little sister's bike was missing too, which would have strengthened their theory.

Oliver Stiles had an account on Sugar Babies For You; it looks like that's how he met Kiara. He was cheating on his wife and some people in the town knew that. Weeks before the crash, Eshana told her friend Larissa that she thought there was a chance Oliver was involved in Kiara's disappearance. There's also the cryptic message on Eshana's Facebook about a holiday without Oliver, and the payment to American Airlines on the bank statement from Oliver's office.

No doubt the police considered Oliver Stiles as a suspect, but he must have an alibi, or they never had enough evidence to make an arrest. They may have dropped the ball with Kiara, but they'll be throwing everything at the Maddison Stubbs investigation.

REID
NOW

GERALD'S BAR IS located between an ice-cream shop and an Italian restaurant. A waiter in a starched white shirt and suspenders greets me at the door. Muted bulbs light the long polished bar. Wax trickles down candelabras set out on each of the small dark wood tables in the dining area. There weren't places like this in Ethelton when I was still around; this feels more like the city.

'Grab a seat anywhere,' the waiter says.

'I'm actually meeting someone.'

'Sure, have a look around.'

I walk past the bar to the booths around the back and find Peyton sitting alone, his phone in hand.

'This seat free?' I say.

He glances up. Lit from below in the candlelight, his cheekbones could cut glass. Again I wonder about the age difference; could he be any older than twenty-five? Maybe I've got the wrong impression. Maybe this isn't what I think it is.

He smiles. 'Beginning to think you might have stood me up.'

I slide in on the other side of the booth and look down at the drinks menu.

'Parking is surprisingly scarce around here,' I say. 'Might have been faster if I'd just walked from Manson.'

'Oh yes, this is the strip. Anything worth doing at night in Ethelton happens here or over near the campus. You know, if you're young.'

'What's it like at the restaurant next door?'

'Fine. I don't eat there much, it's a bit pricey.'

This entire strip has changed. The video store has gone the way of the cable salesman and the TV repair shops. The florist burnt down, and no one's fixed the place back up. Only a few places remain from when I was a kid, when Mom would do the Ethelton women's hair before driving back across the river to Manson.

'So this is the local watering hole?' I say.

Peyton grins. 'Not quite. It's fun though. There'll be a band on that tiny stage soon.' He points over my shoulder. 'It's better than the sports bar, or the student bars.'

'Student bars. You could fit in there nicely, you're barely out of your teens.'

'Ha, that came up early.'

'What?'

'The age difference.'

This *must* be a date. 'Well, how old *are* you?' I ask.

'I turned thirty-one in November. You just assume I'm young because I serve you coffee and like to be clean-shaven.'

Maybe he's right. There might be some bias here.

'It is quiet,' he adds. 'I guess no one really wants to be out.'

'Because of the missing girls?'

He looks at me as if solving an equation. 'I guess so. You ought to be careful – people will be suspicious of out-of-towners.'

Once more I find my gaze drawn to his mouth. Full lips, above which sits the hint of a moustache.

'Well, you're not local either, are you?' I say.

'Local enough. Moved here with my mom as a teenager.'

'Your accent could pass for local, but I had a hunch.'

He smiles. 'You think you can read people. All salesmen are like that.'

The air is warm between us.

A waiter appears at our side. 'Drinks?' he asks.

'I'll have a gin and still water,' I say

Peyton orders a whisky soda. He holds out a card. 'Leave it open.'

Before the waiter can take the card, I push it away and put a twenty-dollar bill in his hand instead.

When the waiter's gone, Peyton says, 'You only pay cash, don't you?'

'It's easier,' I say and quickly change the subject. 'It must be tough waking up to discover what's happened. I wonder if Mrs Stiles remembers being behind the wheel. I can't imagine what that would be like.'

'You're awfully interested in the crash,' Peyton remarks.

'I've heard they had problems,' I say. 'He might have been cheating. Did you ever see any tension between them?'

'It's just rumours. Everyone has heard them.'

I can't pursue this too hard without raising suspicion.

The drinks arrive and I take a good slug of gin. It's not the cheap Gordon's I normally drink; there's some obscure botanicals in it.

'I'm just a true crime junkie,' I say. 'I know you're close to all of this and I shouldn't push you.'

'You're like a dog with a bone, aren't you?' he says, with a teasing note in his voice. 'Small towns are powered by gossip.'

'And the gossip was?'

'Apparently he was a bit of a creep.'

'That's what I heard. He was on one of those online dating sites,' I say. 'A sugar baby site.'

'Yeah, I heard someone saw him in the back seat of his car with Kiara. That's the thing about rumours – even if they're true, you never get the full story.'

'Right,' I say.

'Anyway,' he says, reaching out and clinking his glass against mine. 'It's nice to meet someone who isn't a complete psycho.' He takes a sip. 'You're way less boring than I was expecting too.'

'Do I give off a boring vibe?'

'A little. Mysterious, yes. Boring, possibly.'

I take another sip of my drink, and it's accompanied by that old familiar habit of reaching for a cigarette. It's been weeks since I last smoked. You'd think Mom's emphysema would be enough to put me off the habit, but I still have the itch. It always comes back. Mom quit smoking when I was a kid, but I still remember the patches, the gum. And the little jar above the fridge; whenever she felt like a cigarette, she'd put a quarter in to see how much she was saving. I remember how proud my father was of her, how he would tell her he'd love her forever either way. I remember her spending the entire jar of quarters on a yellow sundress and the way my dad smiled when she wore it. After he died, within a couple months she was back to a pack every couple of days. Perched out in the dark on the porch at night with a coffee and a cigarette. Never in the house.

Peyton and I sit and chat for a couple of hours. I stop at two drinks, despite a pressing urge to let the evening dissolve in gin and too-loud bar music. A hangover will make tomorrow much harder to get through and I need to be on my game.

'Maybe next time we can get a meal,' I say.

As we walk towards my car, I realise a decision has been made. I'm dropping him home.

He gets in the Challenger beside me and I follow his directions. He lives in a unit half a mile away, and when I pull over, I see something that makes me freeze. There's a white Jeep parked out front.

'What?' Peyton says.

'This is your place? This one here?' I point at the unit.

'Yes?' he says slowly. 'Why?'

'What's it like inside?'

He turns to me. 'That's forward of you.'

I force a laugh. 'I guess I want to see where you live. I'm not trying to pull a move.'

'Well, that's a shame,' he says. 'Come on. It's a mess, my room-mate is a bit of a slob.'

'I thought you said you walk to work?' I say, nodding at the Jeep as we pass it.

'Oh I do, I barely drive that thing. Plus my roommate uses it more than I do.'

Before I can react, we've reached the unit's door and Peyton's lips are against mine. It's brief and intense. He grabs my face and pushes me back against the door. I find my hands on his back, pulling him against me. Then as quickly as it starts, it's over. He stops.

'I was waiting patiently all night to do that,' he says, smiling against my lips. He kisses me again. 'Come on, I'll give you the tour,' he says, taking my hand.

The house is empty. Peyton puts a record on, something cool and jazzy, then gestures around him. 'This is the living room.'

No TV, a green velvet couch, unframed art on the walls.

'Kitchen,' he says, pointing through an open door. He puts his hand on another door, closed. 'Brendon's room.'

Brendon. I make a mental note.

He touches the door beside it. 'Bathroom. And come down here, I'll show you my room.'

At the end of the hall, he opens the door into an immaculately tidy room. Bed made, bedside table clear except for a thick book marked halfway and a reading lamp. In the corner is a computer on a desk, with a Swiss ball for a seat.

'It's cosy,' I say.

'You mean small. But it's fine, I like it.' He takes my hand again, leads me back along the hall.

'So how do you know Brendon?'

'Found him online. I couldn't afford to rent the entire place myself, so I listed the room, and he was interested.'

'Seems everyone meets online these days,' I say. 'Except we met in a cafe.'

'That's true. You just kept turning up until I agreed to go out with you. Grab a seat.'

I sit on the couch as he goes into the kitchen.

'Nightcap?' he calls back.

'Would love one but I've still got to drive.' He hasn't invited me to stay, just yet.

'Soda, juice?'

'Water is fine.'

My eyes are drawn to Brendon's door. I need to know more about him.

I stand and go into the kitchen. There's a power bill on the fridge but it's in Peyton's name. He's mixing himself a martini.

He turns and hands me a glass of water.

'Cheers,' he says, and we clink glasses.

'So is he a local, Brendon?'

'Why?' he asks, with a funny smile.

'Sorry. I thought you would have learnt that about me by now, Peyton. I'm a curious man.'

'I'm curious about your curiosity.'

I know I've got to move on. 'I guess I just didn't think people found roommates online. Anyway, he's out for the night, I assume?'

'He messaged me earlier and said he was going to his mom's place.'

We go back through to the lounge; we talk about music and books. He kisses me again, one hand resting on my cheek. The other against my chest.

He pulls away. 'You're a bit distracted.'

Could I tell him what I'm really in town for? That I'm not a salesman but a creepy private investigator, someone who uncovers people's deepest secrets by any means possible. Would he run for the hills? If he did, it wouldn't be the first time it's happened. People don't like to date someone who could find out everything about them. I'm basically a qualified stalker.

'No,' I say. 'Just wish I didn't need to drive.'

'You don't need to drive,' he says, a small smile. 'There's room here.'

It's a tempting prospect.

'Okay, maybe I'll have a martini.'

'Good idea. Dirty?'

'Dry and clean, please. So what does computer science mean?'

'It's always changing. I'm learning about blockchain technology at the moment.'

'Like cryptocurrencies, NFTs, that sort of thing?'

'That sort of thing.'

I can't take my mind off the possibility that his roommate, or someone driving his car, vandalised the memorial. Or, and I can't dismiss this possibility altogether just yet, that it was Peyton. But he's not given any indication he felt that strongly about Oliver. He did mention his roommate didn't like him though.

He drains the last of his martini. 'Dry and clean,' he says, standing up.

'Bingo.'

While Peyton is in the kitchen, I go quickly to Brendon's room. I open the door silently and slip inside. It's dark so I use my phone to look around. On a dresser I see a bong, some vape pens. Clothes on the floor. It's a far cry from Peyton's spotless room. There's a computer set up at a desk with two large monitors. A gamer?

I don't know precisely what I'm after, but a surname would help. Then I see it. A framed picture on the dresser. Brendon is handsome – tanned skin, a big smile. He has his arm around three girls, all younger. And one of them, the oldest of the three, is Kiara King. *Is Brendon Kiara's brother?* If so, does he also know that Oliver Stiles was seeing her? That might be enough motivation to vandalise the memorial. Or to do something worse.

I raise my phone and take a photo, then I go to his computer desk. I don't know what I'm looking for but I scan the surface, then pull open the desk drawer. It's full of cables, an old mouse, the sort of computing paraphernalia you'd expect.

'What the hell are you doing?'

I slam the drawer shut and turn to find Peyton standing there, a martini in each hand.

'I can explain,' I say, but I know it's too late for that now.

'Get out,' he says. His voice is cold. 'Right now, before I call the police.'

'Please – it's not what you think.'

'Get the hell out of my house!'

He steps back to let me through.

I lower my head and walk past him, take my coat from the back of his couch. I pull it on as I step through the front door and turn back to apologise, but the door slams an inch from my face.

'Alright,' I say. 'I had a really good night too.' Then more quietly, 'I just had to go and ruin it, didn't I.'

I cross the lawn, taking another look at the white Jeep. I go closer to peer through the windows into the dark inside. I don't see anything other than an empty chip packet in the footwell of the passenger seat and a Wendy's cup in the centre drink holder.

I get in the Challenger and set off back to the motel. All the excitement of the night has drained out of me, leaving a vacuum of self-pity and frustration.

To take my mind off the endless fuck-up that is my sex life, I think over the case.

Brendon may be Kiara's brother, and he might have spray-painted *CROOK* beside Oliver's memorial. Cody Booth is Maddison's ex, and he harassed Oliver at the restaurant the night of his death. Cody and Brendon. At least one of them is guilty of something.

ESHANA
BEFORE

DANCE SCHOOL IS starting again soon but I'm thinking maybe I won't go along anymore. Embarrassing myself at drinks after the prize-giving ceremony was bad enough, but the gossip about Oli has made matters worse. In fact, the thought of seeing those women again makes me want to crawl into a dark cave and hibernate. I've only seen Larissa once since that night, and she looked at me with sad, sorry eyes. But things have been better between Oli and me lately. We've promised to be more communicative, more open. And I've agreed to trust him more and not jump to conclusions. I am endeavouring to put it all behind me. The police have cleared him. Kiara is probably somewhere in California, writing a screenplay and working at a bar. It's all been blown out of proportion with the rumours and speculation but now things are quietening down again.

Work has been busy, and this morning I drove to meet with one of my colleagues who's in the city for a wedding this coming weekend. It felt good getting out of the twin towns, even if it was only for half a day.

I stopped in to see Clare at her real estate office too. We had a quick coffee, and she asked about Oli. She wanted to know if the police are still talking to him about the girl he helped, but I brushed her off. Oli will kill me if he finds out I told her about that.

On my way back in the late afternoon, I pass through Manson and decide, on a whim, to stop at a diner Oli and I went to a few times when we first moved out of the city. Last time I was here, I had the waffles and could barely get through one let alone two, but they were really good, and for the first time in weeks it feels like I have an appetite again.

I pull up outside beside a truck with a bumper sticker for Trump. It's an old beat-up thing with *Ryley's Plumbing* signage on the side.

When I walk in, the place feels stifling. I peel my scarf off and push it into my bag. Apart from the piped music, the place goes silent. Conversations pause and a thin layer of tension falls over the place.

I head straight for a booth near the corner and look down at the menu. *Why didn't I just go to my usual cafe, across the bridge? Why did I stop in Manson?*

The waitress comes over. She's pretty, her black curls pulled up in a topknot.

'Do you want me to run through the specials?' she says.

'I think I know what I want. Do you still do the waffles?'

'Yeah, we got waffles. That what you want?'

'Yes, please.'

'Sure. And can I get you anything to drink?'

'No,' I say, squeezing out a smile. 'I'm fine for a drink.'

There's a small flicker of argument at a table across the room. I look over and the father of the family is staring at me. He's a big barrel of a man wrapped in a stained flannel shirt, with a faded beige-camouflage cap and a scorching red beard.

I feel heat on my neck – like when my mom saw the snake on the trail. I sense danger, but can't identify from where or why.

I look away. My appetite is gone again.

The door opens and someone else enters. All I can see in my peripheral vision is that he's a tall man. He takes the booth near me.

The waiter brings over my waffles as the family of the staring man rise to leave. But the man's not going towards the door, he's coming around the tables. I look up just in time to see his eyes are fixed on me. They're ugly and mean.

'He'll get what's coming! You both will,' he says. 'How can you stay with him? She was still a girl!'

My heart pounds and I can't keep his gaze. I look past him to his family. A daughter with a birthmark on her neck, and two boys who could be twins. His wife too, her hands trembling by her sides. Does she feel my shame?

'Come on, honey,' she says.

'Hey!' Another man's voice behind me. 'Leave her be.'

The room is silent again.

'Relax, buddy,' the bearded man says. 'Just wishing the lady an enjoyable meal.'

Now the second man comes forward; he's a few inches taller, with strong tanned forearms. 'What's your problem?' he says.

I focus on the grain of the wood in the dark varnished table.

'Alright, Eric. Out you go,' says a third man in chef's whites and Crocs. He must have come out from the kitchen. 'You've said your piece.'

The chef gestures to escort the bearded man out. He shrugs, winging his arms and pushing out his chest.

'I can see myself out,' he says. He carries himself with an easy unspent violence that causes a sort of cold terror in my stomach.

I don't want to leave this restaurant. I'm not sure if my legs would carry me. He could be outside, waiting for me.

'Mind if I join you?' the man from the booth near me says. 'I've just ordered the steak, and I wouldn't feel right if he came back.'

He walks around to face me and I meet his eyes. They're grey and intense beneath his broad forehead.

'Sure,' I say. 'Okay.'

'What's your name?'

'Eshana.'

'Eshana, my name's Jarrod. But my friends call me Sticks.'

He stretches out his great big hand. As I reach to shake it, I find my own hand is trembling violently.

'It's okay,' he says. 'He's gone now. What was that all about anyway?'

'It's a long story.'

'Well,' he says, gesturing towards my plate. 'You can tell me about it while you eat your waffles.'

REID
NOW

ON THE WAY back to the motel, I switch the radio on to clear my head. They're running the news headlines from earlier.

. . . remains were discovered this morning by a couple walking their dog. Police are yet to release the identity . . .

I turn it up. This morning? How did I miss this? I remember the TV crew at the gas station. It makes sense now.

Remains. Not *body*. The distinction is important. Maddison Stubbs has only been missing for a few days. If it's her, she would likely be described as *a body.*

. . . In other news, a key witness has come forward in the abduction of Maddison Stubbs. A child from one of the neighbouring properties noticed a white sedan arrive at the property on the day of her disappearance and leave sometime later. The vehicle belongs to a local mechanic's garage. This comes after police discovered personal effects belonging to Maddison in a shed on a rural property outside of Ethelton . . .

Someone has died. I feel sick for the family. It never gets easier, even after my years as a cop. It's Cody Booth. It has to be. A car belonging to a local mechanic's garage.

I drive to the street where the garage is located. The police must have made the connection with Cody Booth by now. They must have interviewed him when Maddison first disappeared given he's the ex.

I park some distance away, far from the prying eyes of any CCTV cameras in the industrial area. I fetch a thin black balaclava, a pair of gloves and my lockpicking kit from the boot, and set out quickly towards the garage.

It's dark and cool; a gust of wind tears along the street. The two gins have taken the edge off, but I'm still a little nervous. This is unplanned and reckless, but if you need quick answers sometimes it's best to take a calculated risk.

It's all warehouses along here, no movement under the street-lights. A dog barks somewhere in the distance and cars drone along the main stretch one block over, but here, I'm alone. I pull the balaclava over my head, put on my gloves and run towards the entrance of Smith's Auto.

They've got a steel roller door with a padlock; I pick it in a matter of minutes and in that time no cars pass. I close the roller door behind me. I click the switch on the flashlight attached to my wrist and a circle of light wobbles ahead of me as I move deeper into the garage.

In the back office, it's as messy as I'd imagined. Stacks of paper. A nude calendar from the nineties hanging on the grubby wall behind the desk. Pens and tools everywhere, dog-eared invoice books, and an old computer with a shiny new payment terminal sitting right beside it.

They're still keeping manual hand-written receipts and I flick through the carbon copies, scrolling back to the day of the crash when Oliver picked up his car. I find it there. He came by around five in the afternoon.

Drain & clean g/t, replace fuel filter/strainer, flush line.
Darryl

It looks like the car wasn't serviced by Cody Booth at all but someone called Darryl. Could Cody have helped him? Or done something to the car while nobody was watching? Then I look at the invoice amount: $0.00. They didn't charge him. It doesn't make sense.

I take a photo of the receipt, upload it.

I go to the computer, turn it on, but meet a password field. I hear a car rolling by out on the street. I've got to get moving. There could be a silent alarm.

I go through the desk drawers quickly, shining the flashlight in. If I can find some more information about Booth, this will all be worth it but there's nothing else here.

Footsteps outside. I go to the door, ready to run. But the footsteps continue past. I wait a few moments, before lifting the roller door and leaving the garage.

I lock up behind me and rush along the street to my car, pocketing the gloves and balaclava. Then it's back to the motel.

The excitement and energy of the night is replaced by confusion and trepidation when I see the door to my motel room is open. The night is about to take a turn for the worse.

I wouldn't have left the door open. I *didn't* leave it open; I remember locking it.

Looking over at the reception area, I see the lights are off. Of course, they are. It's almost midnight.

I see movement inside my room. Someone's still in there. I need my gun but it's in the air vent inside the room.

A figure comes out, shoving something up their top.

'Hey!' I call.

The figure, a man, turns to me, then runs.

I sprint after him, round the corner of the building. He's heading for the fence. I close in as he leaps to get over it, grab his hoodie and pull him back.

He throws an elbow wildly in my direction.

'Hey, stop it!' I say. 'What have you got?'

He swings again. I find he's all hoodie, no muscle beneath.

I slam him hard against the fence, my forearm resting under his jaw, pressing against his throat. 'You want to be arrested?' I say. 'You better stop swinging.'

'I didn't take anything!'

'I saw you.'

'I said I didn't take anything.' His voice is thin. I take a little pressure off his throat. He stops struggling. I stare into dull eyes, pupils dilated. He's on something.

'You went through my room,' I say. 'Who are you?'

'No one. It was open. I just wandered in for a place to sleep.'

'Bullshit. What did you take?'

'Nothing.'

'You shoved something up your top. You can give it back, or I can have you arrested.'

He looks past me, then reaches into his top and pulls out my headphones, and a few bills. They were in the pocket of the jeans I was wearing yesterday.

Anger swells, I could hit him. 'What else?' I say.

'Just this, man! I promise.'

'The door was open?'

'Yeah, I swear. It was open.'

'Turn around, hands on the wall.'

'No, come on, man, please.'

'Do it.'

He turns to the wall, places his hands on it. I pat him down. He's unarmed and doesn't seem to have anything else on him other than a lighter. Just an opportunistic junkie? It looks like it.

'You see anyone else go in my room?' I ask.

'No. Was just wandering by.'

'Your dealer live here?'

He turns back now. 'Yeah.' The headphones are probably worth a hundred bucks, and there's about twenty-five in cash. I take my headphones and put them in my pocket.

I hand back the cash. He needs it more than me. 'Go buy yourself some food,' I say. 'Don't show your face around here again, understand?' He takes the cash from me, uncertain.

'Thanks,' he says, before running off.

I return to reception and press the bell. Nothing. I press it again and give the door handle a good shake to rattle anyone inside awake.

A bar of light appears beneath the door behind the reception desk. Eventually the door opens, the lights come on inside and the woman who checked me in is standing there. She's got a hoodie on over the top of what looks like a nightgown and is wearing tattered slippers.

'What is it?' she says. 'It's the middle of the goddamn night.'

'The door to my room is open.'

She shrugs.

'I didn't leave it open. I found a junkie in there. Did you see anyone?'

She scratches her neck and sighs. 'What do you want me to do?'

'Would cleaners have been into my room for any reason? I've only been out since seven.'

She shakes her head. 'The rooms only get cleaned between guests.'

I feel a little guilty waking her up and dragging her outside like this, but I need to be sure.

'Would anyone else have keys?'

Her eyes go past me, to the road. 'No, just the set you have, a backup in the safe, and the ones in the office for cleaning.'

Whoever got in might have picked the lock, I suppose. Or it's possible the junkie was lying and he did break in.

'Have you got CCTV?'

'No,' she says. 'Not on the rooms. Just the one camera in here.'

'Right, well, could I move rooms? I don't feel safe knowing someone's gotten in there.'

'You want to move rooms?'

'Is that okay with you?' I say. 'Either that or I'll have to leave.'

She huffs out her breath. 'Alright, come see me in the morning.'

'No, it has to be tonight. How could I sleep in there now?'

She stares outside, her jaw working like she's trying to crush something between her molars.

'You can understand I don't feel entirely safe anymore,' I say. 'The lock is probably broken.'

'You could use the chain?'

'I'd prefer to change rooms.'

She seems to shrink a little as she exhales. 'Alright. I'll be right over with the keys.'

'Thank you.'

I approach my room slowly, listening carefully, trying to block out all other sounds. The road is quiet, but the powerlines out on the nature strip buzz. I move to the wall beside the door, reach one hand in and find the light switch. The single incandescent bulb throws an anaemic glow out through the door. No sound inside.

Someone has wrenched the door open. I can see the marks from the crowbar. The lock is likely busted.

I look once over my shoulder at the motel sign, *Vacancy*. Then turn back and slowly scan the room. I don't know what to expect.

I see the contents of my bags strewn across the floor – underwear, shirts, jeans, hats. Everything. I step my way through the flotsam of luggage and check the bathroom. Empty.

Working quickly before the woman from the check-in desk comes by, I unscrew the vent. My gun and my money are still there. I pack the money in my bag and press the gun down the back of my jeans.

It's almost 1 am by the time the woman brings the keys. I'll pay for both rooms in the morning and keep it vacant for a couple more days in case whoever broke in decides to come back.

I leave my car where it's parked out front of room seven and drag my things to room nine. I lock and chain the door before checking my things to see if anything is gone. Eventually, I discover I'm missing one sock and nothing else. All of my other belongings are accounted for.

I climb on a chair and unscrew the cover of the air vent and push my money in slowly. I've not seen anyone else who's staying here but I've heard them: people talking; a TV turned up loud; the meaty thump and moan of lovers.

I slide the gun just under the mattress on the side furthest from the door.

REID
NOW

IN THE MORNING, I knock on the doors of the neighbouring rooms. No one answers at eight or six.

At room five, a young woman answers the door, holding a baby to her shoulder. 'Yeah?' she says.

'Hi, umm, I was in room seven and someone broke in last night. I was just wondering if you saw anyone suspicious.'

She laughs. 'Suspicious? You know where you are, right?'

'Well, acting more suspicious than usual, outside my door? Anyone with a crowbar or a hammer?'

She leans out to look towards room seven as if it might jog her memory, then shakes her head. 'I didn't notice anything. I mean, there was a nice car parked outside yesterday. That's the only thing I noticed.'

'Was it white?'

She squints, shifts the baby to her other shoulder. 'Might have been.'

'A Jeep?'

She shakes her head again. 'I can't remember. It was probably about eight-thirty, nine o'clock last night.'

'Thanks.'

When I was out with Peyton, could Brendon have come here, broken into my room, gone through my stuff, then gotten the car back to his place before we turned up there around ten?

•

As I drive towards Ethelton, my mind casts back to the day when Stubbs had visited me at home. Soon after my ex, Marco, had published the footage of Cosby breaking the teenage witness's arm in the Amanda Marley investigation, the entire station wanted to put their hands on me

Stubbs had arrived at my place in uniform, except for those cowboy boots he loved. I watched him stride from his car to my front door and felt something fist-shaped blocking my throat, or perhaps pressing down on it. But I was determined I wouldn't show fear.

He knocked, two raps.

When I opened the door, he made his way to the table in the kitchen and sat down, took off his hat.

I fixed him a cup of coffee and one for myself then set them both on the table.

'I always looked up to your dad,' he said. 'When I was your age, he was my age now, and he was a good cop.'

'I don't have time for—'

'Hear me out, Reid.' He took a sip of the coffee, set it down again.

'You're lucky I'm not a bitter old bastard. You're lucky I'm holding them all back at that station, because what they want to do to you would be a whole lot worse than what Cosby did to that kid. It *will* be a whole lot worse. You think you can still work? You think you can still come in? The DA is copping it from all sides.'

He sipped the coffee again, then reached out and turned his hat on the table. 'We looked after your Mama, like we looked after you. You ought to remember that. The law isn't so rigid as you might think.

'Now here's the thing,' Stubbs continued. 'That video never should have been released. As you know, it only shows one side of the story.'

'It shows Cosby using excessive force. It shows a cop with anger-management issues snapping a teenager's arm in an arrest,' I said.

'It shows those things, sure. But it doesn't show that kid spitting at him, cussing him, telling Cosby he's going to kill his family. That boy saw Wojcik drag Amanda Marley by her hair into his car. His statement is *still* credible, irrespective of how he was arrested but the courts don't see it that way.'

I didn't answer.

'You know Cosby's getting death threats now? We've got people down there picketing the station. All of which could have been avoided if you brought your concerns to me instead of sharing them with a journalist.

'I've spoken to the DA and she said Wojcik's going to get off,' Stubbs said. 'The girl won't speak out against him, she's too scared. And the judge is going to say the drug dealer's statement was taken under duress. No jury will accept his statement as reliable. The whole state has seen the footage. So you better hope Wojcik doesn't reoffend. You better get down on your knees and pray.'

When Stubbs left that day, he shook my hand and took my promise that I'd take redundancy and leave town. I'd had enough of the threats, the dead rats left in my patrol car, the bullet on my pillow. I was giving up.

Less than two weeks after Wojcik was released, he abducted Amanda Marley again. This time when he took her out there, he killed her. He should have been in prison. It's my fault he wasn't. I've carried that burden for a decade.

That's why I can't deal with the police here. That's why I have a missing wing mirror on the Camry. I think about how different this investigation would be if I had a reliable contact in the Manson PD. I could find out why the investigation into the crash ended so quickly. The chance of someone falling asleep at the wheel, especially on a short drive with someone else in the car, is statistically very low. And I could get more information on the car too, particularly why the service record shows it was serviced by a different garage right before the crash, and why Oliver wasn't billed.

I have an idea. *Mosley.* I make the call, and listen to it ring through the speakers of the Challenger.

'Here's trouble,' Mosley says when he answers.

We have known each other since before we became cops; and when I made the force, Mosley was the first to drag me down to the bar to celebrate. He's also the only one who was on my side when the arrest tape leaked.

'No, nothing like that,' I say. 'No trouble from me. I'm just back in town on an insurance job. That car crash on the Boulevard in Ethelton.'

'What car crash?'

'Single-car collision with a power pole; one fatality, one hospitalisation.'

'Not ringing any bells.'

'The deceased was an author and an academic at Sandown.'

'Oh right, yeah, I remember that. The crash got lost with the disappearance of Stubbs's girl, and now that body they found out near the dam. They've had a couple of our officers head over to help out. Mostly traffic control near the site, and help searching the gorge and along the stream.'

'Who was it?' I ask. 'They released details yet?'

'Yeah, a local girl. Went missing about six months ago. Kiara King was her name. Dental records confirmed it.'

It's a gut punch, even though I should have known it was coming. I don't speak for a moment.

'They got anything else on it?' I manage.

'I only know what's already in the media. She was buried, the storm washed some of the soil away and a dog found her. They're still investigating cause of death but, given she was moved and buried, I'd say the homicide team are on it.'

'What's the theory?' I ask. 'Do they like a local for it?'

'You're not going to go chatting to any journalists?'

'Come on, man.'

'Alright. Blunt-force trauma to the skull, broken bones in her wrist, hip and chest. There's talk of a fall, maybe from a building, something like that. The water tower's a mile or two from the dam, but they're not so sure about that. They're not going to get much traction on physical evidence alone given the death occurred a while ago. That's the first thing.'

'Suspects?'

'Probably the same ones they had when she went missing.'

'Any of them Oliver Stiles?'

'Are you working this case or the crash, Reid?'

'The crash, but you know how it is. I'm seeing connections here, loads of them.'

'You got something the fine folk at Manson PD don't?' Mosley says, and I can imagine him smiling.

'Uh, I doubt it. I know they didn't sweep the vehicle properly. I found it at the wrecker's; still had some personal effects inside.'

'And of course you've returned those to the police?'

'I plan to,' I say.

'Right, so is this call a confessional?'

'No,' I say. 'Listen, could you just keep your ear to the ground for me? Maybe if you've got the file handy . . . anything on this crash that I could use?'

'To deny the poor widow her insurance payout?'

'Look, read the file on the crash,' I tell him. 'It doesn't make sense. I'm not so sure it happened the way the investigators say it did. It just seems rushed. And I get it – I'd probably do the same. But these people had enemies. There might be a crime here. They might be victims.'

'Enemies? Like who?'

'A mechanic, who just so happens to be Maddison Stubbs's ex, accosted Oliver the night of the crash.' I think through what I've found. 'Oliver was on one of those sugar daddy websites, and I know he had a thing for younger women.'

'How young, and how do you know?'

'I know because he has a school uniform in a box in the bottom of his wardrobe.'

'Shit,' Mosley breathes. 'That's not a lot to go on, but I'm sure Stubbs and his crew will be keen to know about it.'

'I think Kiara King's brother vandalised the site of the crash too, calling Oliver a crook. He drives the same vehicle I saw the night it happened.'

'You've been busy. You should be talking to the police.'

'You know I can't do that, Mosley.'

'So call it in anonymously.'

'Nothing's anonymous.'

'The tip line is. Look, I know you want the cases to be connected. If they are, the boys at Manson will be all over it already, trust me.'

I laugh. 'I'll pass my information on to you and you can do with it as you please.'

'I don't want anything to do with Manson PD,' he says.

'That makes two of us.'

'Well, what do you need from me?'

'Anything the insurance company wouldn't have. Full coroner's report if you have it. Any complaints against the deceased or his wife. There are no convictions against either of them, but I'm interested to see if there are any near misses on their files. Any active legal proceedings against them that I wouldn't find. Any debt, that sort of thing.'

A long pause. 'Shit, Reid, things are different these days.'

'I know.'

'They can see all our activity – who we look up, what prints we run. If they ask me why I'm looking this person up, what do I tell them?'

'That you're responding to an anonymous tip.'

He laughs at that. 'Answer for everything. And what will you do with this information?'

'I'm not about to interfere in Eshana Stiles's life. I'll be careful. She woke up just yesterday. Been moved from the ICU.'

'Call in the tip,' he says. 'Just to cover my bases. Make it anonymous. A burner if possible. Have you checked court records?'

'What for?'

'I don't know. I can check criminal investigations at our end, anything he was suspected of but not charged with. Have you checked what criminal and civil suits he's faced through the courts.'

'No,' I say. 'I'll take a look now. And I'll call in the tip when I get off the phone.'

'Info will come via my personal email. Delete it as soon as you can.'

'Thanks.'

'One last thing, and I'm only doing this because I trust you won't sully my good name. Oliver Stiles worked at Sandown, right? Friend of my wife works there. Go chat with her.'

'Name?'

'Lianne Shaw. I'll send you her number. Tell her you know me.'

•

I pull into a car park up the street from the cafe where Peyton works and call the PD that Mosley's stationed at from my burner phone.

Disguising my voice as best I can, I say, 'Oliver Stiles was seeing Kiara King before she died. He has a school uniform in the base of his closet that may belong to Maddison Stubbs.'

The man on the line goes to speak but I ignore him.

'Make sure you look into the crash and the uniform. There's more to this story than you think.' Then I hang up.

Inside, I wait patiently for that familiar smile, but it's not Peyton who comes over to serve me. It's a man with a Guy Fawkes goatee and an apron tied a little too tight. The chef. I should have guessed Peyton doesn't want to see me. I probably shouldn't have come.

'Food, coffee?' the chef says.

'Ah, sure. Cup of coffee, black. And I'll take the omelette.'

He nods, and a moment later a coffee is dumped in front of me, a little splashing over the lip of the cup. 'Food won't be long,' he says.

I turn to look for Peyton, see him serving another table. I try to catch his eye but I might as well not exist.

The omelette comes out much faster than usual, dumped down as unceremoniously as the coffee. I'm tempted to open it up and check for spit.

Peyton strides past me to the tables outside. *You wasted a good thing,* I tell myself. I was starting to really like him.

I drain the coffee; it scalds on the way down. Then I open my laptop, turning it so no one can see the screen, and read the news stories about Kiara King while I eat.

There's nothing new about Kiara, except the location of the body in the gorge. And some images of police tape looping down to block the path to the dam.

I search the records of a few courts, both local and in the city. It's tedious; you have to search each court one at a time. Finally a record comes back for Oliver Stiles. He's been the defendant in a civil suit. He's been sued by C Mendes. It doesn't ring any bells. It was about seven years ago and I'm sure it's nothing. I keep searching and find something else. Another suit filed by the lawyers for A Stiles five years ago. *A Stiles*. Something clicks. Annabel sued him – was it just part of the divorce proceedings or something else?

I leave a bill for the breakfast and stride out the side door, pulling my cap low over my eyes. I check my phone and find a message has come through from Mosley.

> Hey Reid, good to chat earlier. Let's get that round of golf in soon.

Golf? I'd rather give myself a pedicure with a pair of snub-nosed pliers, but Mosley knows that. This is banter. The message also gives us cover as the reason for my call earlier.

Just as I'm checking my email, a message from sidmosley75@ protonmail.com comes through. A series of images, all a little blurry as if taken in a hurry. The photos show a computer screen with case notes for the crash. There's a transcript of Oliver's interviews when Kiara went missing. So he *was* a suspect back then. Mosley's email also includes notes on Kiara King.

A couple things pique my interest. Oliver Stiles complained about getting threats in the months leading up to his death. And Oliver's alibi the night Kiara disappeared was his wife, Eshana; they both claim he was at home all night with her. What if she was covering for him?

In the body of the email are six words:

> You might be on to something.

I message back.

> Great to chat. My shout next time we get that round of golf in.

REID
NOW

ON THE WAY to the college, I drive past the gorge track. I remember the day I was walking back from the dam with a few of my friends I used to play hockey with, my hair still wet and a towel hung around my neck, and Ricky Olsen was coming towards us with a clutch of pimple-faced older boys.

'Pigs get fried,' Ricky said to me with that sneering mouth of his, talking about my dad.

I often had difficulty controlling my anger after Dad died, and that day it came over me white hot. I landed one or two good punches; I recall the feel of Ricky's nose cracking against my fist. Then me and my friends received the sort of beating that makes you hurt for weeks. It still hurts now thinking about it. Not just a swollen face and fists, but cracked ribs, probably concussion too. But it was worth it just to see the surprise and pain on Ricky's smug face when I broke his nose.

That wasn't the worst thing I did when I was taken by one of those blind rages. The next time it happened I had a hockey stick in my hand and the consequences were much worse.

There's a handful of cars parked near the track out to the dam. The track itself is cordoned off. I park but don't get out of the car.

I just watch. The searchers are mostly cops, no doubt cursing the recent storm that would have washed away physical evidence that otherwise might have remained. The others look like volunteers, or media, or looky-loos.

There are two women standing nearby, one holding the other, who has tears streaming down her face. She's got a tube running to her nose and now I see she's hooked up to an oxygen tank. I guess she must be Kiara's mom. Like everyone else, she probably assumed her daughter had run away. Maybe she dreamed Kiara was somewhere working on a film script for a Hollywood studio, just like Angel at the gas station did. At least she'd been able to hope. Now all hope is gone, as swift as the fall of a guillotine.

I turn the ignition and leave, with that cold numb feeling inside. Second-hand sadness. When I arrive at the water tower five minutes later, there's a patrol car parked off the road, walking distance from the tower, but no cops in sight. Maybe someone's sitting in the car to see who turns up.

The tower is thirty feet tall, with a walkway up the top and a ladder in a cage that was always padlocked to keep kids off it. The layers of faded and indecipherable graffiti up there suggest it hasn't always been an effective deterrent.

The door to the cop car opens and someone gets out and begins towards me. Instantly, I shove the Challenger in reverse, swing around and clear off.

Fifteen minutes later on my way to Sandown, I'm already feeling a little nervous about last time I was at the college. I call Lianne Shaw from my car.

She answers after just one ring. Her voice has a clipped, even tone. Sounds like a British accent.

'Hi Lianne, my name is Reid, Vince Reid. A friend of mine, Mosley – ah, Sid – gave me your number—'

'He sent me a message,' she cuts in. 'Told me you'd be calling.'

'Great. Well, I was hoping we could chat in person, if possible. I'm passing by the college now.'

'I have a class at midday.'

I look at the clock. That's in twenty minutes. 'I won't keep you long.'

'What about later?'

'If you've got five minutes now, that would be perfect.'

I hear her exhale. 'Right, sure. I can meet you outside the entrance of the Haydon building. I'm one minute from there.'

'I'll head there right now.' I park up and stride from the car through the gates. I stop a student for directions. Then jog in the direction she points me. I find a lean, well-dressed woman in her early forties waiting for me at the base of a building. She's wearing black-rimmed glasses and has a sharp, intelligent gaze.

'Reid,' she says. 'Come on, I'll take you to my office.' Despite her short legs, she has a quick efficient stride. 'Sid mentioned this is about Oliver Stiles,' she says, turning to me.

'That's right,' I say.

She stops at a door, unlocks it and shows me inside. 'Grab a seat.'

It's more or less the same layout as Oliver's office, although much tidier.

'What do you teach?' I ask.

'Media Studies.'

She eyes her phone before placing it on the desk, and puts her keys down beside it. I notice she has a small key like the one that was attached to Oliver's thumb drive. I stare at it a beat too long.

She drums the table with her thumbs. 'So, you've got ten minutes. Sid mentioned you're investigating something for Oliver's estate?'

'More or less. I'm just trying to piece together his last few weeks.'

'Well, someone in the English department would be a better contact for you. I didn't know him particularly well. I wouldn't say we were friends.'

Those last few words are charged with hostility and I expect her to explain why she didn't like him.

After a brief pause, I prompt her. 'Not his biggest fan?'

'That's a fair assessment. I think it had something to do with the fact he came from Trident, which I suppose is seen as a more prestigious college. He rubbed some people the wrong way, including me.'

'He was arrogant?'

'That's a word for it.'

'What word would you use?'

'Entitled, superior. He thought he was untouchable. That's how it felt anyway. And you know he had a lot of money?'

I clear my throat. 'Did you ever hear rumours about misconduct with students?'

She nods once. 'I heard the whispers when he arrived, but nothing was substantiated and I don't like to propagate rumours. In my direct dealings with him, he was professional. Then again, I'm probably not the sort of woman to attract advances from men like Oliver Stiles.'

'You're not a nineteen-year-old student, you mean?'

'Those are your words, not mine.'

'Sure. Did you know him to have any enemies? Or if anyone made any threats against him?'

'Other than the prank with the car, I don't remember anything.'

'Prank?'

'If you can call it that. Someone put something in his gas tank. They caught them on the security footage.'

'What happened next?'

'I heard Oliver asked the dean and security not to send the footage to the police. He said he didn't want someone getting arrested for a prank, and he knew who it was and would deal with the matter himself. That was the last I heard of it. The car got towed.'

'When was this?'

She shrugs. 'Must have been a couple of weeks ago.'

It's coming together. The reason Oliver's car was at Smith's Auto the day of the accident was because Cody Booth put something in Oliver's gas tank. That's also why the repair was free – Oliver must have contacted Booth or his boss and threatened legal action. That could have caused Cody to back off. Or he might have dug his heels in and done something worse next time. Whatever it was, it might have caused the crash.

'No other enemies?' I ask.

She stands. 'Not that I know of. I better get going.'

'Thanks. I won't keep you any longer,' I say, also standing. I point at the small key. 'Odd key, that one.'

'It's for my gym locker. Believe it or not, I do spin classes three times a week.'

'I believe it,' I say with a smile. 'Thanks for your help.'

'Good luck finding what you're after,' she says, showing me the door.

I return to my car, fetch the key from the glove box and head towards the gym. I wait until someone scans in and follow them inside. There's a row of lockers in the men's changing room. I try the key in locker 39 and it opens.

There's a duffel bag inside. I heave it over one shoulder then stride from the changing room and through the gym without looking at anyone.

Whatever's inside the bag feels important. The sort of thing he can't keep at home, or in his car.

I pull over halfway between Sandown College and Manson and open the bag. It's full of clothes, as well as containing Oliver's US passport and, by my guess, roughly ten thousand dollars in one-hundred-dollar bills. Hardly the sort of thing an academic would need when he's working out at the gym.

So Oliver Stiles was planning on leaving town. The question is why. Because he murdered Kiara King and the investigators were closing in? Or because Eshana had discovered his affairs, or discovered he'd hurt Kiara and maybe Maddison too? Was he planning on running away from his wife or the law?

ESHANA
BEFORE

HE'S A GOOD listener, with a smile he can turn on in an instant and a booming laugh that makes me look around the diner self-consciously. It's an odd, almost unfamiliar feeling to have fun with a stranger. I notice his wedding ring and recognise the encounter is entirely platonic, which makes me trust him more. He's not an attractive man as far as I'm concerned, but he's a good conversationalist. It doesn't feel like he wants anything from me, apart from a chat.

He eats his steak and mash; I eat most of the waffles and tell him about Oli – how we met, why we moved here. Then I tell him why that man accosted me: because there's a rumour that my husband was involved in Kiara's disappearance. Despite the fact he was cleared by the police; despite the fact he was at home in bed with me when she ran away.

After an hour of just talking, finally I say, 'I'm sorry. I've been talking about myself all this time. What's your story?'

'What do you want to know?'

'Well, what do you do?'

He smiles, looks down and spins his wedding ring. 'Look, this was entirely coincidental, and I'm not working right now, but I'm actually a cop.'

I feel a sudden heat, like a fever. 'You didn't think to tell me that?'

'Hey,' he says, interrupting me. 'I'm off duty, and I'm not a detective. I'm not here to get information out of you. Like you said, your husband was cleared, and I believe a man, or a woman, is innocent until proven guilty. To me, it just sounds like your husband's being punished for his charity.'

'Yes,' I say. 'Yes. That's it. People are sceptical of altruism. It's like Bill Gates. They become targets for the cynical.'

He leans forward to rest on the blades of his forearms and a small gold cross on a chain falls from the collar of his plaid shirt.

'The thing about it,' he says, frowning now, 'the buzz in the station was that your husband was definitely involved. Then one day,' he makes a gesture with his fingers and thumb, '*voila!* He's got a rock-solid alibi.'

'He does,' I say. 'He was home in bed all night. So how could he be involved?'

'Who knows?' He sits back, resting his arms along the back of the booth. 'My boss, Chief Stubbs, he's a good man. He wanted to move on quickly. I don't mind telling you that he more or less closed the case off the back of your statement. From that moment, Kiara King was considered a runaway. Which is fine, right? Because your husband is innocent. Kiara hasn't turned up since.'

'Right,' I say. The mood changes a little.

'And you know,' he goes on, 'it was probably just the stuff with the sugar baby website that made him a suspect in the first place.'

Something chills inside me. My face feels paralysed and my heart thumps. *Sugar baby website?*

'Oh,' he says, a small smile creeping up the edges of his mouth. 'You did know about that, right?'

I feel a flush of embarrassment. That day the police took Oli away – was it to question him about that?

'Well, I better get going,' Sticks says. 'I got some things to do at home. But let me pay for your lunch.'

'No,' I say, but he's already laid bills on the table and is rising from his seat.

He places a card in front of me. 'If you ever want to chat again, not as a cop but as a . . . uh, a friend, I guess, just let me know.'

'Sure,' I say.

Once he's out the door, I stand too, leaving the money and the card where they sit on the table.

I'm sure Kiara's safe, I tell myself as I get back into my car. *She's somewhere far away, happy and living a brand-new life.*

I keep thinking it all the way home, hoping eventually I'll believe it.

●

Late that afternoon, the gate opens, and a taxi comes through and drives all the way up to the house. A moment passes, then the door opens and Oli climbs out, holding his bag and his coat folded over his arm. He looks gaunt under the security light that comes on as he approaches the front door.

'Hi,' I say. 'Where's the car?'

'At the shop. It'll be in for a couple days.'

'What happened?'

'Something with the engine. I got it towed to a mechanic's and organised a taxi. They have a car available for me to pick up tomorrow while mine is being repaired.'

Later, when he gets out of the shower, I notice a bruise the size of a grapefruit just below his armpit.

'Squash,' he says when he sees me looking, but he knows I don't believe him.

'Is something going on?' I ask. 'Are you in trouble? Is it money?'

'No,' he says, smiling, but it doesn't quite reach his eyes. 'Nothing at all to worry about.'

But when we're in bed, he says, 'I'm thinking about upping our insurance. I want you to be taken care of if something happens to me.'

REID

NOW

I HAVE A responsibility to put the duffel bag back and tell Mosley where it is. If I don't, I'm potentially impeding an investigation. It's a lot of cash, double what I've been paid by Crown, but I can't keep it.

If I do hand it in, the police will check the CCTV footage in the area and know I discovered the bag. That will throw me right into the middle of the investigation; not to mention Mosley who referred me to Lianne.

I could take the bag to the Stileses' house. Eshana will still be in hospital. Then I could call in a tip that it's there.

I put the bag in my trunk, then decide I'll put the other items I found in there with it. The thumb drives. But when I look for them, I discover they're not in my bag. I search the room then realise I haven't seen them since I found my door open. I'd checked that none of my things were gone, but that's the problem. *My* things. I didn't even think about those thumb drives. They could have been in the junkie's pocket and I missed them when I patted him down. Well, there was nothing on them worth taking anyway. They're more or less worthless.

I have three things to do before I send off my final report to my contact at Crown Insurance.

I send the girl from the gas station, Angel, a message asking if we could chat. Oli clearly was planning to escape. I wonder if Angel knows more than she is letting on?

Then I get onto the second thing: asking Brendon why he spray-painted the sidewalk at the memorial to Oliver. Peyton will be at work so I can head to his place and hope that I catch Brendon there.

And after that, I plan on visiting Eshana. Now that she's awake, she might be able to answer a few pressing questions, and I can hand over her husband's bag. It would be useful to know who the next of kin is too, who's been handling Eshana's affairs. But Crown haven't released that information to me.

There's no one home at Peyton's, so I head to the King house, thinking that Brendon might be visiting his mom. I notice the large work boots on the front step and expect Brendon to be a giant. But when he opens the door, I see a man of average height and build with dark eyes, a little puffy from either smoke or crying.

'Hi,' I say. 'Brendon, I take it?'

'Man, we're not talking to anyone. My mom's having a hard enough time as it is.'

'The media have been here?'

He looks sceptical. 'What do you think? Vultures have been here every day. She's not doing any interviews. I'm not doing any interviews. So you can just get back in your car and leave.'

'Look, I'm not a journalist. I'm a private investigator looking into the affairs of Oliver Stiles.'

He shakes his head. 'I ain't talking about that either.'

'I know it's a hard time and I'm deeply sorry for your loss.'

He scoffs like I couldn't possibly understand.

'Listen, I lost my dad as a kid. He was murdered in cold blood. I know it's not the same, but I get it. That's why I want to get to the bottom of things. I need to know why you hated Oliver Stiles. Why did you call him a crook?'

His eyes sharpen on me. 'What?'

'You hated his guts, right?'

'I did. But it's not what you think.'

'What do I think?'

He just shrugs.

'I think he was sleeping with your sister, and paying her money.'

He grits his teeth, his jaw knotting. 'What did you say?'

'I know he met Kiara on Sugar Babies For You.'

His nostrils flare and his eyes go wide. 'You've got about three seconds before I throw you off my porch, man. You better clear off.'

'Help me understand. Why was she seeing him? Why was he paying her? Was it just sex?'

He sniffs hard, calming himself. 'I hate him – you're right. I hate him for who he was, and for threatening my sister.'

'You hurt him. You did something to his car.'

'No,' he says, his voice booming. 'We tussled once or twice and he got off light. I barely touched him. But he deserved worse than he got from me. I hate him because I know he's the one that did that to Kiara.' Tears start. He sniffs them back. 'I know he killed her and put her in a shallow grave, and I can't do anything about it. I could have stopped it earlier. Stopped her from dealing with him. But I didn't.'

'You've told the police this?'

'They know what Stiles was doing. They have to know.'

He sighs, seems to shrink half a foot. For a moment I think he's going to breakdown, but then he stands tall.

'I'm glad he's dead. If he wasn't, I'd kill him myself.' He balls his hands at his sides, leans a little closer and speaks slowly. 'Now this is your last warning. Get the fuck off my porch.'

I don't need to be told a third time. I step back down, hands raised. 'I'm truly sorry for your loss.'

'Yeah,' he says, slamming the door.

ESHANA

BEFORE

WHAT THE COP said about the sugar baby website stays with me over the next few days. I'm convinced now that's what the police wanted to ask Oli about when they took him to the station that day. Then the investigation just ended suddenly. *They cleared him,* I remind myself. He's not guilty of anything. So why did that cop mention the website? I find myself hating him, despite the fact he stood up for me in the diner. I hate him for thrusting my mind back into doubt.

I decide to do what I know Holly would tell me to do. Get it out in the open.

I ask him about it in the car on the way to his colleague's place, where we are going for dinner.

'Oli, do you know anything about a website called something like Sugar Babies?'

I turn to him. His face is neutral. Then he smiles.

'Yeah, I do. Remember our fifth anniversary?'

'Yeah,' I say, realising where this is going.

'Well, I used one of those sites to find the woman who came that night.'

'I thought you said she was through an agency?'

'She was. I contacted her through the site, then she referred me to an agency to book her. She just uses the website to advertise.'

'Right,' I say. 'Do you think you could show me the messages? Just so I know? You know how I get worried and suspicious.'

'I know,' he says, reaching for the indicator. 'I can try, but I deleted the account. I'd forgotten all about it until the police brought it up. Looking back, I think that's why they interviewed me so many times. I guess it doesn't speak to my good character that I had an account on that website.'

'How do you think they discovered that?' I ask.

He shrugs. 'Who knows?'

'Maybe,' I say now, 'they thought Kiara was on there too.'

'Maybe.'

•

The following day, my boss and I are on a video conference with a start-up, planning their next three months of hires, when I see the article. Larissa sends it to me. Her message reads:

> I know you've probably seen this, but I thought I'd send it just in case. I'm really sorry Eshana. I'm sure there's an explanation.

I click the link.

SUSPECT MESSAGED SUGAR BABY KIARA KING BEFORE HER DISAPPEARANCE

'Eshana? Any thoughts?'

I look up to see half a dozen faces expecting a reply, but I've completely lost what we're talking about. The cop in the diner was telling the truth.

'I, ah, I agree, yeah. It sounds like a really solid plan.'

Uncertain smiles.

Susan, my boss, frowns. 'You agree? With what point exactly?'

I swallow, try to breathe. 'Could I just have a moment? Umm, something has just—' I can barely speak.

'Okay, sorry, everyone,' Susan says. 'Eshana, take five, and we'll continue on.'

'Thanks,' I say, closing the lid of my laptop.

I go back to the article on my phone.

A former lover at the heart of the investigation into the disappearance of Manson teenager Kiara King had corresponded with her online before her disappearance.

Documents leaked to the *Herald* show that the prime suspect, who cannot be named, was interviewed several times by police as part of their investigation into the disappearance of King. The two met on a dating site called Sugar Babies For You that pairs usually older men with younger women, often in exchange for money. The *Herald* understands that last year the two met for a rendezvous organised via the platform, then continued to see each other on a regular basis.

The suspect was at home with his wife the evening of King's disappearance and has not been charged of any involvement.

I think about that cop in the diner again. Was it really a coincidence that he was there when I was? And who leaked this information about Oli to the press? The *Herald* couldn't print it if it wasn't true.

I drink a glass of water, try to compose myself, but I want to cry. I want to ball up under a blanket and howl. Things will surely get worse around town now. That bearded man at the diner can't be the only one who suspects Oli.

I go to the bathroom, take two of the pills from my therapist. Oli had an affair. But it's over. The girl is gone. *We can deal with this*, I think. *I can deal with this.*

But he's been lying all along.

I feel my heart slowly breaking, cracking down the middle. The pain spreads to my other organs.

I feel shame. A deep, burning shame. Spiked with something else: rage.

REID
NOW

MY PHONE VIBRATES. A message. It's Angel getting back to me.

> I can't talk about it at home. Could we meet instead?

This is a good lead.

> Sure. I can do that. Would it be easier for you to call
> me later, maybe when you can get out of the house?

> No. I cant risk it. I can only talk in person.

I wonder what's so important that she doesn't want to send it through cyberspace. It doesn't sit right with me meeting her alone, but this could be the final piece of the puzzle.

> Sure. Beside the river on the Ethelton side down near
> the picnic area whenever you're free?

There's a walking path there that goes all the way out to the college. It's well lit but used to be a quiet spot.

8 o'clock 2nite? I'll need to sneak out.

Sure thing.

•

I like to scope a place out first so I head over there a bit early. There's a group of college students drinking down by the river. Ten or so in total, mostly boys with a couple girls. They've got beers stacked in formation on a picnic table. The cold has turned the grass to concrete and the fog limits visibility to about thirty yards. I glance over as I pass; most are looking down at their phones. Someone says something I don't catch but they all look in my direction, a couple of laughs. A joke at my expense, but I don't mind.

I continue on towards the public toilets and soon the college kids are just shapes in the fog. It's still a bit early but someone is there. Standing alone in the shadows near the block of public toilets.

'You turned up,' a voice says.

It catches me by surprise. It's not the voice of a teenage girl but a man.

I'm trying to make out who he is when a grenade explodes against my cheek. It sends a shock through my skull, and into my body. I throw a punch back, connect hard, but before I can land another, someone else hits me.

There are voices all around me, but I can't hear what they're saying.

Backing into the light, I get a good look at them. Three men. One with a scraggly ginger beard, who rushes at me again. This time I see the punch coming and duck in time.

I try to slip by, to run for help, but someone else grabs me, wrestles me to the ground. I push him off and stand.

'You're not going anywhere!'

Another blow rocks me. My ear rings. I cover my head as more blows rain down. I fall over but manage to catch a foot and pull, sending its owner to the ground. I roll and land one good punch on him before someone pulls me back by my hair. Every follicle on my scalp screams.

A blow hits my face and the darkness becomes tinselled with moving pixels. A boot hits my ribs. I cough, taste blood.

I push myself up, try to run, but I lose my legs and roll down the bank towards the river. Gasping, crawling towards the water as if I might paddle away, but they're there again, surrounding me.

'Touching up teenage girls!' a mocking voice calls. 'You do the King girl out there in the bush too, huh? And now you're lining up my daughter.'

The penny drops. 'No,' I say. 'I'm investigating.'

The words don't sound like words at all; more of a groan.

Another blow hits me, so hard that I'm breathless. I fold in half. It occurs to me that I might not survive this. These men could beat me to death, or leave me crippled.

'Help!' I howl, rolling over, still covering my head with my arms.

Through a gap, I see boots coming towards me. I scream, but the sound is trapped in my throat.

The pain is all over now, exploding my hip, my back, my face.

So this is it; this is how I die. I taste more blood, feel it all over my face. See red through my squeezed-closed eyelids.

The light of a mobile phone glows in the fog.

'Get away,' one of the men says.

'Or what?' another voice says. It sounds younger.

I open my eyes, see the beer drinkers from the picnic area. There are at least six of them. One is holding a phone up, recording.

'You don't want to interfere here, boy. You better hand over that phone!'

'It's streaming,' another voice says. 'Even if he hands over the phone, the recording's out there. The police are probably halfway here.'

It might be ending, I realise, relieved but also not entirely convinced. Optimism has burnt me before.

'Call the police!' the bearded man says. 'They can take this groomer away when we're done with him.'

I sense the newcomers' hesitancy and keep my arms over my head. Anything could be coming.

Another voice: 'This has nothing to do with you kids.'

'It doesn't matter. We're not going to let you kick this guy to death. If he has done something wrong, the cops can deal with it.'

My head feels light with relief, even though I can barely breathe and everything is spinning. Concussion.

This is why you got the open carry licence, I remind myself. I would only have needed to show the gun and all this would have ended before it started. Then again, what if these men have guns too?

'Alright,' the bearded guy says, to me this time. 'Stay the hell away from my daughter, you hear me? If I see you again, I'm gonna kill you.'

'Still filming, dude,' one of the college students says.

Then the men are backing away. One spits, but it hits the ground a foot short of me.

The college students help me to my feet. Everything nearby around me – the river, the trees, the path – twists in my vision. It feels like there's something broken on my left side. A rib, I assume. Hopefully nothing else underneath it. And my wrist – I landed on it awkwardly when I went down, and it's numb now. Like my face and most of my body.

'What happened?' one of the students asks.

I shake my head. 'They jumped me.'

'Were you doing something to his daughter?'

'No!' My mind is reeling so much I can't come up with anything except, 'Has anyone got a cigarette?' It feels like it's the only thing that would make me feel better. That and a stiff drink.

Someone thrusts something towards me. 'Just this. It's a vape.'

I put it to my mouth and inhale deeply. It tastes like candy.

'Ugh,' I say, holding it out in the direction it came from.

'Keep it,' a girl says. Others laugh. The road emerges through the fog.

I open my eyes again and realise there's blood all over the vape pen, all over my hands.

'There's an ambulance on the way,' someone says. 'And police.'

'No,' I manage. I feel around in my pocket for my keys. 'No, I'm fine.' I know I'm not, but I need to get away.

'What if those guys were telling the truth?' another voice says.

'They're not,' I say. 'It's a mix-up. I'm not into young girls. I'm not into women at all.'

'You're not going, not until the police get here,' a voice says.

I turn and look at their faces, trying to work out who spoke. 'No, no. I've got to get home. I'm not sticking around.'

A beat passes.

'Come on then,' a girl with tattoos and dark hair says. 'You can't drive, not like this. I'm sober. Where do you live?'

'He'll get blood in your car,' someone says.

'We can't let him go?' the earlier voice says.

'What are we going to do? A citizen's arrest?'

'You heard him. He wants to go home. I'll drive. My car is a piece of shit anyway. A little blood won't matter.'

'Drive mine,' I say, reaching for the keys again.

Two of the boys help me to my car. They put me in the back seat, one rides shotgun. Someone else follows behind in a truck. I sense not everyone is sober, but I'm not about to complain.

We pass a cop car coming the other way, then an ambulance whizzes past.

'So,' the girl says, 'what are you then?'

'Sorry?'

'A prison escapee? A mobster? Why are you so scared of the police?'

'Not scared of them,' I say. 'I just don't have time to deal with them. And I don't have insurance so I don't need to go to hospital.'

I notice the two in the front share a look.

'Stop here,' I say as we approach a gas station. I reach for my wallet. 'Here. Fetch me a bag of ice, please?'

The boy in the front goes in and returns with two bags of ice before we head off again.

Five minutes later, I say, 'This is me.'

'Here?' the girl says.

'Yeah, just here is fine. Pull over.'

We're near the motel but I don't want them to know exactly where I'm staying.

'Thanks,' I say as we all get out my car. 'I don't know what would have happened back there, but I know you people saved me.'

Only now do I realise the boy with the phone in his hand is filming me.

'Hey, stop that,' I say.

'Sorry, man,' he says, but he doesn't lower the phone.

After they've left in their friend's truck, I get back in my car and slowly navigate the last half mile to the motel, my body trembling with pain

I stagger to my room, strip off and shower. The hot water stings the cut above my eye and the one on my bottom lip.

Afterwards, I drag the hand towel over the mirror. In the slash of clear glass, I assess my puffed-up face and body, mapping out all the blows with the corresponding swelling and bruises. It's my face that got it the worst. I drool constantly from where my lips are too swollen to close properly.

'Jesus,' I say to the ogre staring back at me.

I reach for my painkillers, grateful that I didn't lose any teeth. Then I divide the bags of ice into smaller ziplock bags, lie on the bed and place some of the bags on the point of excruciating pain halfway up the left side of my rib cage. I rest a bag on each side of my face, then press my elbow against another bag on the bed, and lie there as still as I can, waiting for the painkillers to do their work.

I took a stupid risk speaking directly with a teenage girl. I'm not in town to look into the Kiara King case, so I have no business pursuing it.

My phone pings. I've still got it, thank god.

Slowly, careful not to let any of the ice bags slip, I reach for it. It's an email from Sarah at Crown, letting me know the payment to cover expenses has cleared and there's no need for me to continue pursuing the matter. I check my bank balance. Another seven and a half thousand has landed. They paid the bonus. Does that mean they're not paying out on the policies? *What did I find for them?*

ESHANA
BEFORE

WHEN OLI ARRIVES home, he's no longer a man but a category five storm. He gusts in. The door slams. His bag hits the tiles near the entrance. He tears his sweater off, returns his phone to his ear.

'I want to see some fucking heads roll, Malcolm. I'm giving you a list of these assholes' names and I want you to make sure they're all out of a job by the end of the month. I don't care if it takes every cent in my bank account.'

He eyes me and shakes his head as if to say, *Don't ask*.

I pour him a wine, take it to him.

He slams it back like a shot, then puts the glass on the bench and gestures with his finger for me to fill it once more.

'I want to get the wheels in motion today,' he goes on. 'It's slander. They've got a history of this. Google Amanda Marley and see how royally they fucked up there. If something *has* happened to this girl and her kidnapper or murderer has been free all this time while they've been chasing their tails with me, that's on them!'

Another pause. I imagine Malcolm, his lawyer, trying to calm him down, assuring him he'll do what he can.

'Well, what about my reputation?' Oli demands. 'They've not mentioned any names, but they're implying I had a relationship with her. I've never had a relationship with her! They made that up.'

Another pause.

'Yes, she's here. I'm about to tell her about it. She knows it's not true . . . Alright. I'll email it all through. I want the article taken down first; I want it down tonight. Do what you have to and charge me what you need to.'

He tosses his phone on the couch. 'I'm going to need something stronger than wine.'

He goes to the cabinet above the fridge, reaches for the Macallan and pours it neat into a glass.

'What's wrong?' I ask. I don't want to mention the article after hearing all that. Maybe Oli's got a point. Maybe it's not true.

'You'll see it soon anyway,' he says, 'unless it's taken down.'

'What?'

'Manson PD released private information about me to the local news. It's online already and will likely run tomorrow in print. Not only is the information private, but it's also wrong.' He drinks his whisky in a single mouthful. 'It's bullshit, so I'm suing them all. I'll bankrupt that paper, and have the entire PD sacked.'

'What does it say?'

'Well, you can read it yourself. Before Malcolm gets it pulled. They're trying to turn the twin towns against us, Eshana, but I won't let it happen.'

•

The article is gone by midnight. There's no apology. No retraction. It's just pulled down.

The next day, I go to the newsagent's and buy the *Herald*. It's not in there either.

I need answers so I drive to the police station.

'Hi,' I say to the man behind the desk. 'I want to speak with Officer Stickler.'

His eyebrows rise. He gives me a look of recognition, almost as though he was expecting me. 'Stickland?'

A flash of embarrassment. 'That's right.'

'He's not in at the moment. But you can speak to someone else.'

'No,' I say. 'I want to speak with him.'

'I'll take your details and have Officer Stickland contact you as soon as possible.'

'Sure,' I say. He hands me a pen and a piece of paper; I write down my number and name.

REID
NOW

WHEN I LIFT the bag, a hot barb digs in under my ribs. Straightening up, I feel bones click and joints ache all over. Despite the painkillers, I barely slept last night, and now the sun is yet to rise. I head back to the Stiles house. I can't get sloppy this time. In and out. Drop the bag and go. Eshana will probably still be at the hospital, and whoever I saw there last time is probably with her now that she's woken up.

I drive to the gate first and press the buzzer to make sure no one is home. No answer.

I put the car in reverse then hear a voice. 'Hello, can I help you?'

I recognise it. *Shit.* But this could still work.

'Larissa,' I say. It's only just gone 7 am. She must be helping her out. 'I spoke to you at Ethelton High a few days ago. I'm investigating the crash.'

'Oh right, hi.'

'Is Eshana home?'

'Yeah, she's home,' she says, her voice uncertain. 'She came home last night.'

'I've actually finished my investigation – I wanted to drop something off. Something I found that belonged to her husband.'

'I'll buzz you in.'

I park up close to the house. Larissa's people-mover is parked in front of the double garage.

The front door swings open before I knock.

'Hi,' I say.

She looks shocked. 'Are you okay?'

'Oh,' I say. 'Yeah, I'm fine. Long story.'

Her eyes go to the bag now. 'That's it?'

'Yeah. It was in Oliver's locker at the college. I think it might be best if I take it to Eshana myself. If you don't mind.'

'Sure,' she says. 'Let me go check with her.'

She climbs the stairs and I hear a door open and the murmur of a conversation.

'Okay,' she says, coming back. 'She's tired and not feeling so great, obviously.'

'Where's her family?'

'She's not got much in the way of family. Oliver's sister was here for a bit, but she had to get back to the city. So I've been helping out since then, along with a couple other dance moms.'

'Well, I'm sure she appreciates it,' I say, following her up the stairs. Each step brings a new wave of pain through my body.

'She does, I know. I sat on hold for two hours for her.' She laughs. 'That's friendship.'

'What for?'

'Oh, her insurance. It's all sorted, but because I wasn't an authority on the account, they insisted on speaking to her. They didn't realise how zonked out she was from her medication.'

I stop halfway up the stairs. 'You spoke with the insurance company? What about?'

She stops too, turns and sees my alarm. 'Is something wrong?'

I feel like a stiff breeze could tumble me down the stairs. 'Life insurance? Medical?'

'Both,' she says. She tilts her head a little. 'What is it?'

'Crown Insurance?'

'Sorry?'

'You spoke with Crown?'

She gives me a small, tight smile. 'Sorry, what are you talking about?'

'The insurance company? Crown Insurance? You called them to help with Eshana's claims.'

'No.' She says it like a question. 'I've never heard of Crown Insurance. I was speaking with State Farm.'

Larissa turns and continues up the stairs. I find I'm gripping the handrail so hard my forearm aches.

Pull yourself together, Reid. I take another step, then another, but my head is swimming. *State Farm?* Is it possible Oliver and Eshana had separate insurers?

'This was for Eshana but not Oliver?' I ask Larissa. 'The call to the insurer?'

She pauses again. 'No, it was for both. Is something wrong?'

I shake my head. 'No.'

But my head continues spinning. I was never hired by the Stileses' insurer to investigate the crash. I was hired by someone else, and I need to know who. I'm an idiot. I should have followed up. The money was too good.

She is tiny and bandaged, but alive and awake. There are balloons, flowers, cards around the room.

'Hi,' I say. 'My name is Vince Reid and I've just been investigating a few things around the cause of the crash.'

'Oh,' she says.

Investigating, I realise, is a vague term and I can't say I've been working on behalf of the insurance company because now I know it's not her insurance company that I've been dealing with. I would never have taken the case if it was simply a private matter to investigate a woman in a coma.

'I've recovered your husband's bag,' I tell her.

'You look like you're in worse shape than me.' She pulls herself up onto her elbows, wincing. I place the bag on the foot of the bed.

'I had a run-in with some unfriendly locals. I'm okay now.'

'That's his gym bag,' she says.

'The bag is full of money,' I respond. 'Along with your husband's passport. Were you aware of any plans he had to leave?'

She looks to Larissa, then back to me. She swallows hard. 'I don't want to talk about this.'

'So you didn't know he was planning on leaving?'

'He wasn't going to leave. He—' There are tears now. 'Please just go.'

'Eshana, is it possible you learnt something about your husband? Something unforgivable? Is it possible you were angry—'

'No!' She says it like she's in pain. 'No! Just leave me alone. Please.'

'Stop it right now! You're upsetting her.' Larissa has her hands on her hips and is staring at me. 'I think you should go.'

I leave, my mind racing. There was something about the way Eshana looked when I told her about the money, the clothes and the passport, as if she already knew what was inside. And now I can't stop wondering, *Did she cause the crash deliberately?*

•

On the drive back, I'm thinking about the information Larissa told me. State Farm, not Crown. I was duped. I feel my phone ringing in my pocket. I see Peyton's name and exhale.

'Oh god, tell me you're okay?' he says as soon as I answer.

'What do you mean?'

'I mean what those guys did to you, Reid.'

How does he know? Before I can form any theories, Peyton has answered the question.

'The attack. You're all over TikTok and Instagram, not to mention the news online.'

I exhale slowly. I have the phone on speaker and should probably pull over but I just want to get to the motel and leave this place.

'I'm fine.'

My reflection in the rear-view mirror is an ugly thing. The swollen lips, the puffy eyes. I must have been a sight for Larissa this morning.

'I saw what those assholes did to you,' he says. 'That's assault – you should be pressing charges. Everyone knows who did it too.'

'You think the police have seen this?'

'If that's the case, they'd be about the only people in town who haven't.'

Shit. That's just what I need.

'One of the guys who attacked you has defended it on Facebook. Telling the *whole story*. Which I know can't be true.'

'It's a misunderstanding,' I say. 'I was investigating something; the girl said she had information.'

'Investigating? You told me you're a salesman.'

'Well, that wasn't exactly true. I'm a private investigator. It's a long story, but I was hired to look into the crash and I quickly realised Oliver Stiles and the missing girls have all sorts of links, and the crash itself doesn't make sense.'

'Brendon said someone turned up at his mom's house. Was that you?'

'You probably think I'm a stalker,' I say.

'Probably.'

'Did Brendon tell you he vandalised the memorial for Oliver Stiles?'

I hear him sigh, imagine him rolling his eyes. 'He didn't tell me that actually. What are you going to do?'

'I'm heading to my motel to grab my things then I'm leaving.'

'Where to?'

'East of here.'

'Pretty vague,' Peyton says, a current of annoyance in his voice.

'I'm going back to the city.'

'Well, before you go, can I see you?'

Just go home, I tell myself. *Don't do it.*

'I'll be back there in five minutes,' I say. 'If you can come by?'

'I'll come now.'

I check the time. It's 8.20 am.

'Comfort Inn in Manson, room nine,' I say. 'See you soon.'

•

While I wait for Peyton, I watch the assault on my phone. One of the college kids has superimposed himself over the video and is explaining what happened. Then there's another video of me in the back of my own car, bloody and rambling. This is bad enough, but something else is annoying me even more. Who was it that was emailing me? Who was it that called me to convince me to take the job?

I open my email and read through the correspondence from Crown Insurance. I see something I should have noticed the first time around: the agent's address is Sarah.Jennings@crownisurance. com. That missing 'n' – it's such a small detail, so easily overlooked.

It means someone's gone to the trouble of registering a domain name that looks almost identical to Crown Insurance's, and then impersonated an agent from there to hire me. Whoever it is clearly has money: they paid half my fee upfront, then that bonus along with the rest of the fee when they told me the investigation was over. Whoever it is faking the job knows I'm a private investigator, which means they'd also know there was a chance I'd realise they're not really from an insurance company.

I assume they've covered their tracks: the payments will be anonymous, I'm sure. And their emails encrypted.

Why go to all this trouble? Why not just hire me in their own name? Because they didn't want me to know what I was really searching for, that's why. And now that they've ended the agreement, does that mean I found it for them? Was it a piece of information in one of my daily reports?

It's probably not worth my time investigating. Equally, I know I won't be able to let it go. Like I said, I need to understand. I have to know the truth. I think I've found my next job. *Who hired me?*

There's a knock at the door. Peyton. That was fast, I think, getting up and opening it. I freeze.

'Hello, Reid.'

My heart rises like an uppercut into my throat. My legs go weak and something prickles at my hairline. I'm staring into the eyes of the man who was once my boss. He's older now, but no less imposing. *Chief Stubbs.*

'Nice place you got here. Going to invite me in?'

My eyes shoot past him to the patrol unit beside the Challenger. The two cops sitting in the front seats.

'What's this about?' I ask.

'Well, for starters, you're the victim of a crime.'

'You're not here for that.'

'Come on now,' he says. 'I don't get out of bed this early for nothing. Are you inviting me in, or shall we do this down at the station?'

I know I don't have a choice. I step back, sit on the edge of the bed.

'That your red Dodge out front?' Stubbs says.

'Yeah.'

'Thought you were in a white Camry?'

'Not me,' I say.

'You know they're still gunning for you. Should have seen the buzz in the station when a few of the older boys got wind you were in town. That Wojcik saga hasn't gone away. Every anniversary, every time something like this happens with my daughter and the King girl, people talk about our incompetence.'

Up close, I can see the way the last decade has worn him down: the deeper lines about his mouth; the slight stoop.

'You'd be doing yourself a favour clearing off, because they'll get you for something. They'll make your life hell.' He draws a breath. I see a deep sadness in his eyes. 'My little girl is missing, Reid. I thought if you're doing your private investigator work, you might give me a call at least to let me know what you found instead of calling in tips to another PD.'

'I'm sorry about your daughter, but you made it pretty clear you never wanted to see me again.'

'We interviewed the kids who gave you a ride back. They told us where they dropped you and it was easy enough to work out where you were staying.' Stubbs purses his lips and his nostrils flare. 'You've had key information and you didn't come straight to me. I've not slept properly since Maddie disappeared. I keep having these dreams – all the violence I've seen, the bodies.' He exhales. 'I keep thinking, what if something happened to her, just like Kiara King? What if there's a connection?

'Then when I pulled those boys in last night, the ones who left you with a face like a squashed peach, I asked them why they did it. And they said you were *grooming* a young girl. So of course, this piques my interest because I happen to know it's extremely unlikely you would be grooming a young girl.'

'I'm certain that Oliver Stiles had something to do with Kiara King's disappearance,' I say.

It's not just the fact that Stubbs is a finely tuned bullshit detector that I tell him the truth. It's that the truth is the only thing that might keep me from ending up in handcuffs.

'We investigated Stiles at the time,' Stubbs says. 'He had an alibi – he was with his wife. I didn't buy it, but it was airtight; we didn't have any evidence to the contrary. The damn wife stalled the investigation. He was with her.'

'All evening?'

'That's what she said. Yeah, we found correspondence between him and Kiara online. We know he'd planned to meet her but then the lead went cold.'

'So he had an alibi when Kiara went missing,' I say. 'But what about Maddison?'

The blood rushes to his cheeks; his eyes go wide. 'What are you saying? You think my daughter was doing the same thing as Kiara? You better be careful what you say, Reid.'

'I'm just saying Stiles could have gone to your house. It looks like he had the Smith's Auto loan car at the time because his car was at the shop.'

Stubbs shakes his head. 'I just don't see what motivation he would have for visiting my home.'

The thing is that he knows there's a hole in this theory, just as I do: there was some missing cash and jewellery too. But Oliver was rich, he wouldn't need to steal valuables.

'Now you're running around town, breaking into offices, getting in fights, because you think we didn't get things right the first time around,' he says.

'I know the crash investigation was rushed,' I say.

He laughs. 'Rushed? It took the crash investigators ten minutes to work it out. You don't know more than them. The wife lost control. She wasn't speeding or over the limit; the road was wet. It's a simple story but a sorry one.'

'How did she lose control?'

'She dozed off at the wheel. And when she woke, she jerked the wheel down. Anyway, you're not the one asking the questions here, Reid. Tell me how you came to be in contact with Angel Ryley?'

'I recognised her from social media and found out she was friends with Kiara. I asked her about Oliver Stiles when I got gas. She handed me her phone number . . . and, well, you know the rest.'

He looks at me long and hard. 'You leaving town?'

'Today.'

'That's a good idea. But if you have anything else to tell me, anything that will help me find my daughter . . .' He looks tired. 'Look, it's not with the media yet, but an interstate truck driver was picked up driving erratically last night. Driver says he gave a girl a lift when he was passing through Manson on Monday. He took her as far as the city. She was scared, her top torn, a little blood beneath her ear. He says he thought she was running from a bad relationship and wanted to help her out. We're holding him until we can confirm his story. Who knows where she was for the three days between when she disappeared and when he picked her up.'

'You buying it?' I ask.

'He picked her up near the shack where we found her socks and things. There's plenty of CCTV around where he supposedly dropped her in the city. He said she was going to catch a bus. She told him she was running from someone, but wouldn't say who. She didn't have her phone; it was found in her room at home. You can only go so far these days without one.'

'Mmm,' I say, suddenly feeling for the man.

'You get out to Pottsville Hospital,' he says. 'Get some X-rays done. And after that I suggest you head back to the city.'

'That's it? You're not taking me in?'

He starts towards the door. 'You've finished your business in town. But if you come across anything else, or have any ideas, I want you to speak to me first. My number's still the same. Got it?'

When Stubbs turns again to leave, I feel relief rinse over me. But I can't help myself, I have to say something else.

'So Cosby made deputy chief. What will happen when you retire?'

He stands at the doorway, half in half out, his head turned to the side. 'Cosby will take up the mantel, I guess. He's doing a good job in my absence. I'm still on leave but I'm heading to the city today to help search for her.'

'And you're okay with that? Cosby taking over. A principled man like yourself?'

Now he turns around to face me. 'I am a person who believes in second chances. You know that about me, Reid. So if a kid makes one mistake, it shouldn't ruin their life. I thought you of all people would agree.'

REID
NOW

NOT LONG AFTER Stubbs leaves, Peyton arrives. His eyes run the length of me and the exhaustion on his face turns into a sort of terror in an instant. Then I'm in his arms, in the doorway.

It takes me a moment to wrap my own arms around him. When he squeezes, I feel like another rib is about to break.

'Sorry,' he says. 'Did that hurt?'

'A little.'

He lets go. 'You need to call the police.'

'They were just here. I need to get on the road.'

He steps back. 'So you filed a complaint?'

'No. They've already brought the guys in anyway. It's all recorded, so I don't need to do anything.'

'Can I come in for a moment?' he asks.

'Sure,' I say, turning to let him through.

He sits on the edge of the bed and I take the chair in the corner. I feel warm under my arms, on my spine. I can't help but flick my gaze to the parking area outside. This isn't exactly how I'd imagined I would end up in a motel room with Peyton, but here we are.

'So you're a private investigator and you used to be a cop?' Peyton says. 'I read about it online. It was brave what you did.'

'Brave? I didn't even mean it. My ex stole the footage.'

'But you showed it to him. Part of you must have wanted it to get out.'

I think about this for a moment. I knew what I saw was wrong. It was police brutality. Maybe I did want it to come out at some subconscious level.

I find my eyes moving down to Peyton's arm, where the edge of his white sleeve clings to his bicep. *Pull yourself together.*

'I don't mean to pry,' he says.

'It's fine. The result of the leak was the key witness's testimony was deemed to be given under duress and excluded. Wojcik got off, reoffended and a girl died. That wouldn't have happened if not for me.'

'It's not your fault,' Peyton says. 'No one ever really knows what's going to happen.'

I close my eyes, let my breath seep out slowly. I hate the fact that I've given this up about myself. Vulnerability can sometimes feel so much like claustrophobia. I stand and blood seems to rush to my head. 'Listen, I've really got to get going.'

He reaches out to hold my hand and it's such a delicate, kind gesture that it somehow makes me feel even sadder. Looking up at me with his slightly wet eyes and sorry expression, I can't let go.

'So did you find what you were looking for – for the insurance company?' he asks.

'Long story. I didn't find anything that helped. I thought I was making inroads, but I wasn't. And to make matters worse, I was played. It wasn't an insurance company that hired me; I don't know *who* hired me. The only thing I found was a thumb drive in Oliver Stiles's car with the world's worst poetry on it. And someone broke into my room and stole it.'

Peyton laughs, laces his fingers through mine. 'Poetry, huh? Well, he was a writer. What do you mean about the insurance company?'

'Whoever hired and paid me was impersonating an insurance agent. Fake email address, website, signature, everything.'

'Wow,' he says. 'Who would bother going to those lengths? And why would anyone steal the poetry?'

'Oh, I don't know. It was just a dozen or so words in a document on the thumb drive.'

He's frowning. 'And someone stole it? What were the words? Did you write them down somewhere?'

'Why?'

'Are they written down somewhere?' he asks again.

'No,' I say. 'Why?'

'Can you remember them?'

'I searched them online – they might be in my history.'

'Check,' he says. 'Quickly.'

I get my laptop out and search my browser history.

'Here, look,' I say.

Peyton reads them over my shoulder.

child practice feeds shame never open despair stream path again sheet maple

'That's not poetry,' he says. 'That's a seed phrase.'

'A what?'

'It's sort of like an address for a wallet.'

This isn't making sense. 'What do you mean?'

'You know what cryptocurrency is?' he asks.

'Of course I know what cryptocurrency is.'

He rolls his eyes. 'So those words, they're like an address and a key to access a cryptocurrency wallet. Crypto is stored online on the blockchain. You don't just carry it around with you.'

'I have no idea what any of this means,' I tell him. 'Are you speaking English right now?'

'Here let me show you.'

He takes my laptop and opens another website. He types the words in and presses enter. When the screen loads, it's showing something that looks like account details.

'Zero,' Peyton says, pointing at the balance. 'There's no crypto in here.'

'So what does that mean?'

'It means the wallet is empty.'

He clicks on a tab that says *Transactions*. Then presses his fingertips to his lips.

'What is it?' I ask.

'That . . . it can't be right.'

'What?'

He opens the calculator app and punches in some numbers. The screen shows 6,235,419.35.

'What's that?'

He seems almost dazed. 'Reid, that's how much money was in this wallet until 11.12 pm two nights ago.'

I feel dizzy. 'That's a terrible joke, Peyton.'

'I'm dead serious. Someone broke into your room and stole just one thing. That's because they knew what was on it. They used the seed phrase to access the wallet and transferred all the crypto out.'

'Transferred it to who?'

He closes the calculator app. 'Impossible to know. We have the wallet address and that's it. They could have transferred it to another wallet, or converted it to another cryptocurrency, or sold it for US dollars.'

'You're telling me I was holding the key to six million dollars and now it's gone?'

'Shit,' Peyton says, closing his eyes. 'You were rich and you didn't even know it.'

'I was never rich. It never belonged to me,' I say. 'It belonged to him, Oliver Stiles. It should go to his wife, or whoever he left it to if he had a will.'

It happened at 11.12 pm on the night my door was open. I didn't get back until midnight, so maybe the junkie was telling the truth. Someone came, got the thumb drives, then left in a hurry, leaving my door ajar.

Then it hits me. I'd included a note about it in my daily reports but hadn't told them what the words were.

So that's what this was all about. Someone hired me to track down Oliver Stiles's fortune, and now that person has it all.

ESHANA
BEFORE

I HEAR FROM Stickland that afternoon. He calls when I'm working through a contract for a client and we arrange to meet at a cafe in town. He looks different in uniform and he's clean-shaven, his stubble gone.

'It would be easier if we did this at the station,' he says.

'No, I just want to see the proof.'

'Sure.' He opens a folder and slides a sheet of paper across the table. It's a printout of screenshots of my husband's communications with Kiara King on Sugar Babies For You.

'How do I know this is real?' I say.

He shrugs. 'I'm not about to fabricate evidence to convince you. I'm here because I know your husband was involved and he got away with it. I really hate to see the bad guy win.'

'Okay,' I say. 'Fine.'

I read the messages. The girl, who the police have identified as Kiara, asks Oli what he wants. He responds that he wants a friendship first, then maybe a girlfriend he can see once or twice a month and who will potentially go away with him on trips. He does go to the city sometimes, and to conferences and writers' festivals interstate. It's him, I know it. The messages read like him. He arranged to meet her, then I suppose they took things offline. I should have trusted my intuition months ago. Worst of all, he lied so easily, and was so convincing. Every time he told me nothing happened between him and Kiara, he was just lying through his teeth.

'Thank you,' I say.

'He's an asshole,' Stickland says. 'You can do better. We can't put someone away for communicating online with a young woman. It doesn't even qualify as grooming if she's told him she's eighteen and he believed that. But I know your husband was involved. Maybe he was at home with you like you said, or maybe he wasn't. Either way, he's got something to do with her disappearance.'

•

When Oli picks me up for dinner at The Pearl, there's a faint mark on his neck just below his jaw.

'I want the truth,' I say. 'I don't care anymore – I just need to know. I've stood by you – I *will* stand by you – but only if you tell me exactly what happened with Kiara.'

He exhales. 'I didn't hurt her. I promise you, I didn't hurt her.'

'But you did have sex with her?'

'No. No, I didn't.'

I laugh. 'You're still lying, all the way to the bitter end.'

'I'm not lying!' There's an edge to his words.

'What about the messages you sent her on the Sugar Baby website, Oli? I've seen them. Are you going to deny that too?'

He takes a moment before speaking again. 'Okay, I tried, yes. I just wanted something else and I thought it was harmless. I wanted to meet her.'

The tears come. 'You bastard. You've been lying this entire time.'

'No! I told you everything I could. Her mom was sick, the money was for her treatment. We met through the site, but I promise you we didn't sleep together.'

'You didn't do anything else with her?'

'No,' he says. 'No, I promise. Not a kiss, not a hug, nothing.'

'So why are you leaving me?'

He looks shocked.

'The safe is empty, Oli. Your passport, the money. It's gone.'

'I'm not leaving.'

'Don't lie to me, please. I can't take any more lies.'

'Look, I thought I would have to leave, but it's okay now. I've sorted it out. We're fine. There were threats, and . . . well, I didn't think I could stay in town. But listen, if something does happen – if I do have to go or, you know . . . anything happens to me – I want you to know you'll be taken care of always. There's a thumb drive in the glove box; it has my crypto-wallet address on it. There's six million dollars in bitcoin there. And the house, of course – you can keep that.'

The car suddenly feels cold. My husband is in deep. This is bigger than a fling with a younger woman.

'Oli, what the hell is going on?'

'Just don't tell anyone anything, okay? You don't know anything about what happened. You'll be fine.'

REID
NOW

I PASS BACK through Ethelton one last time before heading towards the hospital. It's 10 am and cold out, but the sun is shining. Every turn of the wheel brings a fresh wave of pain to my ribs and shoulder. I'm rolling through Ethelton slowly when I notice a few cars parked up near St Paul's Church.

A wedding, or a funeral? I remember something. The memorial service for Oliver Stiles. It's today. I park up on the street and walk to the church. Inside, the memorial has started. Someone is talking about Oliver's time at Sandown. It must be one of his colleagues.

I see a few familiar faces, and it reminds of my mother's funeral a little. Just a small crowd of mourners sitting in the pews.

I suppose with everything that's happening with Maddison and Kiara, most people wouldn't want to be seen celebrating the life of Oliver Stiles. I stand there at the back for a few minutes, listening in. After a short while, I leave again through the doors, closing them silently behind me.

Walking back to the Challenger, I notice something that stops me in my tracks. A white jeep. Not Peyton's jeep. This one is different, it's newer and cleaner. *This is the car I saw.* I'm certain. It must belong to someone inside. *Let it go*, I tell myself. But I can't. This is bigger than I thought. Six million dollars stolen.

I sit in the front seat of the Challenger and I wait.

Soon the church doors open. I see Larissa departing with a few other women I recognise from the dance school. Eshana is among them. There are some people who could be colleagues from the college, by the look of them. A couple others I don't recognise. I watch them all, noticing which cars they walk towards. Then I see a face in the crowd I haven't seen since the start of my investigation. Dark hair, dark eyes and tanned skin. She's in a body-hugging dark dress. I wonder how Eshana feels about her dead husband's ex-wife turning up at the memorial service.

I know what's going to happen before it happens. Annabel Stiles walks directly to the white Jeep. She unlocks it and climbs in.

I start the Challenger, move forward and swing in to cut across the Jeep, blocking her in the park. Then I get out and walk to the driver's window. I must be a sight, with my disfigured face and injured body hobbling along. But I make myself smile. She'd told me she drove a Mercedes. But here she is in a Jeep.

She looks scared and when I signal for her to drop the window it only comes down an inch.

'Hi Annabel,' I say. 'We spoke on the phone.'

She swallows, turns forward to look through the windshield but there's no getting past the Challenger. Other mourners are looking over as they depart but I ignore them. I've got her pinned.

'So why did you do it?'

She looks guilty. 'Do what?'

I smile. 'Let's not play games. Why are you even here at his memorial?'

'I'm here to pay my respects to my ex-husband.' She swings for indignant but it falls flat.

When I laugh, she flinches. 'Your respects? That's funny. Where were you the night of the crash, Annabel?'

'I was at home,' she says, turning now to look me in the eye. 'Look, I had nothing to do with any crash. Okay?'

'I saw what you did that night, to the flowers? Spray-painting the sidewalk.'

She sighs. A moment passes before she speaks again. 'You have no idea what he put me through. *No idea.* That man embarrassed me. He disregarded me and moved on.'

'Whose car is this?'

'It's my partner's. He likes me to be safe on the drive out here.'

'And you're here to keep up appearances? Or is this personal with Eshana? You want to rub her nose in it?'

She lifts her jaw as if offended. 'I just wanted the town to know what he was like, what he was really like. I did that with the spray paint before the news came out. Everyone was celebrating him – the news articles made him sound like a saint with his school program, his philanthropy. I needed them to know.'

'And if I point the police in your direction, you're telling me you have a rock-solid alibi for the night of the crash?'

'Of course I do. I wouldn't do anything to hurt them. I can be relieved he's dead, without wanting to kill him. And it was an accident, right?'

I turn back. Most of the mourners have gone.

'I'm not so sure.'

'Well,' she says, before running her tongue under her top lip. 'If you're looking for suspicious people, I wouldn't be looking at who's here at the memorial.'

'What do you mean?'

Now she smiles. 'I'd be looking at who *isn't* here.'

Maybe she has a point.

'I came,' she continues, 'because I thought Clare would be here. But perhaps she couldn't stomach it.'

'Clare Stiles?' *Why hadn't I checked her out more?* I knew he had family in the city.

'Clare Mendes,' she says. 'She used to be married.'

Mendes. Something else comes to me. The lawsuit against Oliver years ago. C Mendes. It was his sister suing him. They've got bad blood. 'They didn't get on?'

'Ha! You have no idea, do you?'

'Enlighten me.'

'He *hated* her. And she probably hated him even more.'

I'm still processing it when she speaks again.

'Now can you move your car? I have to get to work in the city.'

Without another word, I get back in the Challenger and drive off towards the hospital.

•

I think about Clare Mendes the entire time I'm being scanned, poked and prodded at the hospital. I leave an hour later, two thousand dollars poorer, with my arm in a sling and a stronger class of pain medication. Those bastards cracked my collarbone, and a small chip of bone in my elbow came away, but other than that it's mostly bruising, and just the smallest crack in my ribs. The human body's durability is a marvel sometimes.

Could it have been Clare who was staying at the Stileses' house, taking care of Eshana's affairs? If so, then it was her I heard on the phone that day. The woman said, *He's not found it yet.* She was talking about me, and the seed phrase. Who was she talking to? Her mother? And I realise now that she saw me from the window, she knew I was there but she never called the police. It must have been Clare. She didn't want me arrested. Maybe because I was working for her.

Back in my car, it takes ten seconds to find Clare Mendes online. *Clare Mendes (née Stiles)* at the top of a LinkedIn profile for a real estate agency in the city. Shaw & Co Realty.

Shaw & Co – that rings a very loud bell in my head. I've done a job for them.

I tracked down someone who'd signed a contract on a home, paid a deposit, then disappeared. It was tough; it took me a couple weeks, one of which was spent in Puerto Rico.

It must be Clare behind the fake Crown Insurance emails. She probably hired me for that previous job and knew she could trust me to hand over anything I found. She wanted me to investigate the car crash as a way to get to the rest of her brother's affairs. She wanted me to find out how to access his finances. Her plan worked brilliantly.

I know where the agency's office is located, so I head in that direction. I'm not supposed to drive, but I've no way of getting the Challenger back to the city otherwise. I stop once for gas and a bite, then before long I'm turning off the I-76 towards the heart of the city.

'Hi,' I say to the receptionist at Shaw & Co. 'I'm here to speak with Clare Mendes.'

She looks up, smiles. Then her eyes linger on my bruises, the sling holding my arm. 'Sure. Is she expecting you?'

'I don't think so,' I say. I reach into my pocket awkwardly, pull out my private investigator badge and flash it. It does the trick.

'One second,' she says. She rises and disappears up a corridor behind her desk.

The office is blighted with glass; privacy is dead in the modern workspace, I think. I see the receptionist go to a woman sitting in a glass booth. I recognise Clare Mendes from her photo on LinkedIn. When she looks past the receptionist and sees me, her mouth falls open. It's just a second before she's composed herself again, but in that moment she's told me all I need to know.

I could call the police. I *should* call them and tell them what I've discovered. Clare Mendes broke into my motel room and stole something that belonged to her brother and his wife. But what proof do I have? I have to play this just right.

I start recording on my phone as Clare comes out with the receptionist.

'Hi,' she says, reaching out her hand. 'Vanessa said you're a cop?'

'Just here to talk to you about your brother's sad passing last week,' I say, avoiding the question.

'Oh. Yeah, sure.' It's a pantomime, the way her mouth turns downwards, the sad look in her eyes. 'Come on through to my office.'

She leads me, her heels clicking on the polished concrete floor. 'What did you say your name was?'

'Vince Reid,' I tell her. 'But you already know that.'

I sit in front of her desk, and she closes the door then takes her own seat in the leather office chair.

'You found me,' she says, her lips twitching as if she's resisting the urge to smile. 'I suppose I should have expected that.'

The façade may have gone, but for the benefit of her colleagues she keeps her body language and expression neutral.

'And you found what you were looking for, didn't you?' I say. 'Six million dollars in cryptocurrency.'

She raises her jaw slightly, fixes her gaze on something above my head. 'I don't know what you're talking about, I'm afraid.'

'One of the thumb drives you stole from my motel room. The one with the address of a crypto-wallet containing millions in digital assets.'

'Sounds like an interesting story. But I can't help you with it. Did you meet Eshana?'

'I did.'

'She really loved my brother, even though he was a selfish, cheating rat. Sometimes I feel bad for her, but she'll be fine with that house and all the insurance money.'

'You caused the crash, didn't you?' I say. 'Then you couldn't find the wallet address at the house, so you recruited me to help.'

'I had nothing to do with the crash. I'm not a monster. I'm pretty certain it was an accident. But after the crash, I needed some help to figure out where my brother kept some important things. I won't bore you with the story, Reid, but my brother effectively stole money from me. He never paid me what I was owed.'

'You left the note on my car too,' I say. 'I saw you in the cafe the same day.'

She sits up straighter. 'Look, I had nothing to do with the accident. I was in the city the entire week of the crash. I was actually a little sad when he died. My mother was upset too.' She flicks her hair with her fingertips. 'If you ask me, Eshana snapped and steered the car towards the pole. I spoke to her a lot on the phone and she was depressed. I'm sure she suspected he was cheating on her, probably going to leave her. It's a lot for someone to take. Anyway, you're not charged with finding out. You've been paid, and you're free to take another job or have a break. A bonus for your work must have been nice too.'

I smile. Five thousand dollars is nothing compared to what she gained. She's good at this, giving me answers in a way that maintains plausible deniability. She's effectively told me she stole the money because she saw it as a family debt. She's denying killing her brother, and I can't help but believe her.

How would a real estate agent know how to make a crash happen, and make it look like an accident? Maybe the simplest answer is the right one. Maybe Eshana did doze off for a second. Or with everything on her mind, she experienced a lapse in concentration. Or maybe she did snap and deliberately drove towards the pole. I can't prove anything either way and I don't need to. I'm not employed by the insurance company. This was all a private matter.

'Why choose me?' I ask.

'You did an impossible job for us last year, and you were so professional and dogged. I needed someone with integrity. Who else was I going to use?' She digs a thumb in at the side of the bridge of her nose, clearly growing tired of this conversation. 'At least the girl turned up.'

'Turned up dead,' I say. 'Hardly a good result.'

'Not her. The other one.'

REID
NOW

I SIT IN my car outside of Clare's real estate office and check the news on my phone.

I knew Maddison Stubbs was a good-looking girl: blonde, all American, with her father's intelligent eyes and her mother's small, upturned nose. But on the screen, in motion, she's somehow more striking. Even with the tears building in her eyes and an unsmiling mouth. She stands behind her father on the podium holding her mother's hand. Mrs Stubbs dabs at the corner of her own eyes.

'We are extremely grateful for the efforts of all investigative bodies involved in helping to bring Maddie home,' Chief Stubbs says. 'We're so relieved to have her back. She's had a rough time of it, and now we just want to go home as a family. I'm not here in any official capacity, so I'll pass it over to Deputy Chief Cosby to give a brief statement and field any questions.'

He steps back to stand beside his daughter, putting his arm around her shoulders.

'I'll take your questions shortly,' Cosby says. 'But just to give an overview of the situation: Maddison Stubbs was at home last Wednesday when Oliver Stiles arrived at the property sometime between three and three thirty in the afternoon. Investigations are continuing, however I can confirm that Mr Stiles entered the property and abducted Maddie. He bound her wrists and put her in the back of a vehicle loaned from a local mechanic's shop, where his own car was undergoing repairs. Mr Stiles was armed throughout the encounter. He drove Maddison to an abandoned shed on Adams Road, where he locked her inside. Later that afternoon, at around 5 pm, Mr Stiles returned the loan car and collected his car.'

He pauses and clears his throat. 'Maddison remained locked in the shed for three days, during which period Mr Stiles passed away in a vehicle collision. Eventually she managed to break through the wooden door and made her way to the nearest main road, Moore Road, and followed it until she hit the Manson bypass. An interstate truck driver stopped to offer her a ride and Maddison rode with him to the city.'

I notice tears streaming down Maddison's face.

'Mr Stiles had flights booked to leave the country for Mexico; his US passport and approximately ten thousand dollars in cash were missing from his home safe. I can confirm we are not seeking to speak with any other persons of interest in relation to Maddison's disappearance. I'll take a few questions now.'

The room erupts with a chorus of interjections as the journalists all raise their hands. Cosby points someone out, rather awkwardly. It's clear he's not used to the limelight.

I can't quite hear the question, but I can figure it out based on Cosby's response.

'I can confirm that we are currently investigating Mr Stiles in relation to the Kiara King case as well.'

He points out another reporter. Again, I can't hear the question, but when I see who's asking it, I feel something cold stir inside. It's my ex, Marco.

Cosby recognises him too and sounds irritated at giving him airtime. 'We have uncovered a plot by Kiara King to extort money from Oliver Stiles. Other than that, I won't be speaking about that particular case.'

I catch a word in the next question. *Motivation.*

'As I said, we are hoping to get a fuller picture of the crime in the coming days. Maddison confirmed in her statement that she'd had very little interaction with Oliver Stiles, although she had in the past seen him engaging in a sexual act with a woman in his car when she was out running. Maddison believed this person to be Kiara King, and when she contacted Miss King sometime around July, Miss King suggested that she was afraid of Mr Stiles. Maddison advised Miss King to tell Mr Stiles's wife or employer about the affair, which would enable her to end it.'

In the background, Maddison sweeps her fingers across her eyes to wipe away the tears.

'Can you comment as to why Maddison didn't come home earlier?' another journalist asks.

'Maddison was terrified, as I'm sure anyone in her position would be,' Cosby says. 'Mr Stiles made his intentions clear when he abducted her.' He pauses, swallows. 'Maddison believed that her life was in danger, and after being taken from her home she could no longer feel safe there. This is a very common reaction to home invasions and abductions. Maddie ran away, I think most people in this room would do the same thing. She didn't think the police could protect her. I won't repeat the things Mr Stiles said to this strong young woman behind me, but it's clear he instilled an extreme level of fear in her. Understandably, and under intense pressure, Maddison made the decision to flee.'

Another question.

'Maddison stayed in a women's refuge in the city for one night under an alias, then she slept rough in a city park. Officers had been searching parks and shelters in the city for Maddison since receiving information from the truck driver that he had dropped her off. She was found around noon by local officers.

'It's an extraordinarily tough time for Maddison and her family. We ask that you respect their privacy. I will not be taking any further questions, however Maddison has prepared a brief statement to share.'

Maddison's parents come with her as she approaches the bouquet of microphones. Stubbs says something into her ear and rubs her back. She bites her lip and nods. Then begins to speak.

'What I witnessed those long months ago in the back of that man's car has changed my life forever. I didn't know Kiara well, but I recognised her, and I didn't speak up. I didn't tell anyone what I'd seen. I wanted to protect her, but didn't realise that in doing so I was protecting him.' She swallows, and looks back down at her written statement.

'I could have stopped him if I'd told my father what I saw, but I didn't and now I have to live with that forever. I'm sorry, Kiara. I let you down. I let your family and friends down. I wish I could go back and change things. I wish I had more courage. I wish you were still here. I will carry you with me and honour your life by living my own, by being strong and speaking out. This has been the hardest time in my life. Without my family—' She blocks a sob with the back of her hand. 'My friends—' Another pause as she composes herself. 'And the Ethelton community, I would never be able to survive this. Thank you to everyone who has reached out.'

She bows her head and turns away. Her parents wrap their arms around her. The room erupts with questions, but Chief Stubbs is already guiding her from the podium.

Cosby, looking frustrated, steps up, his hands raised as if placating a wild beast. 'Alright, alright, that's it, people.'

I close the screen on my phone and sit back. The truth, I see now, is a bubble trapped in mud. Eventually, one way or another, it will rise. It will break open at the surface.

Maddison Stubbs is home safe. There's just one last thing to do.

I start the car, shoot a message to Peyton and set out back towards Manson. I've got an old white Camry to get back to the city, and a dodgy mechanic, Cody Booth, to speak to. There's still something that doesn't make sense.

•

I arrive back in Manson around lunchtime. Passing by Fenton Park, I think about Dennis again. Tossing the football back and forth. Then I see him on the floor of Mom's room, the pool of blood and splintered wood. Blood on her hands and face. Always the same images from that night come back. The police and ambulance arriving. Mom in handcuffs. I think about it all as I navigate my way toward Smith's Auto.

Soon, I park up on that same side street near the garage. As I wait for Cody Booth to come out, I try to focus. I need to forget the past and focus on the task at hand. Why am I still pursuing this? I've been paid, but I always want the truth. What is it about *this* case? I've carried the guilt around for a decade because of what happened to Amanda Marley. In some small way, is this absolving me? Do I feel better knowing I might be able to help find exactly what happened to Kiara? I just know that I can't leave it behind me, I owe it to the town. Eventually I see him walk to his Honda Civic, get in and drive away. I start the Challenger and follow.

I read the bumper sticker again: *Don't get too close, your daughter is probably in here.*

Cody must have been angry at Oliver because when they were going out together, Maddison told him what Oliver had done to Kiara. But I can't get past something he said during our first encounter. *Tell him it's over. This has got to stop.*

Who did he mean by *him*? And what exactly was it that had to stop?

I follow the Civic to a set of lights. When the light goes green, I'm two cars back and Cody races off, but I have a good idea where he's heading.

The Civic is parked outside Dunkin' Donuts, the same place I found him last time. I park behind his car, blocking his exit, and open the Challenger's door. I should probably just leave town like Stubbs said, and leave this all behind me, but that impulse to understand is too strong.

Cody comes out with a tray of coffees. 'What the fuck, man? I'm in a hurry!'

'Hi Cody,' I say with a smile. 'Remember me?'

He looks irrationally afraid, even taking into account my bruises, cuts and scrapes and the sling. I didn't think I could still have that effect without a uniform and a gun strapped to my hip.

'Look, man, we're straight now,' he says. 'I'm not going to say or do anything, alright. You guys have got to back off.'

'You guys?' I repeat. 'Who exactly do you mean?'

'You can't arrest me. I haven't done anything wrong.'

Cody thinks I'm a cop. I suppose I did interrogate him last time.

'You're scared of the PD,' I say.

'I'm not scared. Just sick of it. You scared my mama though, and she's got nothing to do with any of this. I kept my side of the deal – you can't keep running up on me. I'm not about to say anything.'

'Cody, just tell me one thing. What is it you're not allowed to say?'

He looks at me now. 'This is a trap. I told Stubbs I wouldn't, and I haven't. I won't.'

Stubbs? It looks like my old boss has put the fear of god into this kid.

'I just need to hear it from your mouth,' I say.

He looks around him. 'I can't talk about it. Me and Maddie broke up.'

Something clicks in my mind, like the moment you pick a lock. 'And why did you break up, Cody?'

He seems to sag, like a man who's lost it all on what he thought was a sure thing. ''Cause of what she did. But I'm not going to "sully her good reputation" and tell the world that she was screwing Stiles.'

Oliver Stiles and Maddison Stubbs. I feel the earth shift beneath my feet, a sudden coldness at my core.

'It's not fair to Kiara,' Cody continues. 'She didn't do anything wrong except see them together. Maddie and Stiles. But he's dead now, and so is Kiara, and that's none of my business. I've moved on.'

'Kiara saw Maddison and Oliver Stiles together,' I say, speaking as though it's a known fact. 'Kiara wasn't screwing him.'

'No. But everyone thinks she was. And Maddie is just this good girl, caught up in it.'

'You accosted Stiles that night at the restaurant,' I say.

'You would have too. Anyone would have! I didn't hear from Maddie for months after she dumped me, then out of the blue she messaged me – on the day she disappeared. She said Stiles had driven her to the cabin, and they were supposed to go away together, then he had a change of heart. He told her he wouldn't go.'

'She called you after she was supposed to be missing?'

His Adam's apple bobs. He looks down at the tray of coffees. 'Yeah, I guess.'

'And you told the police.'

'Of course. I called her dad straight away.'

And Stubbs told you to keep quiet, I think. He wanted to protect his daughter's reputation.

'Maddie was in tears, distraught. She told me she was going to confront Stiles, tell his wife, tell the town what he did. I still cared about her, so yeah, I was mad. I thought she might do something crazy – hurt herself. I was searching for her when I saw him and his wife sitting in the window at the restaurant.'

'Did you find Maddie?' I ask.

'No,' he says. 'No, I didn't hear from her again.'

'Listen, Cody,' I say. 'I'm not a cop.'

His eyes go wide.

'I can help you. I used to be a cop. I have a friend in a PD outside of the twin towns. Or you could go higher.'

He shakes his head. 'No, I can't. I'm not doing anything.' He clams up. He won't say another word.

I move my car to let him leave. Kiara saw them. So that's how she got the money out of Oli? Did Brendon King know?

ESHANA
NOW

CAN YOU EVEN begin to imagine what it's like to wake up into this world only to discover you killed the love of your life?

It's been a week since the crash and I was unconscious for four days of it, while doctors worked to reduce the swelling in my skull. When I found out he'd died, I wept for two days. The drugs helped but still the sadness was all-consuming. I can't remember much of the day of the crash, but Larissa has helped fill in the blanks.

I welcome the visitors who come and take my mind off things. Clare was here earlier in the week. Becky and some of my friends from the city came by or sent flowers. The dance moms have all been. And the private investigator who returned Oliver's gym bag full of money.

There was also a visit from the police. They know what Oli did. Teams of them scoured through the house, boxing things up and taking them away. They found the school uniform that girl left after the threesome, the one Oli liked me to dress up in.

Larissa has done a good job of shielding me from the brunt of it all. I've been offline since I woke up, closing the world out to recover and mourn my husband.

I do wonder what Oli's actions mean for me in this town. I can't imagine staying here; wherever I go, people will know me as the woman who married a monster. I could sell this house and move back to the city; use the insurance money to buy a nice apartment and begin a new life. But I have my doubts about starting afresh. Will I be forever tainted? Maybe I'll wear my husband's crimes for the rest of my life, like an odour.

Larissa is sitting on a stool at the kitchen bench. As I pass her, I see that she's scrolling through a news site on her phone. An image of a girl comes up onscreen.

'Who is that?' I ask.

Larissa locks her phone screen and turns it over. 'Oh, nothing. Just scrolling.'

'Larissa, show me right now.'

She turns on the stool to look directly at me. 'It's just the girl who was missing. They found her.'

'Show me.'

Reluctantly, she unlocks her phone and opens the browser. She shows me the girl. The article names her: *Maddison Stubbs.*

My eyes fix on the necklace she's wearing. I recognise it. It's the one I assumed Oliver had bought for me for my birthday. *I know you,* I think.

A flash of memory comes back from before the crash. Oli asking me to pull over not long after we left the restaurant that night. When I did, he told me he'd been seeing someone else, someone younger. He told me that he'd ended it with her and he was sorry. He begged me to forgive him and stay with him.

It hurts so bad remembering this.

And other moments from that night come back too, in bits and pieces, like something resurfacing from the depths of the sea.

REID
NOW

PEYTON IS WORKING, so when I knock on the door of the unit it's Brendon who answers.

'You,' he says. His eyes are red-rimmed. He's been crying.

'Can I come in?'

'Why? So you can go poking your nose in our business again?'

I let my breath out and it sounds more annoyed than I was intending. His eyes narrow a little.

'Look, I'm trying to work out what happened to your sister,' I say. 'The cops in this town haven't done a very good job with the investigation.'

'Well, they know who did it now. It was him, Stiles.'

'Maybe, but I'm not so sure.'

He folds his arms, giving me a chance to continue speaking but not letting me in.

'I know Oliver Stiles had a relationship with Maddison Stubbs too. A source has told me that he heard from Maddison *after* she was supposed to have disappeared. She told him that Stiles was planning on running away with her but changed his mind. He said Kiara was never in a relationship at all with Stiles.'

'She wasn't,' Brendon says. 'I told you that the first time. But no one is going to believe that, are they? She was on that website, she met him, she was messaging him.'

'So why was she doing that?'

'For the money. For my mom.'

'What was she being paid for then?'

He clenches his jaw.

'You're not going to get in trouble,' I say. 'Just tell me the truth.'

He grunts. 'I know that. What could I be charged with?'

'Conspiracy to defraud,' I say without missing a beat. 'Extortion. Blackmail. You might have misinterpreted me. When I say you're not going to get in trouble, what I mean is you're not going to get in trouble if I choose not to contact my good friends at the Manson PD to tell them my suspicions. You and your sister plotted to extort money from Oliver Stiles.'

He looks at me like he's about to take a swing. 'You think you can just stand there and threaten me?'

'I'm not threatening you. I'm just clarifying what will happen if you don't tell me the truth.'

'And what are you going to do with the *truth*?' he says.

'I just *need* to understand. I can't tell you how important it is to me. It's a hazard of the job. And who knows, maybe it will unlock something for me. Maybe I'll get to the bottom of my own case.'

'And what's your case?'

'Did Eshana Stiles deliberately crash the car the night her husband died?'

He looks skyward, places his hands on his hips. 'I was so angry when I found out what Kiara was doing. All those profiles of her looking like a cheap whore. Using those sites to try and find married men. She thought if she became a sugar baby, she could find someone to pay for Mom's medicine. I only found out because I was at their house one day and saw her messaging some old guy.

I got the truth out of her in the end. I hated them – all these creepy old douchebags exploiting young girls like my sister, who was only seventeen. I wanted to call the police on this guy so Kiara told me she'd stop. I watched as she deleted the accounts and blocked his number. Then a few weeks later, after doing a bit of reading up, I realised these old men were mostly married and mostly rich.'

'So you thought of a better plan to squeeze money out of them?'

'Welcome to America,' he says with a sad smile. 'What would you do to save your loved ones?'

I think about my mom and dad. 'Well . . . anything.'

'That's right, you would. Anyone would. So Kiara went on the site again, and when she went on dates I was always nearby, watching. If anything untoward happened, I'd step in. But then she met this Oliver guy and, well, that was it. We had a plan. We couldn't just blackmail him, he was careful. He never sent nudes or anything incriminating. So Kiara called it off with him and had the idea to follow him instead, knowing he'd try it with someone else. The problem is, I work out of town – four days on, three days off. So we took it in turns to keep tabs on him. Eventually, Kiara saw him in a car with her. She got a picture on her phone.'

'Maddison Stubbs?'

'I guess so. We didn't know who she was at the time though. So we got in touch with Stiles, told him he had to pay us. That's why he did it,' he says, his eyes watering, his words softening. 'That's why he killed Kiara. To get rid of his secret.'

'What about the photo of Maddie and Stiles.'

'I don't know what Kiara did with it, it was on her phone.'

'But Oliver knew that you knew. He didn't get rid of his secret.'

'Yeah, he did. I went to the police and told them he killed her, but they wouldn't listen to me. I'm just a low life according to the cops in this town. I smoke a little weed, used to do other drugs and have been arrested a few times. I'm hardly a reputable source. They just told me he had an alibi.'

'His wife?'

'Yeah. And I couldn't tell anyone else cause they'd just think I was just trying to protect my sister's reputation.'

'And he always paid up?'

'Yeah, I was going to start getting more money out of him, maybe enough to help out with food and bills at home. Then Kiara disappeared. I wanted to believe she had run away, but now I know.'

'And did you ever tell his wife?'

'I planned to. But no, I didn't tell her. I knew we would get in trouble too for blackmail. And the police were already investigating Oli. But his wife knows now. Everyone knows Stiles is a killer.'

'So you're convinced it was Oliver who killed her?'

'I can't be more certain. That alibi is a lie.'

Eshana holds the key to this investigation.

'Thanks,' I say. 'And, Brendon, I really am sorry about your sister. From what I can tell, anyone who actually knew her really loved her.'

ESHANA
NOW

AFTER LARISSA'S GONE, I go to my work laptop and search online for Maddison Stubbs. She's everywhere. Big-eyed and innocent-looking, a girl from a good, wholesome Christian family. Her father is the local chief of police. She speaks well, enunciating clearly, but I know she's not telling the truth. She's made herself the victim. But why? To protect her reputation? Or for some other reason?

It makes my head spin. I feel my organs tense, as if at any moment I could be sick.

I read another article, this time about the investigation into Kiara King's death. Police divers have found Kiara's phone in the dam, and her bike. Recent messages on the phone confirm that Oli lured Kiara to the water tower using an anonymous app called Frenz.

The comments on the article are horrible. The media has made a monster of my husband and many are celebrating his death. Some insinuate that I knew about his affairs and that's why I crashed the car. Some of them are certain that Oli planned to kill Maddison too.

Just then, the bell chimes. Someone is at the gate. I look out the window but don't see headlights.

I go to the intercom. 'Yes?' I feel brittle, like spun glass.

'Hi,' a voice says. 'I don't know if you know me. My name's Maddie. I knew your husband.'

My heart thumps. 'Yes,' I say. 'Hi, Maddie, of course I know you.'

'Can I come up?'

'What's this about?'

'I have something to tell you, but I don't know if it's the sort of news I should share over the intercom.' Her voice is small and innocent.

Is she coming to tell me that she was having an affair with my husband? Because I already know that. Or maybe she's here to tell me that the news stories have twisted the truth? Except I heard it from her mouth: Oli kidnapped her at gunpoint, locked her up in a shed and left her to starve.

I close my eyes for a moment. My husband was a lot of things, I know that. But a kidnapper, a violent man, he was not.

'Mrs Stiles?' Maddie says.

I press the key symbol on the pad and the gate slides open. I watch her walk up the driveway towards me.

This feels awkward already and I'm really not in the mood to do this with her now. I suppose I want to know why she lied about Oli abducting her at gunpoint.

'Hi, Maddie,' I say to her at the door.

'Hi,' she says. 'This is a beautiful house you have.'

Something feels off suddenly. She's holding her handbag close to her side.

'Thanks,' I say, looking at her with curiosity. 'But, umm, you've been here before, haven't you?'

She smiles. 'Have I?'

'Yes,' I say. 'Yes, of course you have.' I study her features. 'That night – it was our anniversary. I knew I recognised you. You were the girl he chose.'

A subtle shift of her lips. 'I was wearing a lot of make-up. Still you remember me?'

'I do. So you just continued to see each other after the ah—'

'Threesome? Oh, you have no idea what he was like, do you? We met before the threesome, Eshana. Then we kept seeing each other after. I liked him. I thought I loved him.' She lets her breath out slowly, staring at me. 'It's a shame you remember me. You know, I've been reading online that people can have memory problems after a head knock. Because you were in a car crash, right?'

What game is she playing?

'I was,' I say. 'A week ago.'

'It's a miracle you survived. I was looking for you that night, and Oli. I knew you were at dinner. He changed our plans. We were going to run away together. He bought us flights, he had it all planned.' She pauses. 'Do you remember that? Do you remember seeing me?'

I step back, press myself against the wall. I have that feeling again – the snake on the trail, my mother's urgent voice. I'm in danger.

'He promised me we'd run away together, but it was just words. He was lying like usual. He told me we could continue to have sex, but that's all it would ever be. He wanted to drop me home, but I wouldn't go anywhere with him after that.' Her voice is mean now. 'You married a chinless, spineless weasel, Eshana.'

'I'm going to have to ask you to leave,' I say.

'Oh, I can't leave,' she says. 'Not now. You remember me. But you don't remember the crash?'

'That doesn't matter,' I tell her. 'Your secret is safe with me.'

She smiles, but there's no joy in it. Her head shakes almost imperceptibly. 'No secret is ever safe if it's shared.'

'Maddie, please leave my house. My friend will be here shortly.'

'Oh no, she won't be back for a while yet. She only left half an hour ago and she lives across the other side of Ethelton, right?'

A spear of ice passes through me. She's been watching the house.

'That said, we better be quick,' she adds. 'My dad will kill me if he has to tidy this up.'

'You were never missing, were you?' I say.

'I was hiding.'

'And Kiara?' I'm almost too paralysed by fear to ask. 'You killed her, didn't you?'

She shakes her head. 'I knew what she was doing to him. I knew what she was holding over him. It was never going to stop. Oli was using an encrypted app to message her about the money – it was easy enough to start another account and I got her contact details off his phone. I messaged her pretending to be Oli late one night and told her it was too risky to deliver her monthly payment to her house. I said I'd left the money stashed in a bag up the top of the water tower instead and she could pick it up in the morning. She said it was too risky and anyone could stumble upon it. She said she would have to sneak out and collect it that night. I didn't think for a second she'd actually come, but people do things for money they never would do otherwise. She didn't realise how risky it would be, a young woman riding her bike all the way out there alone. But people take risks when they're desperate. She got there and climbed up to collect the money.'

'Then what?' I whisper.

'Then she fell.' That's when Maddison pulls her hand from her bag and I see the gun.

REID
NOW

THE LIGHTS ARE on in the Stiles house. I press the intercom at the gate. No response. I press it again. No response. Do I wait? She might be sleeping.

I buzz one more time. Still no response. I peer towards the house and see now that the front door is wide open. This isn't right.

I take my handgun from the car, strap it to my hip, then cursing that my arm is still in the sling, I awkwardly pull myself up over the fence. Aching all over, I run towards the house, alert for any movement inside.

When I get to the door, I don't call out in case something *is* wrong, in case someone else is here with her. Then again, there could be another explanation for the open door. Maybe someone just left.

I listen to the house. It's still. I move through the place silently, clearing each room individually. Then I look over the lawn and the gardens. She's gone. Somewhere out there in the dark night.

There's only one clue to what she was doing before she left. A cup of tea, half empty and almost cold, sitting beside an open laptop.

I step closer and see a number of tabs open on the browser. They're all stories about Maddison, except for one article about divers finding Kiara King's bicycle and mobile phone in the dam. The police have confirmed that messages were exchanged between Kiara and Oliver Stiles that night to organise a meet-up at the top of the water tower to exchange money. The message was sent on an app called Frenz. I've come across it before. It's an app for cheaters – all anonymous, simple to make an account.

I check Eshana's search history and find that just a short while ago she was searching Maddison's name obsessively.

Maddison Stubbs escort
Maddison Stubbs Sugar Babies For You
Maddison Stubbs Kiara King
Maddison Stubbs Ethelton College
Frenz app
Make Frenz app account
Maddison Stubbs address

What if, after scrolling through all these articles, Eshana flew off in a rage to confront Maddison and her family?

Even though I don't want to face Stubbs again, I better get over there. Anything could be happening. I open the gate from the house, then race down the driveway as fast as my broken body will take me. I get in the Challenger and set off.

I press my foot to the floor. And wonder why it feels like Eshana is the one in danger, not Maddie?

•

Stubbs lives on the other side of Ethelton on a small farm that's walking distance to the Boulevard and not so far from the water tower either. The epicentre of everything that's happened in this town the past six months.

I race down from the hills, taking a switchback a little too quickly and feeling the tyres give up a bit of traction. It takes ten minutes before I'm pulling into the track that leads to the farm. I can see Stubbs's Manson PD car parked up near the house.

I get out, open the gate – it's manual, unlike the one at the Stiles place – drive through, then close it again. I park up beside the police car, look in through the passenger window. The chief's hat is sitting on the front seat.

Eshana's car isn't here. She must have gone somewhere else.

I hear a sickly knock from up beside the house. Something cracking. It happens again. I put my phone in my coat with the microphone on and facing out.

I creep up the driveway and then I see him: Stubbs chopping wood. A security sensor comes on, throwing a cone of light on the gravel before me.

He turns, squinting. 'Reid. That you?'

'Chief.'

He looks towards the house, then back at me. 'You better have a damn good reason for turning up at my home. I thought we agreed you were leaving town.'

I step closer. 'You also said that if I knew anything else about your daughter I should tell you.'

'Well, we're not looking for Maddie anymore. She's home safe.'

'This feels important, Chief.'

He puts another piece of wood on the block. 'So,' he says, resting the axe over one shoulder, 'what is it then?'

I swallow. He must know his daughter was seeing Oliver Stiles. That would explain why the information never reached the media. What about the rest of the PD? Do they know? It would kill him knowing his staff had that over him. Most people these days probably wouldn't care so much, but I know Stubbs. He wouldn't like it one bit. If nothing else, he's a committed lawman. He knows right from wrong.

Does he also know that Oliver never had a relationship with Kiara King?

'Well?' Stubbs says. He turns and the axe crashes down. The log splits. He bends and positions a piece to split it again. 'You just gonna stand there and watch me cut my wood?'

Where to begin?

Crack. Another piece splits. Then he lays down the axe. 'Hold on, I think I can hear my phone ringing.'

He heads inside. It's clear he hasn't issued an invitation to follow him.

He comes back out a moment later. 'You better make this quick. Tina's on her way back with dinner.'

'I've been doing a bit of my own investigating, as you know,' I say. 'And I started to see all sorts of connections between Oliver Stiles and Kiara King. Then I spoke to Kiara's brother, Brendon.'

Stubbs rolls his eyes. 'Yeah, we interviewed him. He's a druggie. Lies through his teeth.'

'Does he?'

'Yeah. He's a known bullshit artist. Why? What'd he tell you?' He bends to stand another piece on the chopping block.

'Well, that makes more sense now,' I say. 'Because he told me Maddison was the one in a relationship with Oliver Stiles.'

Stubbs straightens. 'Reid, don't come to my house and repeat the lies of a desperate man. He lost his sister and I'm sorry for that, but grief makes the mind believe all sorts of crazy things. He doesn't want his dead sister to have that sort of reputation. And I understand, but smearing my daughter ain't bringing her back.'

'Yeah,' I say. 'That's what I thought.' I turn to leave, then pause. 'Except this is the part I don't get. He told me he and Kiara were blackmailing Stiles. And Stiles was paying them, because they were going to tell the town about his affair with Maddison.'

'There was no affair!' Stubbs booms.

'No, of course not. But in this story Brendon told me, the reason Stiles killed Kiara was because of the money. But I discovered that Oliver Stiles had millions of dollars. I don't think paying Kiara a few thousand dollars a month was going to cost him dearly.'

'So there you go,' Stubbs says. 'The story is clearly a falsehood. I don't know why you're even telling me any of this.'

'Yeah, I thought that too. But then I wondered what happened to the school uniform.'

'What are you talking about?'

'The school uniform I found at the base of Oliver Stiles's wardrobe. The one I rang the tip line about. It was never mentioned in the media, and there's been no explanation about why it was in his bedroom.'

'It was Kiara King's uniform,' Stubbs says.

'It was an Ethelton High uniform. Kiara went Manson High.'

'Oh, right,' Stubbs says. 'Well, maybe Stiles took it from the house when he kidnapped Maddie. He must have grabbed the uniform then.'

It's an obvious lie. If that were the case, the uniform would have been mentioned in the media and police reports. It would have formed part of the investigation.

'Is it possible the police didn't know the uniform was missing in the first place because Maddie gave it to Stiles before any of this happened?'

He steps closer. 'What are you saying about my daughter, Reid?' He prods my chest. 'Just say it. Get it out.'

'You were protecting her.'

A twitch near the right side of his lips. Then he swallows. 'The teenager's brain isn't fully developed, not until well into their twenties,' he says. 'Like I said, I believe in second chances. I gave you a second chance.'

He's talking about the Amanda Marley case. 'It wasn't a second chance, Chief. You made me leave town, you made me promise I'd never come back.'

'I'm not talking about *that*.'

It dawns on me. My skin tingles.

He smiles. 'You remember now, Reid?'

'I was sixteen. I just wanted to protect her.'

'Your mama begged me, *begged* me to arrest her. And this is the thanks I get?'

REID
NOW

I'M BACK THERE that night – Dennis in the kitchen, me in my bedroom. I can hear his sly comments about Dad. He hated my father because he died a hero; because he was a better man and my mother missed him. So many times I fantasised saying that to him. Imagined how he would react. But I didn't say it. I sat on my bed like a coward, listening to the bickering, imagining him wearing Dad's medal. It went all night and I just couldn't block it out. The anger grew and grew until it seized me. Then, at around 1 am, I heard Mom's screams in the bedroom. That's where I black out. The memory is gone, but I know what took place.

The old hockey stick Dad had bought me was beside my bed. In a blind rage, I grabbed it and raced up the hall to Mom's room. I didn't stop swinging until the stick broke. Then I started stomping, and didn't stop until Mom threw herself onto Dennis's bloody form.

'Just go, get out of here,' she told me. 'Look what you've done to him. You've killed him. You've *killed* him.'

I didn't hear her words at the time. I was trying to drag her off Dennis's body, to keep going. It turned out she was right.

Stubbs's voice snaps me back to the present. 'This is how the law works around here, Reid. We don't let it get to the judge if we know in our hearts that there's a better way to serve justice.'

'Oliver Stiles really was at home when Kiara died,' I say. 'Eshana was telling the truth. You protected your daughter. You tidied up her mess.'

'Just like I tidied up yours,' he snaps back. 'Just like I've done for so many others in this town. The mother of five who's driving just a *little* over the limit. The farmer growing a bit of his own weed out in the hills for his sick mama. That's what law enforcement is really about. Community, looking after each other.'

'What about Kiara, who looked after her?'

'It was an accident. They were talking at the water tower. Kiara fell. Maddie called me, distraught. I drove out there and put the body in the gorge. You know everyone hates searching out there. I thought that would be the end of it, but the storm, and those dog walkers. She was about four yards off the path, which would normally be far enough. Maddie doesn't deserve to go to prison and through the courts because of *an accident*. And let's not forget that Kiara King was extorting money from Stiles.' I think about the phone in my pocket and move a little closer to him.

'So that's why Maddie ran away to the city?'

'You wanted to make detective, Reid, but you still haven't figured it all out?'

'She was here,' I say.

'She really did disappear that night at first. I reported it, then she called me. She needed somewhere to hide, so she was out in the shed when the detectives came by. Then we picked up a trucker on amphetamines. He reported having a girl in his cab but he couldn't remember who. We ran with it. Then when Kiara's remains turned up, I thought it best she lie low for a little longer.'

'I took her down the city last night. The cops found her this morning.'

The missing jewellery and cash, the common tyre tread and boot prints. It was the perfect crime scene for an abduction because it was all set up by a man who has seen almost forty-five years of crime scenes.

'Where is she now?' I ask.

'She said she was going to catch up with a friend.'

'Does Eshana Stiles know about the affair?'

He lets his breath out slowly. 'I suppose it's possible. Maddie said that Stiles was going to tell his wife that night that he was leaving her.' He stops and looks towards the house. 'Oh, sorry, Reid, that will be Tina again. Give me a moment.'

He lays the axe down and heads towards the back door. Except I didn't hear the phone ring the first time, and I definitely didn't hear it then.

There's a siren in the distance, growing louder. I look towards the road and see flashing red and blue lights cutting through the darkness. Has Stubbs called the police on me? But why?

I unclip my gun, watch the corner Stubbs disappeared around.

'Reid?' A voice comes from the front porch near where I stand.

I turn and see the gun. Then it fires.

ESHANA
NOW

SHE'S SITTING DIRECTLY behind me. I imagine the gun pointing at the back of my head, or maybe at my spine.

She's directed me to take the bypass. I guess it's because we won't see much traffic this way and there are no lights to stop at. No one will see us.

'Maddie, you don't need to do this,' I say.

'Do what?'

'Point a gun at me. Make me drive you. Whatever it is you're planning.' Tears rattle my voice and I draw a breath to steady my nerves. 'I'm not going to tell anyone that you had an affair with my husband. I won't be able to convince anyone you had anything to do with Kiara's death. We can just go our separate ways. I'll leave Ethelton.'

'I don't think that's going to work.'

'I promise you,' I say, hearing the desperation in my voice.

'But what if you try to do it again?'

I focus on her words, trying to parse some hidden meaning. 'Do what again?'

She ignores me. 'What was it like when you woke up?'

I choke back a sob. 'Horrible. It was the worst moment of my life, realising my husband was dead. And all the physical pain. I felt so trapped.'

'I didn't mean it to happen that way,' she says.

A shiver passes over me. 'Maddie, what are you saying?'

'You really don't remember?'

'What happened?'

'I just wanted you to stop. That's all.' She sounds sad.

I feel a spike of rage. 'What did you do, Maddie?'

'What did I do? What did *you* do? You killed him! You killed Oli.'

'It was an accident.'

'No,' she says, and there's an undercurrent of rage in that one single syllable that could sweep me away. 'I knew you were out for dinner; I knew when you'd be driving home. I waited in the freezing rain until I saw his car coming, then I stepped out and waved you down.'

I can see it now. Not a memory, but it's easy to imagine. It's right there in front of me. A girl in a sweatshirt and jeans, waving both arms.

'I thought he was driving,' she says. 'I wanted to confront him in front of you so you would see he broke my heart. But that's just it, Eshana. The car swerved, and then . . . the crash. I saw Oli on the hood, the blood everywhere. I thought you were both dead and I knew I couldn't be found at the scene. When I heard another car coming, I rushed back to the shed. And I hid there.'

My eyes sting. I realise I'm crying again. I think of Oli, his smile, our wedding day, all those memories over the years. He wasn't perfect – no one is – but he didn't deserve to die.

'Turn off here,' she says.

I realise we're heading towards the water tower. She's going to kill me just like she killed Kiara.

'Listen,' I say, 'I have millions of dollars in bitcoin on a thumb drive. I can give it to you. Just, please, let me go home.'

'Keep driving,' she says.

I stop at an intersection. 'Just hear me out.'

She opens the window and the gun fires. The explosion is so loud, my entire body recoils.

'This gun is loaded,' she says. 'Keep driving or I'll shoot you in the back of the head.'

I try again. 'Six million dollars. You could do anything. You could leave Ethelton, buy a mansion somewhere. You would never need to worry about money.'

'You're lying,' she says.

The thumb drive was in the glove box of Oli's car; the car I crashed. I've no idea where it is now. The safe at home is where Oli kept his gun. If I can get to it, I can defend myself.

'I'm not lying. That's how Oli made his money. He kept the wallet address on the thumb drive and said if anything ever happened to him I'd be taken care of. But I have the house and my insurance money. I don't need the six million.'

'Drive,' she says. 'I'm not changing my mind.'

I see headlights coming along the road at the intersection.

'Okay, just listen. I'll give you the code for the safe. You can go there and get the thumb drive yourself.'

'What is it?' she says. 'What's the code?'

The lights are closer now. They're flying along. I could flash my headlights as they pass, but they probably wouldn't even notice.

If I turn the hazard lights on, they might stop to help. Then again, Maddie might pull the trigger.

'The code is . . .'

The lights get closer. I can see they belong to a truck. It's big; the sort of vehicle that always comes out of a collision better off.

If I time it right, so the truck clips the back of the car, it might roll or tip us. I could get out.

My foot hovers over the accelerator. I clench my jaw and brace. This could be the end.

Just as the truck is about to pass, I press the accelerator and move into its path.

REID
NOW

STUBBS FIRES OFF three rounds from about fifteen yards away. Miraculously, none of them hit me as I dive.

'Come on now, Reid. Come out.'

I hear his boots coming down the porch steps. I press my body against the side of the Challenger. My pulse slams in my ears as I shuffle towards the driver's door. I pull my arm out of the sling, and moving it brings a sharp pain to my collarbone but I've got no choice.

I fire my own gun blindly over the hood. The recoil almost causes me to lose my grip. It's been a while between drinks and I don't get to the range much these days.

Stubbs returns a shot that claps off the hood so close to my head I feel its turbulence.

I reach with my free hand for the car door and open it. Then I fire one more shot over the hood.

As I reach into the car and start the engine, another shot rings out. The windshield cracks. A high-pitch whine fills my head.

I pull myself into the Challenger, stay low under the dash, shift the car into reverse and jam the accelerator down with my palm.

The Challenger flies back towards the gate and crashes hard against it, partially breaking through.

More shots. Holes appear in the windshield. The cracks web.

I keep pressing the accelerator but it won't go. I shift the car to drive and it moves forward. Another shot whistles over my head.

I find reverse again and press the accelerator to the floor. This time the Challenger breaks through the wooden gate.

The sirens are still sounding; the cop car is right there. I lift my head enough to look back and see an officer crouched in behind his door, gun aimed in my direction. I have to take a risk.

I slam on the brake, rise to grip the wheel and turn it to straighten up on the black top. I put it back into drive and accelerate. More shots hit the car.

After a few seconds, I get up on the seat, just in time to swing around the first bend. I flick the lights on.

The cop car is racing along in my rear-view mirror now. The scene ahead is broken up into panels where the glass has cracked. But these old roads are just as familiar to me as they are to the cops, and the Challenger has the speed to outrun any cruiser. I remember the years of joy-riding with friends around here. It's like second nature.

After a few bends, the cop car hasn't drifted away, and I know they'll be radioing for others. I reach for my phone and make a call I would never make in any other circumstances.

It's 10 pm so I'm shocked to hear his voice instead of a recorded message.

'Reid?' He says it like a question. He's still got that husky voice. That and his made-for-TV smile are what drew me to him in the first place.

'Marco, hi. Listen, I need to make this quick in case something happens.'

'I haven't heard from you in a decade,' he says. 'I'm surprised you still have my number.'

'Don't say anything. Just listen,' I tell him. 'I've been investigating the Maddison Stubbs-Oliver Stiles case. I found out that they were in a relationship. And it was Maddison who pushed Kiara King off the water tower.'

'You're telling me Maddison Stubbs killed Kiara King?'

'Yes, and her father covered it up.'

'I'm assuming you have proof.'

'I'm going to send you a recording right now. Stubbs told me what happened – he was buying time for his officers to arrive. Then he shot at me. It's a long story. Just listen to the recording.'

'Okay, okay,' he says. 'Send it now.'

I hang up and keep my foot to the floor, barely slowing to take the bends. I need to get as far away from Stubbs and the Manson PD as possible. I think about Eshana. What if she's with Maddison? But I can't help her now. I can't do anything but expose Stubbs. I've always respected him, but a desperate parent will do anything for their family. Mom probably would have done the same for me.

I keep pushing the Challenger as fast as it will go, and in each straight I can see I've gained more distance on the cop car. Then there are two of them. Soon there will be more. As much as I know these roads, I'm outnumbered. There will be spikes and a roadblock set up soon. It's over, I realise. The police can arrest me, but Stubbs can't stop what's coming.

I pull over to the side of the road and take the keys out of the ignition. I send the recording to Marco, watching the upload bar grow as the sirens become louder and louder. Then I start a new recording, this time I place my phone upright against the tyre of my car. You can never be too safe. I kneel at the side of the road with my hands on my head, in full view of the camera streaming to my cloud storage.

The first cop car slides to a halt, its headlights cutting through the dark like blades. Both doors open and the cops are screaming at me to lie face down, keep my hands on my head. Their guns are trained on my centre mass.

I know the drill. No sudden movements. I lie down and wait.

Then the cuffs are on and they're hauling me up, searching my pockets. I'm thrust in the back of the car and we're heading for the police station. It's all over.

ESHANA
NOW

I SEE A bright light. The truck's horn blares. Maddie screams behind me. I squeeze everything inside, bend my knees and slip lower into my seat.

I hear an explosion. The gun. The windshield cracks.

Brakes scream and somehow we sail by in front of the truck. The car tips where the road drops away, and rolls. I see black and red. My face crashes into the steering wheel and I bite my tongue, taste blood.

I can hear Maddie howling, and the truck's horn sounds as if it's coming from inside my head. But nothing is as loud as my own heart, punching its way out of my chest.

It takes me a moment to reorient myself. I'm pressed against the roof. I can hear Maddie scrabbling around on the roof too, but I don't stick around. I manage to get the window open and drag myself out.

Red tail-lights ahead. They're stopping. I get to my feet and run towards them.

A man is marching back in my direction, fists and arms swinging at his sides.

'Help!' I call.

Then I hear another gunshot. I drop.

The man suddenly looks fearful. He turns on his heel and rushes back to the truck.

Another shot. The gravel kicks up beside me. I'm a sitting duck.

I sprint to the truck but the tail-lights are moving away from me. He's leaving!

I scream, 'Help! Please!' I pick up a stone and hurl it, knowing nothing will make him stop.

Turning back, I see Maddie crawling out of the car.

I'm weak and sore and can barely run at all, but I keep pushing through the pain.

Another shot. It misses, but it's only a matter of time before a bullet hits its mark.

'You're not getting away,' she calls after me.

I can hear her getting closer. My lungs sear. I slip on a loose piece of gravel and roll down into the ditch. Desperately scrabble to my feet.

The truck is gone. In the distance, my car lies on its roof, steam rising from its belly, its two headlights shooting out into the trees beyond the road's edge. Another shot cracks through the silence of the night. She's coming closer.

I see her silhouette. The gun raised in my direction.

Then there's another sound. In the distance, growing louder. It's a siren.

The relief makes me so light I could float. Then I realise it could be her father. She's so close now, up on the road, aiming the gun down. I tense everything and wait. The gun lets out an impotent click. Then another one. She's out of bullets. I exhale.

A car becomes visible on the straight, its lights flashing. Then another. The truck driver must have phoned them.

'Maddie,' I say. 'It's over.'

'No,' she says, and I hear tears in her voice. She throws the gun down towards me and runs in the direction of the coming cop cars. She's going to play the victim.

I'm seized by a new panic.

It'll never work, I think. The cop cars slide to a stop, their doors open and the officers train their guns on Maddie.

'Put your hands in the air!' one cop screams. 'Hands up right now.'

She stops, looks around her as if confused.

'Me?' she says. 'No, she kidnapped me. It's her.'

'Get down on your knees and keep your hands up.'

I crawl back up to the road and watch as the handcuffs go on. I hear her protests. She begins crying, howling as if in pain. They lead her to the back of the police car.

An ambulance arrives, sirens wailing. Then the cops come for me.

REID
NOW

'EXPLAIN IT TO me again,' Cosby says. 'But this time, Reid, make it make sense.'

The one thing I can count on in this world is my ex's ruthless ambition. The story is a huge scoop and I need him to get it out right now. The recording is the only thing keeping me from going to prison. I know Marco will likely try to maximise the benefit for him, but surely he realises the perilous position it puts me in if he takes too long.

'The recording is on my phone, you can listen to it yourself.'

Cosby is taking less pleasure in this than I would have expected. He knows that if I'm telling the truth, then his boss, mentor and friend is in big trouble. Would they destroy my phone to try cover it up? Maybe Cosby knows more than he is letting on, maybe he knew all about Maddison and Oliver . . . and Stubbs. I remember how afraid Cody was of the police; they were bullying him into silence. They must have known something was going on. Cosby also must have sensed Stubbs was quick to close the investigation into the crash, and quick to discount Oliver Stiles as a suspect in the Kiara King disappearance. Stubbs likely knew that the longer his detectives investigated Stiles, the more likely it would be that they'd discover the truth: Oliver was seeing Maddison not Kiara. It's impossible that some of them don't know the truth.

'Well, the chief is telling us that you went there with a gun. He said you were deranged. He also told us that you yourself killed a man, and let your mama take the fall for it. Is that right?'

I feel hot suddenly. There was always a chance this would come out, but they can't prove it. It was almost twenty years ago. But I know that there's no statute of limitations on murder. Stubbs said on the recording that my mom begged that he arrest her, but he didn't say why. Hopefully I've not incriminated myself.

'That would mean the Manson PD covered up a historical crime,' he says.

There's a knock on the interview room door and Cosby steps outside.

I sit there. After a few excruciatingly slow minutes, I stand up, move around the room. I can't stay still but I know this will only make me look more guilty.

Eventually the door opens again.

'Take a seat,' Cosby says.

I do.

'I see you're still friends with that journalist.'

The story has broken. It's all I can do to keep from smiling but he still has something over me. *Dennis.*

'Looks like we are going to have to let you go.'

I don't trust him. This must be a trick. 'What about what you said? About Mom and ah—'

'Well, I'm not sure if we can take Stubbs's word for it. Not after this.' He pauses, looks me in the eye with open contempt. 'Don't you ever believe I'm doing this for you. We're not looking into it. Too much time has passed and if it was covered up, well, I don't want to drag our reputation through the mud again. But just know, I'm not doing this for you.'

'So I can go?'

'We still need a formal statement and more details. But you're not under arrest.'

Stubbs will be well and truly deep past retirement age when he gets out. And even if he wasn't, with multiple felonies, he'd never wear a uniform again. Still, I'm not looking forward to the day I have to face him down in court when I'm called to give evidence.

By the time the police have taken my statement and I've been officially released without charge, it's early morning. The cold outside the station shakes the fatigue and exhaustion from my bones.

A cop drives me to the garage where the Camry was repaired and I wait in a cafe nearby until the garage opens. The police are holding the Challenger as part of the investigation before it too will have to be repaired. I cringe, thinking about all the bullets that hit the car.

It feels good getting behind the wheel of the Camry. It's the type of car you wouldn't look twice at, especially with a forgettable man behind the wheel.

Over the next few days, I learn what happened with Eshana. Maddison will be going away for a while too. Murder, kidnapping and attempted murder headline the show, but there are a whole host of other charges. It was her father's revolver she'd used to kidnap Eshana. Even her mother will be lucky to avoid incarceration because she knew Maddie hadn't been abducted. The news hits the national media, and Marco is the star for breaking the story.

•

This morning, I leave the city before dawn, to catch Peyton as he opens up.

'Hello stranger,' he says. 'You've been the name on everyone's lips the last few days.'

'I'm just here for the omelette,' I say with a smile.

'That's a shame. I thought it was for me.'

He unlocks the door and goes inside. I take a seat. The chef is already in the kitchen, preparing for the day.

Peyton fires up the coffee machine.

'So I was thinking,' he says. 'Say I visited the city, and wanted a drink, where would you suggest I go?'

I smile at that and catch his eye.

'It depends,' I say. 'What day are you thinking?'

'I'm off Thursday. So I could come along Wednesday night. I just need to find somewhere to stay.'

'I'm sure we can find you a bed in the city,' I say.

·

After leaving the cafe, I head to the cemetery where Mom and Dad are buried, side by side. I think of those years, the first seven of my life. I was a happy kid; we were a happy family. It's odd seeing the photo inset of Dad, still such a young man beside the photo of Mom, whose photo shows an old woman with kind eyes and a warm smile. I'll never be able to leave this place forever, I realise. I'll always be drawn back one way or another.

I sit on the grass in the quiet of the cemetery. A new day has begun. For everything that has gone wrong for me here, there are still a few moments of light and joy. There's Peyton, and the memories of my mother and father. There's still something.

ESHANA
AFTER

THE AMBULANCE BRINGS me back to the hospital for assessments and scans. I didn't hit my head too badly when my car rolled, but I'm bruised and bloodied from the broken glass.

Officer Stickland comes with a detective to interview me in the hospital. I tell them everything: what I remember about the affair, Maddie stepping out on the road the night we crashed, then how she turned up at my house with a gun.

'What's going to happen to her?' I ask.

'She's being charged with kidnapping, unlawful possession of a firearm and attempted murder, along with other minor charges,' Stickland says. 'And the detectives have got enough evidence to charge her for the murder of Kiara King.'

Later, at home, Larissa and a couple of the dance moms come to see me, probably for the gossip, but it's nice to have company.

A couple of days later, Clare is coming up from the city. She calls me on her way to check in, and it's nice to know I still have her as a friend. Her and Oli are not as different as he used to think. She can be kind and supportive.

'I'll be there around five,' she says. 'I'm not working anymore but I can help you set the place up for inspections and the sale.' She doesn't need to be this nice to me, I remind myself.

'Thank you so much, Clare. I really don't know what I would do without you.'

'It's my pleasure. Anything for family,' she says.

'I'm looking forward to just getting out of here, back to the city. Maybe you can help me find a place to live.'

'Of course,' she says. 'You can even stay at my place. For now.'

'And you said you quit your job? Did you win the lottery or did you meet a super-rich man?'

She laughs. 'Something like that. No, it's just time to take a break. I've got a lot in savings. I'll think I'll be fine.'

'Well, I'll see you later on. Feel free to stay, I still feel so lonely in this house at night by myself.'

'I'll pack a bag and bring wine. I can help you go through Oli's things if you like.'

There's just one thing I can't get off my mind. My memory of those last moments with Oli has been coming back, slowly but surely. I resist it, but it's always there, growing clearer and stronger. There was something Maddie said when she kidnapped me.

'What did I do? What did you do? You killed him! You killed Oli.'

'It was an accident.'

'No.'

Oli had just told me about the affair with Maddie. I was crying, my vision blurry.

'Shit,' Oli said, as I drove us along the Boulevard. 'That's her. She's gone off the deep end.'

I could see a figure on the road through the rain; a girl, waving her arms.

I pressed down on the accelerator.

'Eshana?' Oli said. Then with more urgency, 'Eshana! What are you doing?'

I pushed my foot down to the floor. I could see her, trapped in the headlights. She tried to run but she wasn't getting away. She was going to pay for this, they both were.

'No!' Oli said. I braced for the collision, but he reached over to the wheel, pulled it down. We shot past the girl with an inch to spare. I tried to wrestle back control of the car. The wheels screamed. The power pole came at us in an instant.

Then there's only darkness.

ACKNOWLEDGEMENTS

MANY THANKS TO the usual suspects but in particular to Pippa Masson, Dan Lazar, Gordon Wise, Paige Tracy, Lynn Yeowart, Tiffany Plummer, Rebecca Saunders, Emma Rafferty, Emily Lighezzolo, Tania Mackenzie-Cooke, Mel Winder, everyone else at Hachette Australia and Aotearoa, and Adrian Minson.

Thank you to the Pomare and Tracy families for all the support. And, finally, an extra special thanks to R.W.R. McDonald.

Welcoming strangers into your home is a
dangerous game . . .

Ever have the feeling you're being watched?

THE

LAST

GUESTS

THE NUMBER ONE INTERNATIONAL BESTSELLER

J.P. POMARE

A wife finds herself racing for answers when the decision to rent out her family vacation home takes a deadly turn in this twisty thriller from the number one internationally bestselling author.

Available now.

How far would you go to protect your family?

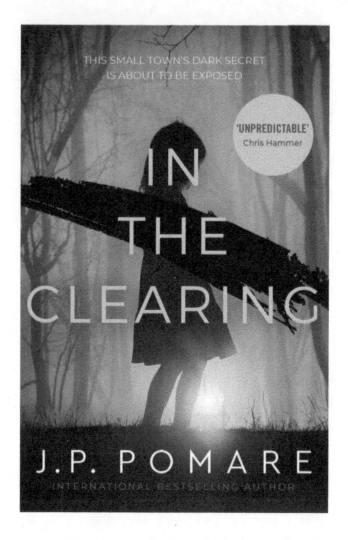

Set against a ticking clock, this haunting and atmospheric thriller pits a ruthless cult against a mother's love, revealing that our darkest secrets are the hardest ones to leave behind.

Available now.

Have you uncovered Evie's secret?

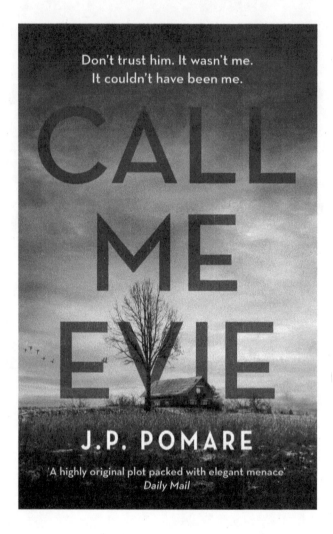

Don't trust him. It wasn't me.
It couldn't have been me.

CALL
ME
EVIE

J.P. POMARE

'A highly original plot packed with elegant menace'
Daily Mail

A seventeen-year-old struggles to remember the tragic night
that changed her life forever in this twist-filled psychological
suspense novel.

Available now.

THRILLINGLY GOOD BOOKS
FROM CRIMINALLY
GOOD WRITERS

CRIME FILES BRINGS YOU THE LATEST RELEASES FROM
TOP CRIME AND THRILLER AUTHORS.

SIGN UP ONLINE FOR OUR MONTHLY NEWSLETTER AND BE THE FIRST
TO KNOW ABOUT OUR COMPETITIONS, NEW BOOKS AND MORE.

VISIT OUR WEBSITE: WWW.CRIMEFILES.CO.UK
LIKE US ON FACEBOOK: FACEBOOK.COM/CRIMEFILES
FOLLOW US ON TWITTER: @CRIMEFILESBOOKS